BEHIND the GREEN DOOR memoir of a time traveler

ann m. andrashie

INDEPENDENT BOOK PUBLISHERS ASSOCIATION ibpa

Spring Harbor Publishing~an independent clean read publisher.org

 Published by Spring Harbor Publishing-an independent clean read publisher, Madison Wisconsin. Printed in the United States of America
springharborpublishing.org

ISBN: 978-1-7370479-4-0 hard copy
ISBN: 978-1-7370479-5-7 e-book
First Printing, 2023
10 9 8 7 6 5 4 3 2 1

ACKNOWLEDGMENTS

I wholeheartedly thank
My editor, mentor, and friend,
Barbara Ann Philleo
My sister Mary Beth, brother Michael,
Jerry, my children Adam and Mariah,
and the ever presence of my, Lord and Savior.
Your support and patience, and guidance
are the winds beneath my pen (keyboard).

DEDICATION

To my most beloved grandchildren both near and far,
and all my family
both alive and those who made it Home
Our Circle Will Never Be Broken

She Wrote It On The Bus

BEHIND the GREEN DOOR
memoir
of a time traveler

THE BEGINNING

All stories begin somewhere and all end somewhere usually far from their beginning. So it was the day I arrived in Timber Town, an old northern Wisconsin town that has no meaning to anyone unless a person is born there, raised and, upon death, placed to rest in its dark fertile ground. It was the late autumn of 1892 that I was escorted to Timber Town by the spinster, yet remarkably fashionable, Miss Gavin. It was that day I rode with Miss Gavin in Shamus' Gentleman's Brougham carriage. The coach was older, yet still fit and in good repair for the once fine doctor Shamus P. Fitzgerald. And if I close my eyes, now weary and worn, I can still see the trees rising in the distance on that chilly October night as we neared the good doctor's mansion on the northern outskirts of Timber Town. I was to work taking care of Shamus P. as his caregiver. But, as it turned out, Shamus had other plans concerning his future and mine.

CHAPTER ONE

We were nearing the turn of the century and most everyone was excited to see what further changes would occur in the coming years. Up to that point in time we'd seen such wonderful inventions come into existence such as the gasoline powered car per the Duryea brothers, Charles and Frank; and the motion picture camera created by Thomas Edison, and of course his famous light bulb, just to name a few.

All these new contraptions were deemed miraculous by some, yet others were considered to be works derived from the Devil's own hands. For me, the phonograph was the serpents' finger, shall we say, that lured me into the future. But alas, one machine, an irresistible monster of a machine, was overwhelmingly seductive that it remains unknown to society even as you read this now. For if left in the wrong hands it would be used as a foolhardy way to live one's life. A life that not a machine but only God Himself renders the right to create, navigate, and take back in His own name and time. Though I admit arguing to God that He Himself is merely the cruel obsession for the weak-minded, not a machine. That was before my adventure that I am writing to you about. And quite the adventure it was.

And truth be told I would not blame you one iota, not a single one, for not trusting what I have written within these pages. But I guarantee you what I have written is the truth, every last word. You see, at my age one has nothing to gain from holding onto lies and deception, and for some, even conspiracies.

But alas, my once dramatically mastered voice has grown graveled and thin, leaving me with no alternative but to pray my words will hold strong and vibrant on these pages. And so it came to pass that I, Camarilla Rae Berkelman, must tell you my story. And perhaps, just perhaps, it is still being written somewhere beyond The Green Door—the door which was once forbidden to be opened, let alone passed through.

I had just turned eighteen and was ready to begin my first voyage away from the comforts of Pine Brook institution and the people that, for the past ten years, had become my family. This was extremely hard not only on me but my Little Margret Jean as well. You see, during those years spent at Pine Brook, though older, she was not only my roommate but the closest person ever in my whole entire life to become my sister, though the same blood ran not in our veins.

Although I loved her so, for Little Margret, living with me outside of Pine Brook would have been a monstrous crime forced upon her. A transgression she would not be able to bear. For the walls of Pine Brook were built to keep someone specially made as my Little Margret, safe from the glares of ridicule from those whom from the moment of conception had been formed so perfectly, and with a good measure of health. Cruel and uneasy as it is to say, truth be told, that little munchkin of a woman, my dearest of all, Little Margret Jean, could easily have been mistaken for some sort of woodland elf.

Yes, she was small and awkward, and by man's standard considered deformed to the point of causing one to stop in their tracks and take a polite little gasp. So you see, life for Little Margret Jean outside of our Pine Brook home would have imposed her great emotional harm.

Our beloved Doctor Bruce Bayshore brought up the subject before Miss Gavin arrived the first time. Our conversation led my common sense to agree.

He was a father to me, Doctor Bruce was. And it was by his good judgment that I should learn a trade before departing from Pine Brook and his care. And so I was prepared to take on my role as a caregiver thanks to him and Nurse Price. But no amount of training could possibly have equipped me for the life that lay waiting ahead for me.

It was a life only a handful have been privy to, one that I dared not share with anyone, not even my Little Margret Jean. For, to do so would have taken away that life and justifiably placed me once again in Pine Brook. Though I loved the old place and everyone there, to return to the institution I once considered home would have meant disaster, especially if I were to return committed as a person truly insane. For the story I'm about to tell, no one would believe, not even Little Margret Jean.

You see, the way I came to Pine Brook was not conventional to say the least. I was nearing my eighth year of age and traveling on holiday with my parents and older brother, Huston. Father decided we should spread our wings and investigate the east coast of the United States, New York City to be exact. It was a long way from southern Wisconsin.

We were to visit mine and Huston's only uncle, my mother's brother of whom she was so proud. It was to be the first time for Huston and me to meet him. We arrived at his quaint little timepiece shoppe only to find it apparently abandoned. We each looked into its windows. From my view as well as Huston's and Mother and Father's, it appeared my Uncle Edward hadn't been much of a shopkeeper after all as Mother claimed. The single room of his shoppe was laden with heavy dust. Its four walls of clocks no longer ticked nor tocked, their hands stuck at all different times. A dark scamper caught my eye.

"Father," I said, "see, see the mouse?" I was forever captivated by such tiny creatures, and Mother was equally forever scolding me for such an infatuation. I watched it nibble the last bit of a crumb in its tiny claws. It then scampered away before Father took a peek.

"Well," he said turning to Mother. "It looks like Edward had some tough times come about."

"Yes, he did," a small stunt of a woman chimed from behind us. To this day I do swear on Huston's grave she was a witch. Her hunched back and long crooked nose, and hair so unkempt, was a snarl of a mess. Mother gasped at the sight. *'Rats nest,'* I heard her say in my head. Rats nest. Often times she called my own hair such a name after a long day of play outside. I looked closer into the witch's mop of gray hair. Perhaps if I'd looked closely enough I might have caught a glimpse of one or two pairs of beady little red eyes. No, no luck. No rats.

"He wouldn't have financial woes if he'd stay put," the witch lady said, sweeping dirt only she could see from the walk. "He could be back tonight, tomorrow or next year. No one can keep track of him.

Comes and goes as he pleases. He hasn't had a decent customer for months and months. Last one he had was—" she yanked a dirty piece of cloth from her pocket and coughed, wiping a spittle of witches drool from her mouth and knotty chin.

"—was that tall, awkward looking fellow. I suppose some might think him handsome but not me. I see beyond a person's good looks and manners. It was after him that your brother started disappearing, leaving his fine clientele—"

She coughed and spat again, then wiped. Father reached for his coin purse and handed the old crow a nice handful of coins and a card. Her gnarled fingers eagerly snatched them as she smiled a wondrously blackened tooth smile that only true witches have. I immediately took shelter behind Huston, grabbing his hand, refusing to let go till we boarded the carriage.

"Well," Father said, "our name and address is on that card. When he arrives back, please give it to him. Let him know we were here and think of him often and do wish he would pay us a visit when possible."

There was nothing more we could do and, with Mother broken-hearted, we boarded the carriage and talked of heading home to Wisconsin.

That's when it really all started. My life inside and out of Pine Brook. In my mind's eye I still hear the whinnies, the cries of the horses as we turned the corner of Uncle Edward's shoppe as we left. I still see the carriages, ours and theirs. Theirs, a black carriage and it was charging straight at us., nearly tipped over as it turned the corner. Father tried pulling our horses back, it was no use. They reared up as did the horses belonging to the other carriage. Long black legs and those of white thrust forward, high in the air, pushing the others away. But it was to no avail. They tangled, forcing themselves to the ground and onto their sides. Their cries sounded as I had never heard an animal caterwaul before. Those few moments seemed to last forever.

We were much too stunned to react. So I thought. I later learned it was the horses and carriages that held us down, trapping us while we struggled, holding us in that nightmare until help arrived.

Huston and I were severely injured and in need of immediate medical attention. But for Father and Mother, there was no need.

We were placed in the hospital. And under Huston's insistence we shared a room; my bed next to his. Ever so faithful as he was, he upheld the last instructions Father and Mother spoke to him.

"You must take care of your little sister. No matter what. See to it that she is well provided for. She is now your charge."

I, being unconscious, was not aware that those were the very last words they would ever speak. Nor was I aware of their passing, or the days and weeks that turned into months. I was told during that time Huston had taken me to Wisconsin and admitted me to what would become my home for the next ten years: Pine Brook mental institution.

Now, to call it an asylum was forbidden (by Doctor Bruce anyway). He being its only physician, superintendent, headmaster, bookkeeper and top psychiatrist, saw it differently. Not as an institution that held and housed the mentally deranged and those cursed with severe physical deformities; but as a fortress of protection for those whom not life but society could not tolerate. People like my Little Margret Jean, and the old Colonel, Mr. Hawthorn, and Molly May Junction, and so many more. Doctor Bruce saw to it that they all found a purpose in life, though meager as it would seem to those in the outside world. For under Doctor Bruce's care, they truly did have value, each and everyone, and so did the many others who passed through the doors of Pine Brook who called it home—even if for just a short time.

And so, as I came out of my unconscious state, I too, had developed a worth just as the rest had. And even if I hadn't regained my senses, there was a very good chance that those caring for me still would have found some purpose for me being alive and breathing even if it only meant keeping the dust from falling onto the corners of the floor in my and Little Margret Jean's room. But as it turned out my purpose was, or might I say, is a mite stranger than the others.

"She's coming around, Doctor." Those were the first words I heard for over a year. "She's coming around." Later I recognized the voice belonging to Nurse Price, but the hand that held mine was none other than that of my Little Margret Jean.

I awoke not knowing I was actually nine and no longer eight anymore. One whole year older than when the accident had occurred.

Yes, an entire year had passed. And truth be told, if Huston hadn't placed me into the merciful hands of Doctor Bruce, and his nurse, Nurse Price, there is a great chance that you would not be reading this, for I would not be alive to tell it.

So, as you now understand, the way I arrived at Pine Brook was not under ordinary reasons, but how I left was.

Huston was wise and had used the money left by Father and Mother as instructed in their will. It was that funding that allowed me to reside at Pine Brook instead of being forced to live in an orphanage for the next ten years. Oh, the horrors of such! But after that length of time the money had run out. At that point, with no money, I was indigent, and with Pine Brook's meager budget I was left with no place to go. And without a means to further my schooling on my own, I had only a few choices. Either leave Pine Brook and strike out on my own or barter my services as a caregiver for slightly substandard shelter and food in my belly and nothing more.

You see, in those days unmarried women without proper education had few choices of self-support. If they were fortunate to have a bit of schooling, and lucky enough to have known someone who needed a helper or companion, it was likely they found employment of some sort (outside of washing floors and chamber pots); store clerks, and secretaries, or perhaps a caregiver of sorts. But for most, we women were groomed to become the best possible wife and mother we possibly could be. After all, to capture a good man was a guarantee of having a real home.

"Make your husband proud, that is a real woman's occupation," more than one old hen would not only encourage, but demand of me when Nurse Price and I rode to Spring Green to replenish our midweek supply from Thornton's Dry Goods.

I had not the heart, and nor was I courageous enough to announce that, for myself, marriage was not a possibility. For, who in their right mind would want to engage with a female who, for most of her life, lived in an institution and to boot, one that spoke with a stutter? It would be out of pure desperation that a man would ask for my hand in marriage. And to this very day I do bless Nurse Price for sharing not those facts but allowing those outside of Pine Brook to believe I was not associated with the institution in any way other than being hired help.

And so, it was settled. Through Shamus P. Fitzgerald, via Miss Gavin, I would receive room and board, a sensible stipend, plus the opportunity to further my schooling. And as promised, housekeeping and other chores would be shared between me and Mrs. Thompson, Doctor Fitzgerald's faithful housekeeper. After all, Shamus P. Fitzgerald was at one time a medical doctor, and though he no longer practiced, his knowledge was invaluable to me and he was willing to share it. It was under his employ I was given the key to go beyond The Green Door— the door only privileged servants were allowed to pass through in order to provide care and service to their families.

But beyond Shamus' green door a totally different world waited, different than anyone knew. And perhaps, just perhaps, Pine Brook had a few doors of its own.

CHAPTER TWO

It was Miss Gavin (sent from Shamus P. Fitzgerald himself) who came to meet with Doctor Bruce. She came to discuss and finalize the details of my hirement as Caregiver to Shamus. So naturally she was the one who was to personally deliver me to him. And I tell you true, undeniably that day was an extraordinarily special day; for it was also the day I left Pine Brook. It was also a day of heartbreak and confusion, and the beginning of a whole new life and adventure. It was so long ago yet feels as if it were just yesterday (as most ambiances of time do for older folks.) And I do recall it quite clearly.

It was early morning. And since it was my last morning with Nurse Price (and Little Margret Jean), I took advantage of every minute as we prepared breakfast. We started with one of our daily conversations, one that now I chuckle at and hold near and dear to my heart, being a young woman and all.

Our special girlish conversations began one day when Nurse Price started accidentally receiving the new fashion tabloid, Harper's Bazar. It was full of beautiful women all of whom were pictured with beautiful hair, wearing *the* most beautiful dresses, and carrying outrageously colorful, matching parasols from France. And their gloves. Oh, how

I adored their arm-length gloves, with all those pretty ribbons and bows! I imagined how delicious they must have felt, all that silky satin caressing the skin.

I promised myself the first time I received any sort of pay for taking care of Dr. Fitzgerald, I would buy myself one of those fancy outfits, including the matching umbrella and gloves to boot. I would also get one exact outfit for Little Margret Jean and one for Nurse Price (even if she didn't want one). I would do it just to be nice so as to show my appreciation for all she and Little Margret Jean had done for me. And who knows, once she had it on, maybe Nurse Price might change her mind concerning certain, *'Ladies' Things, and What-Nots,'* as she referred to women's high fashioned underthings. They were needed, of course, in order to wear *Harper's* clothing properly in style. 'Course it would take an awful long time to save that much money. But I was sure I could do it. After all, I was only eighteen and I did have my whole life in front of me.

See, our dresses at Pine Brook were, long, drab, and plain gray. And every morning in the kitchen, Nurse Price would say, "I'll stay with these, thank you!" while glancing at the fashion page of *The Courier* newspaper, with the *Harper's* next to it, a sad envy in her eyes.

And that morning I left was no different. For a brief moment Nurse Price stopped stirring the huge bowl of thick mixture of eggs and flour and milk. Her gnarled fingers, from too many years of work, tapped the pictures and then rested on the sizes and price given for the dresses and underthings. Flustered, she started stirring again, almost frantically. You see, Nurse Price was a rather large woman, and the clothing offered was not.

"At least we don't waste time and good money having to get into all those nasty layers of proper undergarments... just to turn around and complain how our petticoats and 'What-Nots' are suffocating us. Why, they even sell smelling salts right next to them for when those fool women fall unconscious due to lack of proper oxygen."

What-Nots, I thought, listening to the hiss of pancake batter pour onto the black cast iron griddle. *Oh, to have just one of those What-Nots.*

"Women forcing themselves into those god-forsaken corsets stiffened with whale bones... suffocating themselves. Well, they can have all that fancy wear."

Flip-flip...flip-flip...one pancake, two pancakes, three.

"We don't have time for all that nonsense. Besides, we coordinate just fine with our surroundings, just fine. We don't need any extras to do so."

Though Nurse Price frequently laughed at her made-up jokes as to how we matched most of Pine Brooks interior construction, it did nothing to help ease my curiosity and want concerning those petticoats and, What-Nots (and the smelling salts that went with them).

Nurse Price's disdain for the fashion world sat in my mind which grew doubt I would ever wear anything but simple, dull, gray dresses that matched Pine Brook's floors. And I was doubly sure the only other color I would ever adorn would be the stains of various foods covering our once-bleached white aprons.

I expressed my secret fashion desires only once to Nurse Price. That is all it took for me to never mention it to her again. But inside myself, it was a different story.

You see, it was Christmas time, and at that time I was fourteen and growing into becoming a young woman. I was hoping my small, meager gift that year would be something a bit private and more on the feminine side. I naturally wanted to know how it felt to complain about the need for smelling salts and fainting couches; all of which were due to what Nurse Price diagnosed as: "those godforsaken, organ crushing, What-Nots." The ones that, "push and move a woman's innards where they are not meant to be moved or pushed. And all for the sake of looking like a curved, walking letter S. Foolish. Simply foolish!"

But I, I would sigh, *Stylish! oh, just so stylish*. In my head of course. Sometimes I would practice expressing such complaints, including pretending faint with Little Margret Jean at my side.

I tucked that memory of Pine Brook deep inside myself along with all the others, and took them with me into my and Little Margret Jean's secluded hallway that some ten years earlier we had decided to claim as our very own private getaway retreat (unofficially, of course) since it was very seldom used by anyone at Pine Brook. The hallway held many memories and secrets.

The object of one particular game was to walk in small tight circles and stare at the gray tiled flooring until the black blotches within melted together, which made one large, connected circle. It was the repetition of the movement that helped soothe my ratty nerves and ease my stutter (especially during one of my wide-awake nightmares) both of which I had developed after the accident.

Doctor Bruce explained my prognosis in medical terms only he and Nurse Price understood: Absorption Psychosis. Then one day while preparing breakfast Nurse Price put it to me in simpler terms.

"You have an overactive imagination, my love, and you tend to run away with it. The difference between you and the old Colonel Mr. Hawthorn and Molly Mae Junction and the others is that you know better. You know you're not an old Colonel unlike Mr. Hawthorn who truly believes he is even though he isn't, and from the Civil War no less. And Molly Mae. Why, the old gal thinks herself to be a locomotive engineer on one of those fine, steam powered iron horses which everyone knows can't be true and never was true, not being a woman. "But you, Camarilla, you know who you are and who you are not... where you are and where you are not. That's the difference between you and them. Your little game of you and Margret walking in that circle is well... well, it's merely your way of trying to undo what was done."

"But what if it is true?" I asked her one time. "Wh-wh-what if

Mr. Hawthorn truly *is* an old Colonel? Wh-wh-what if Molly Mae Junction *was* an engineer on a steam horse before she lost her mind? Who-who says it can't be true?"

We would argue this nearly every day, and each time it ended the same. Nurse Price clucking her tongue and sighing.

"Well then," she said. "We are honored to be taking care of them, aren't we? Besides, I've watched you and Margret plenty of times fooling around in that hallway of yours to know it isn't..."

She tsked again. "Spinning in time. But you always manage to come back, don't you?"

And somehow, I always did, no matter where and when I traveled to. But that day I knew I wasn't to come back. Ever.

So naturally that day I was more nervous than usual and focused even harder on the tiles as we trotted faster and faster in our circle, watching the blotches connect, making one single blur.

Finally, Little Margret Jean and I stopped walking. We slumped onto the floor, and studied the large, spinning black fragments in the tiles.

"I-I think I'm gonna' bust open with a case of the spins," I stammered. "I-I am—I'm gonna' bust open!"

"You want me to get Nurse Price, or maybe Doctor Bruce?" Little Margret Jean asked.

"I-I'm fine, I-I'm fine," I watched the swirls slow and untangle, turning back into plain old speckled tiles. "I hope Mrs. Thompson is just like Nurse Price, but with fashion sense."

"I sure am going to miss you," Little Margret Jean said and patted the curls on my head. They were dark and long, just as my mother's had been. But my nose belonged to my father. It was longer than most girls' my age. I gave it a twitch, sniffing back my tears.

My stomach filled with a miserable wave of guilt as my words echoed down the hall, for I knew they were just as empty as that corridor and would never come true.

"One day, when things get right, I-I I'm coming back to get you, my Little Margret Jean." Little Margret smiled that innocent look of trust I had grown to cherish. I knew she heard me. Worse, I knew she believed me.

"Maybe Frieda or Molly Mae Junction will play dolls with me," she said softly, holding onto her knees, rocking back and forth. The tick-tock of the wall clock's pendulum swung back and forth filling the silence of our last moments alone. I looked at its hands.

"I-I'll remind them," I stared at her, forcing her elfin-like image to stay forever burnt in my mind.

"Little Margret, I-I hate to be the one to say this, b-but it's time. We need to go."

"Eight o'clock? Eight o'clock already?"

"Yep," I nodded. "Eight o'clock. Miss Gavin and D-d-doctor Bruce said b-b-be ready at eight-th-th-thirty... sh-sh-sharp."

Little Margret closed her eyes tight. I heard the lump in her throat squeeze its way down her windpipe. My own lump held its place, not going up or down. It hurt.

It was hard to believe in God, especially since the accident, and then the death of Huston. So for Little Margret Jean's sake, I said my prayers, but to those I knew truly did exist at one time.

"Momma, Daddy, Huston, help me to do a good job for Doctor Fitzgerald. And since I'm not going to be here no more to watch over Little Margret, if you can, please watch her for me and keep her safe...Amen."

"Amen," Little Margret said, dipping her head low.

We headed to the door, thick and constructed well from the dark wood from the walnut trees lumbered from the back acreage of Pine Brook's very own property. Placing my hand on its knob, I held my breath for a moment and took in our hallway and its tile.

This is the last time I will ever see it, I thought as Little Margret placed her tiny hand on mine. Her touch held us there for a bit longer. We looked at each other, my heart sinking with hers. We both knew my promise to come back and get her was not to come true. Ever. It couldn't. Little Margret understood the reason why. And that broke my heart even more making my eyes fill with tears. After all, being near sisters as we were, we did discuss the possibility of one day boarding together outside of Pine Brook. And now my day had come. Hers never could.

"We have one last adventure together," I said forcing a smile. "Will you help me spy one last time, on Doctor Bruce and Miss Gavin?"

A grin spread across her face. "Yes! Yes, I will, my big Camarilla Berkelman with lightening bug green eyes. I will do it one last time."

I took a deep breath. *And this is the last time I will chase my Little Margret Jean.* "Are we ready?" I asked.

I'll never forget pulling open that dark, solid door for the very last time. Least of all, I will never forget the sight of that little sprite of a woman scampering past my legs. The little lady I called friend and sister.

CHAPTER THREE

Little Margret Jean stood on my shoulders and tugged the pulley-rope attached to the glass window above Dr. Bruce's office door. She peeked through the glass, watching, listening, while I waited patiently for her to report back to me—in whispers, of course, as to who was doing what. That's how we did it every time we went spying on the good doctor and any guests he might be receiving. Little Margret on my shoulders, repeating who said what and how, until she managed to pry open the top window without so much as a single tiny squeak. Then down came Little Margret off my shoulders. From there we would share turns peeking in the gaping keyhole—which never worked as far as keylocks were concerned. Hence, if we were quiet enough we could hear every word said within Dr. Bruce's office. And so it was that day.

"Miss Gavin just wiped her face again with her fancy handkerchief," Little Margret told. "Now she's twisting a gold ring on her finger. Is she married?"

"Left hand, or right hand?" I asked, closing my eyes, picturing Doctor Bruce's thick, nightcrawler lips spraying Miss Gavin with each word he spoke. His sputters of spit weren't his fault by any means. Like most of us living at Pine Brook, Doctor Bruce also had his problems. He said it mattered not to him what he looked like, or sounded like, to those on the 'outside,'" he'd say patting his big burly chest with his large, over-sized hands emphasizing the meaning of, "inside, where it really counts." He said it helped him connect with those around him, "it's all here, inside and out none of us are perfect.

"We all have some form of abnormality. If we didn't, we would be round pegs trying to fit into a board full of square holes."

That was what Doctor Bruce reasoned with everyone coming through his doors.

"On her right." Little Margret held her hand up just to make sure. "Yep. That's right. Her ring is on her right hand."

"It's unfortunate that Pine Brook isn't equipped to give Camarilla the adequate education a young woman her age should have, especially in this new day and age."

Little Margret pulled away from the keyhole. "Your turn," she whispered. "She must be a widow," I said, as I put my eye to the hole. I could see Doctor Bruce reaching for his glass of water sitting on the edge of his desk.

"But who knows," he continued. "Maybe one day women will have the very same advantage to obtain an education as a man.

The way they are fighting for their rights I wouldn't be surprised to see that come true even in my own day."

He sipped his water, then blotted the age spots speckling his balding head.

"But putting all that aside, I have personally watched Camarilla grow into a rather bright young lady. I can assure you, we're all going to miss her."

I turned from the door's keyhole. It was Little Margret's turn. Within a moment or two she turned to me and laughed. "Looky... look..." she said, pulling herself away to let me see.

I stuck my eye against the keyhole, smothering the laughter inside my mouth with my hand, I watched Miss Gavin lean her bony body away from Doctor Bruce. She nearly choked with shock as he clamped his ample lips onto the rim of his water glass. His jowls jiggled and swayed with each dispirit gulp like a fat, round baby suckling from his mother's teat. Then, very gently, in a most sacramental manner, he placed the empty glass back on his desk.

Both Little Margret Jean and I had seen Dr. Bruce suckle not only glasses of water in such a manner, but sporty little cups of tea topped with shots of bourbon and other spirits, as well. All in secret, of course.

On dull days we would amuse each other with contests to see who could give a better performance of Doctor Bruce: Little Margret Jean, or me, Camarilla Berkelman.

Then, just like that, Little Margret turned serious as I. For she was hearing what I was.

"I have to be honest," Doctor Bruce was saying, "I wasn't sure if releasing Camarilla into your hands to become a caregiver was the ideal situation. However, after hearing you out about this Doctor Fitzgerald, I had to reconsider. It just might be best for her. And with his housekeeper there, I am sure Camarilla will not be overtaxed with work."

I heard him sigh as he poured himself yet another glass of water. "And for Pine Brook," he added, holding the pitcher for Miss Gavin.

"No, no thank you," she said, putting her hand over the rim of her glass. "I realize it must be hard for you to see her leave. But giving her a chance to further her trade is far better than having to turn her out onto the streets, isn't it? I mean, with no real need for her to be institutionalized that is what would happen, is it not, or—god forbid—worse. And yes, Doctor, Mrs. Thompson is looking forward to having Camarilla with her. A woman always enjoys another's company."

She darted her eyes about the dreary little office. "Be assured,

Doctor Fitzgerald's generous offer certainly will help not only Camarilla as you say, but Pine Brook as well. And just think how far she might be able to go in life learning under the Doctor's own personal care. Maybe one day she will become a nurse, or possibly even a doctor herself."

Miss Gavin's generous words must have been hindered by Doctor Bruce's fat earlobes, for he pushed my files to the side and narrowed his eyes into nothing more than mere slits. As if to reassure himself, he repeated (in his own terms) what Miss Gavin said.

"Well, Camarilla's situation certainly leaves me with no choice. With no physical abnormalities, and having no real psychological issues other than a mild case of Absorption Psychosis; or as laymen put it, she has an overactive imagination and a mild speech impediment. I have not enough legal grounds to keep her here, especially with no further funding of support. No, I'm afraid that the state just won't allow it. I could have lied and claimed she has more wrong with her than what...but I fear claiming that she is institutional bound for life will hinder her future in a worse way.

"Sad to say, they will not add a provision of any sort to include her on their payroll as a housekeeper. They claim if they do it for one, they would be bound to do so for all. I've tried everything." I watched him reach into his pocket and pull out a fresh, clean handkerchief. He wiped the sweat from his brow and frowned.

"Huston," he grumbled, folding his kerchief over, giving his forehead another sweep. "He's the one who should have given her the love and protection she needed. He could have given her a real home with all his money. But, no. Instead, he chose to dole it out to some institution for unnecessary mental health care while he ran all over kingdom come."

I was shocked at Doctor Bruce's words. For not once during my ten years living at Pine Brook did I hear him say one sour word about anyone, especially Huston. A pit of sick sank down into my stomach.

It burned. After all, I held no malice against Huston. How could I? He was my brother. Confused, I looked back inside the keyhole hoping what I heard was wrong.

Doctor Bruce opened his kerchief, searching its folds as if looking for any age spots that might have rubbed off from swabbing his forehead.

"Why, he'd send her care payments months in advance from all over the world promising he'd be here on a certain date to bring her home; but as those dates drew near, we would receive another advancement with yet another note excusing his absence. He was either one selfish son of a..."

Doctor Bruce looked down at the papers sitting on his desk. His face reddened. So did mine with anger and shock as he continued talking against Huston. I did not want to listen any longer, for I almost loved dear Dr. Bruce as I had my own father, and to hear him say such things against Huston broke my heart.

"Please excuse my tongue, Miss Gavin," he said. "Huston was running from something, that's for sure."

Miss Gavin tapped her finger against her pencil thin lips. It took her a minute or two before she spoke for she searched her words wisely. And I was relieved at what I heard. It was as if she knew I was outside the door wanting to speak out in Huston's defense but could not. She was doing it for me.

"Doctor, I understand your concerns," she began. "But perhaps Huston did try his best to be a responsible young man. After all, he was a young man, and having one's younger sister underfoot, well, more than likely, Huston himself simply couldn't deal with the death of their parents. After all, he and Camarilla were very fortunate coming out of that carriage accident alive."

"Yes!" I whispered a cheer repeating Miss Gavin's words. Little Margret Jean nodded smugly in agreement.

I watched Miss Gavin twist the gold band on her left hand. She was not a homely woman but rather plain and ordinary. Imagining the opposite sex finding her attractive was not impossible, but improbable. It had to be her sound and sensible attitude that would have drawn her a man, rather than her looks.

"It is rather strange how Huston ended up departing from this life in the same manner, isn't it?" she asked. "Carriage accident, traveling across Europe. Don't you think so, Doctor?"

Doctor Bruce looked down at my files and squeezed them, saying nothing but for the nod of his head.

"Anyway," Miss Gavin continued, "I have Camarilla's account set up to receive her stipends in a trust fund. She should do quite well." Doctor Bruce heaved a heavy sigh. "Yes, I know," he managed. "It is time to let her go. But there is one last thing, Miss Gavin," he said, giving her a grievously stern look. "If for any reason, any reason at all, Camarilla is unfulfilled, I expect you or Doctor Fitzgerald to contact me. Immediately. Are we clear on that?"

"Of course," Miss Gavin said, plucking the pen from Doctor Bruce's desk, signing the last of the agreement papers. "Of course.

CHAPTER FOUR

I inspected the coach Shamus sent Miss Gavin to fetch me with. It was older yet still fit and in good repair as also was the once fine doctor Shamus P. Its construction was good and solid made of thick wood, painted black, wiped down clean except where the neck high rubber tires rode through a mud puddle or two. A crimson spray of muck had splattered clear up to the gaslight along the carriage door. Miss Gavin saw the fret on my face. And I saw the accident. I could not help it. I knew it was only dried mud, but I saw it as blood. My parent's blood. Huston's blood. My blood. The blood that left me orphaned.

"This carriage is a Gentleman's Brougham carriage," Miss Gavin said encouraging me, reaching her white gloved hand down for me to take hold helping me into the cab. It looked like the hand of an Angel. An Angel I did not want to touch. Instead, I held tight to the shoebox I cuddled in my own hands, a small box filled with precious memories, some of which I remembered, some that I did not.

"It's alright Camarilla. This is an excellent carriage, a carriage designed for those who have had the privilege of obtaining a rather fair career, such as a medical physician like Doctor Fitzgerald," Miss Gavin explained. I held my shoebox even tighter. I stared at her hands and wondered how my father and mother's Angels' hands felt as they reached out to them that day they came and took them away, and Huston's on his last day on earth.

I wanted to tell Miss Gavin our carriage was also fit for a king, but did not. It was something I rarely talked of, the accident, that is. Along with God and His Angels, since I doubted their existence.

The horses were restless and whinnied. Their long black legs shifted anxiously causing Miss Gavin and her hand to move forward. I jumped backwards away from the sound of the creaking wood and horse hooves clumping about.

"Wait," Miss Gavin hollered down at me. "Netsel, he'll help you up."

I had no choice. After all, I had to get aboard and being only five feet-even, made the steel step much too high for me to attempt on my own.

I took a deep breath and held onto my straw 'sailor' hat left behind from a former patient. By no means was it fit for a queen. But with a few sewing notions and a most beautiful pheasant feather Nurse Price had given me, it wasn't half-bad. Not *Harper's Bazar* quality, but not bad at all. With that, I gathered my courage and looked up at Miss Gavin sitting inside the carriage.

Leather upholstery the color of, dark coffee-brown padded the cab's single seat and its ceiling and sides. Any sunlight finding its way through the front and side windows was instantly sucked up making the inside of the cab dark as its outside.

The flooring constructed of rich mahogany was small but not too tight, and to make it comfortable the seat held two folded blankets of soft black fur laid ready for use for what would be the chilly ride to Shamus'.

"Use your carriage step, Miss," a man's voice instructed behind me.

A pair of strong hands appeared from nowhere and firmly wrapped about my waist and lifted me effortlessly up. Miss Gavin grabbed my hand and tugged me inside. I stuck my head outside the carriage door and looked down at the man.

A very large and tall black hat rested on his slouched shoulders hiding his head and face. He glimpsed up at me revealing the face of what would have been considered a very good-looking older man, if not for what Nurse Price always called, "a pure shame," due to his ruddy complexion.

He had the same markings of so many of those his age. Nurse Price and Doctor Bruce referred to the dark, reddish little dips and dents scattered about his dark olive cheeks and forehead as scars of the Chicken Pox.

"It always leaves its mark either by death or on the face," they explained early on as I began questioning such appearances of those poor unfortunates coming into Pine Brook. For Netsel I was glad it was his face, and not death that marked him for I instantly liked him.

"Th-thank you, N-Netsel," I stammered, bashfully. I gave him a reassuring smile that said I truly understood the power of shame.

"You are much welcomed, Miss," he said, glancing at me, duplicating my smile.

Before he turned for the front of the rig, I winked at him confirming our new friendship. He winked back letting me know it was for sure a sealed deal.

I watched him walk away. He was no taller than what my grandfather had been, but not as round or nearly as soft. For Netsel was built stocky, and though older, was obviously still firm and very strong.

The horses recognized him and gave a soft whinny. His presence comforted them as well as myself.

Miss Gavin smiled gently, handing me a fur. I placed it on the seat next to her and sat down, closing my eyes. Taking a deep breath, I fondled my shoebox to calm myself. I heard a snap and opened one eye and peered at Miss Gavin who was pulling a lacy handkerchief from her floral tapestry purse dotted with fancy accents of tiny red glass beads. The hankie had been dipped in rose water, for the heavenly scent filled the small cab. She put the hankie to her nose and gave the tip of her nostrils a dainty little pinch, then delicately snapped the kerchief back inside her clutch. I knew one day I too would have a beautiful clutch and such wonderfully refined manners.

"Have you ever been to Timber Town," she asked knowing very well I hadn't. It was her way of filling in the empty spaces meant for speech and conversation.

I sat up tall and straight and looked out the side glass window of the cab. "N-no ma'am," I said. "I have not ever been to T-T-Timber Town."

Just as I got the words out, Netsel shouted, "Haa! Haa!" The horses gave a soft whinny as the ever so slight sound of leather slapped gently against their backs, jolting us forward. I held tight to my box as we rolled slowly ahead.

Yes, I was scared and unsure, yet a part of me was also so very excited and full of hope for a whole new future that was surely to be as bright and cheery just as Miss Gavin described to Doctor Bruce. But then I saw Nurse Price standing on the porch, her apron pulled to her eyes wiping away what I assumed were tears of mixed emotions. Both tears of pride for all she had done for me, and tears of grief one feels when having to let go of those we love. Her free hand rested protectively on Little Margret Jean's shoulder.

Little Margret waved ever so bravely over and over again as she held onto Mr. Hawthorn's invalid chair. He, being the good soldier, placed his army colonel's cap next to his heart whilst his other hand gave me an attentive salute. I pried my hands from my box and waved back; all the while my heart aching to not let go of not even one of them. But as Pine Brook's residents stood on that miserable old porch as if watching a parade march by, I knew I had to let them go. For in my mind, I also saw a procession of my many years living at Pine Brook. And as I took in my surroundings for the last time and sorted my thoughts, I welcomed the deep silence that came between me and Miss Gavin.

The institution seemed so small compared to when I first set foot on its grounds calling it home those some ten years before. The stately oak and walnut trees Little Margret Jean and I played in and walked among for countless hours seemed to have grown miraculously overnight. My eyes watered with tears that forced me to look away from those wonderful old trees and my odd little family, for if I hadn't, I might not have traveled on.

I so wanted to stop the lump in my throat from growing any larger. I tried distracting myself by softly blowing at the feather dangling from the rim of my straw hat. It worked for a while until I noticed that one of the most important persons in my life (up to that point) was nowhere to be seen. Doctor Bruce. I wanted to thank him one last time for all he had done for me, despite the fact he spoke so ill of Huston.

Why wasn't he there? I thought. *Him, of all people.*

"M-M-Miss Gavin, w-where is Doctor Bruce?" I asked, forcing the words up over the ball nuzzled tight in my throat.

"My dear, I assure you, Bruce is very upset with you leaving and he felt that perhaps it would be best if neither of you saw each other. He felt it would make it easier for both of you. I am sorry. Nevertheless, he wanted me to reassure you that you do have quite an excellent life ahead. And after a while it will be as if you had been with Shamus all your life. You'll see, I promise."

Once again, the quiet grew between me and Miss Gavin as we turned off the driveway and onto the main road. Spring Green was to the left. I traveled that road countless times with Nurse Price, taking our weekly shopping trips into town. To turn right seemed unnatural for it was never done before.

"Is-is it far? T-Timber Town?" I finally asked again despite the fact that I already knew.

“Yes, and no,” Miss Gavin quickly answered over the creaks and squeaks and groans of the carriage. The smell of her fine rose water was long gone. In its place, the spicy, crisp autumn air filled the coach’s cabin.

“It’s a full day’s ride,” she continued, anxious to fill the void of conversation. “We should arrive at the estate some time tonight.

Netsel doesn’t believe in overdriving his horses so we’ll be taking a few stops. And we girls can always use the stops to our advantage.”

She grinned at me and pulled out a box from under her foot-rest. With a girlish giggle she opened the small wooden container and pulled out a roll of very thin, damp, cottony paper.

“Wh-what is that?” I asked.

“This, dear Miss Camarilla, is called, toilet paper. It’s a fine paper doused in a solution of aloe-vera lotion. This particular brand was invented by Joseph C. Gayetty in 1857, to be exact. Quite expensive, you know. Doctor Fitzgerald was quite adamant that our trip be made as comfortable as possible.”

“Oh,” I said. “I have heard of it before, you know. I-I-I got to use it a few times actually. When w-w-we were still a family, when w-wwe visited my uncle in New York. But not with a-a-al, a-a-la verna.” I blushed wishing I hadn’t said anything.

“Aloe-vera, dear,” Miss Gavin corrected, staring mournfully at me with her small brown eyes. I knew she expected me to make one of two comments concerning my parents’ death and Huston’s. But I couldn’t. I just plain, outright could not. For them resting peacefully in the arms of our good Lord till his next arrival, with no worldly cares to toss and turn them about in their graves, hadn’t given me one ounce of condolence. The pastor that buried them came up with the idea, not me. And in that very same breath he told how Momma and Daddy were taken in order to be trained up to be one of God’s own angels. *Rubbish,* I thought. Pure unadulterated *rubbish.*

That’s when I started figuring things out for my own self. I figured if the Almighty needed them more than what I or Huston needed them, then I did not want Him, God. For He would be a weak God for doing so.

"Rags," I spat out, steering our conversation away from all that, and back onto the subject on hand. "That's what we used most back home." And that was all Miss Gavin was to get out of me.

Of course, I did care about high-priced paper soaked in some naturalistic medicine called aloe-vera used to clean certain parts of one's body after doing a certain deed. One day I would use nothing but. So I promised myself. And I made one other promise that day. To be like Miss Gavin.

I looked at her, so simple and plain, yet so very refined. A new sense rose inside me; I believe it was that strange twinge of the feeling of growing up.

And so, we rode on.

The bare branches of the trees lining the long straight road were a canopy of bare sticks. The morning sunlight danced among them catching my eye. Though I knew Pine Brook was well behind us, I still tried to hear Nurse Price and My Little Margret Jean and all the others shouting goodbye. None of that came. From that moment on, all the sounds and waves of farewell were to be played only in my memory.

I opened the lid of my box and stared inside. The contents made me both happy and sad at the same time. I was happy to have what was inside that little box, yet so very sad it was all I had. Still, I smiled and then shut it carefully, hugging it with my hands so Miss Gavin (who pretended to study the scenery instead of me) wouldn't see its contents or the note Nurse Price left me.

Dear old Nurse Price. She knew all along the importance of my shoebox and what it held for me. She made sure it was wrapped all nice and neat, and used what she called, 'the least usable and wasted page of the *Courier* newspaper.' I can't help but chuckle when I think back to it. Unbeknownst to me, she knew of my secret yearnings for obtaining high fashion. For the paper she used to wrap that miserable little box with was none other than, the fashion page. The note she left inside read:

'It will give you something to look at along the way, I suppose. Something other than your traveling partner, and all that dried up grass, and woods. And the behinds of those horses.

God Love you forever-

Nurse Price.'

I wondered if in Timber Town the sun was scattering its light, flickering in and out the tree branches. Different trees, different branches, *but it is the same sun after all,* I reasoned.

I focused on a great oak similar to the one Little Margret and I climbed and sat in. Our private tree. I blinked, hiding the tears once more slipping from my eyes.

"How-how far did you say it is to T-T-Timber Town?"

Miss Gavin patted her tight gray bun and adjusted her riding bonnet. Again, she twisted the gold band on her finger.

Again, she answered, "a full day's ride."

CHAPTER FIVE

If I close my eyes, now weary and worn, I can still see the trees rising in the distance on that late October day as we neared the good doctor's mansion on the northern outskirts of Timber Town. The trees, adequately undressed for late autumn, stood like black naked sticks against the dreary gray sky of October. Leaves that clothed the trees through summer had long ruptured into every imaginable color and now laid in their damp, chilly graves we call dirt and earth. But their death is different than any other. For, in death they do not smell of putrid rotting decay associated with the dead, nor encase our morbid and ghoulish thoughts that come creeping into our nightmares. Rather, the death of summer has a rich and full aroma of wild spices, and a sweet knowing that come spring, those crumpled brown leaves lying about the roots of the trees will serve a great purpose. To bring about life once again. And little did I know my purpose, my true purpose for serving Shamus, was like that of those deceased leaves.

"We're here," Miss Gavin said softly. It had grown dark, bringing the night's chill. She and I (and Netsel) had ridden along quite content watching, calling out names of birds and small forest animals scattering about the bare trees. I was sure by now they were nested deep within their burrows, drawing comfort and warmth from one another. I, on the other hand, had to be content with the fur Miss Gavin had given me. My nose tingled from the crisp air that had emerged with the risen moon, the same chill and bright harvest moon that belongs to all long, late autumn nights.

The horses whinnied, clearing their throats and nostrils. The clop of their hooves slowed the carriage to a full stop.

"Doctor Fitzgerald believes October to be the most forgotten month of all months," Miss Gavin said as she lit the cab's reading lamp next to her head. She peered into the mirror alongside the lamp and glanced at our reflections.

"Why, you look like a scared little raccoon," she said lightly. I snuggled deeper into my fur blanket not wanting to move. I wished the horses would have picked up their pace again if for just awhile longer. But I knew they would not. From what I had witnessed, I knew Netsel wouldn't force them to take another step until it was time to lead them to their stable. There, he would clean and blanket them and see them properly fed and watered before he would do the same for himself.

I listened to Miss Gavin blather on as to how well I would do for myself, and how wonderful everything was going to be, "with the help of the Doctor," of course.

The nervousness involved when meeting someone new flared a wave of queasiness inside my belly. Nevertheless, the meeting had to be done.

So, I put forth all the advice and preparation Nurse Price and Doctor Bruce had given me over the years for such occasions, which had been rare indeed.

Straightening myself, I pulled off the fur, tucked my shoebox under my arm, and put on my courage.

"We can wait a moment," Miss Gavin said, tucking the few gray hairs that had come loose back into her bun. "Netsel will help us off.

"Netsel," she called through the long communication tube connected between the cab and Netsel's seat. "Oh Netsel, would you mind bringing my traveling case, please?"

She hung up the rubber tubing and said in a low voice how Netsel would bring it but only after he first comforted the horses.

"Oh, he so does love those horses" she said, "He counts them as his own, you know. Like children almost. And as well he should. He is forever lecturing how we are all able to fend for ourselves, but animals cannot. Well, some can, but some can't. The ones we use to help us, anyway. Like horses and such. They can't. It's a shame how most creatures don't get treated as well as what he treats those horses." A thud on the ground from the front of the rig let us know Netsel had jumped off the driver's seat. The horses sneezed a few times in anticipation. For what Miss Gavin said was true. Indeed, he did walk to the front end and give the horses solace before bringing her travel case.

"Ee-ya, ee-ya," he comforted them, "We be home. Yup, we be home."

Within a moment, he was standing outside the carriage door, Miss Gavin's case in hand. She took it and thanked him. Through the low glow of the cab's gaslight, I watched as she preened herself in the mirror next to her head. Yes, she was a plain looking woman with nothing remarkable about her at all, except for her good manners, and gracious ways which caused me to admire her all the more besides her wonderful fashion sense.

She opened her hatbox, smiled, and pulled out *the* most magnificent bonnet I had ever seen in all my mere eighteen years of life.

It had three beautiful peacock feathers that floated this way and that in the air, like large blue-green eyes searching out their whereabouts. I stared at them, blowing at the plain brown pheasant feather flopped over the ridge of my straw hat. It rose for one glorious moment then plopped down resting on the side of my cheek showing just how lifeless my own wear truly was. For my wonderful straw hat hadn't enough spark to withstand even one day's carriage ride. I sighed. Instead of watching Miss Gavin groom herself, I looked out the carriage window and caught sight of my new home. I swallowed deep and hard.

For even under the harvest moon, I could see that the enormous house was beyond my imagination.

A cloud of silver fog floated like one massive ghost about the mansion's roof. I counted nine chimneys, each stack chugging out a haze of smoke that danced with the sweet smell of wood burning in the fireplaces below within the mansion. All but a few windows of the mansion's three floors shone bright from the gaslights within. Needless to say, it looked ever so warm and inviting.

"Jeepers-Creepers," I said, not able to contain myself.

"It is impressive, isn't it?" Miss Gavin answered with such pride as if she herself owned it. She pulled out two fresh pairs of plain white gloves from her purse.

"Doctor Fitzgerald, he...the Doctor understands..." She looked down at the gloves. Her thin lips tightened. "No, I'm sorry, there is no other way to say it. And I do apologize for that. But Doctor Fitzgerald, bless his heart, understands the underprivileged. He's seen plenty of its consequences in his day, but he will not tolerate a woman being, being, well, being what he considers under-dressed."

She held up the gloves. I stared at them wanting nothing more than to feel them on my hands.

"You have to understand Camarilla, he is older and from a different generation. He's a bit, well, Victorian as many men his age are, not like the younger, more modern Edwardian men coming up in society. But Shamus is delightfully so. You'll see."

I wanted to tell her I was not at all upset concerning the implications of her statement, but rather delighted. I wanted to tell her how simple, girlish pleasures of style were far from Pine Brook's means for such attire, and that I appreciated the doctor's generosity. And due to such generosity, it would be the first time I was to wear real dress gloves since I was a child. But, minding my manners and preferring not to sound one bit ungrateful for Pine Brook's upbringing, nor to sound desperate for a few luxuries, I kept my thoughts to myself.

Miss Gavin gently flagged the gloves. I took them, placing them on my lap just as she had done, and as I remembered Mother doing with hers. One last time she straightened her hat with its wonderful peacock feathers then slipped on her gloves. I did the same to my own hat, lopsided feather or not. Miss Gavin smiled. I smiled too, slipping on my new gloves.

"Well now," she said with a breath-filled sigh. "Are we ready for you to meet Doctor Shamus P. Fitzgerald?"

And so it was, under that bright October moon that Miss Gavin and I walked up the brick path leading to the front porch of the mansion.

We journeyed up a flight of steps and stood on the porch. It was a fine porch. And unlike most, it appeared to be surrounded with white picket guard slats.

Two gaslights blazed strongly on each side of the door. A deep floral design forged within its thick golden oak showed the owner had wealth. I found it odd we were not using the back entrance in the usual manner as I heard Nurse Price tell her tales of hired help rules. So, I inquired Miss Gavin of it.

"It's not customary for all hired help to enter a home via the back door," she said, watching herself fidget with her hat in the door's glass window. “Not here in America anyway. That’s more of a British thing. Most domestic’s rules are British, you know, not American. Although

Shamus does enjoy a good many of them.”

She looked out into darkness. Except for the contented whinnying of Netsel’s horses in the distance filling the quiet, it was the same darkness of night swaddling Pine Brook. I could barely make out the full size of the stable, though I could tell it was much closer to the mansion than our stable, and cleaner. For the smell of manure did not linger in the air.

“Look, it’s snowing,” Miss Gavin said.

I turned my face upward. Chilled flakes of delicate white fell on my face.

“Netsel will be coming soon with our baggage. I assume he’ll be as tired as we from such a long day. And hungry.” “Y-y-yes, I suppose he w-will,” I stammered.

A plaque sat under the gas-lamps next to the door.

I ran my finger along its inscription written in gold with the strictest of precision:

Shamus P. Fitzgerald, M.D.

Nora R. Fitzgerald Nurse

Nurse Society of Philadelphia

I had not seen a display announcing one’s self to the world since the plaque attached to my uncle’s small timepiece shop in New York City. I shall never forget the writing on his simple, stone business plaque:

Green Door Original Timepieces

Established 1865

Edward Olson, Proprietor

With the remembrance came my mother’s screams that filled my head. I pushed them away and concentrated on the gold lettering in front of me.

"H-h-his wife..." I said, reaching out touching her name. "Nora, Nora R. Fitzgerald."

"Nurse Price told me a-about the N-Nurse S-Society of Philadelphia and how if sh-she would have had a way to attend sh-she s-s-so would had done so very w-willingly."

"Yes. Yes, Nora did." Miss Gavin answered. "Shamus informed me that the Philadelphia School of Nursing was the only school of nursing on the whole continent of the United States of America, leaving it the only formal source of learning the true art of nursing. But there were three other means to learn the craft. Under a medical physician, or an already practicing nurse. Or the other not so desirable method: self-taught, with all the trials and errors and horrors thereof."

"Th-that's what Nurse Price told me, t-t-too."

I knew Doctor Bruce was right in placing me as a caregiver at that wonderful huge mansion under the direction of someone as wealthy and remarkable as Doctor Shamus P. Fitzgerald, instead of being cut loose to serve some undocumented landlord, or worse.

It behooved me to think of all the intelligent young women (and men) performing duties much beyond a normal day's work for pay so little and meager; their room with board hidden away in some obscure room. Their labor too many times gone unnoticed unless not done at all. Complaints oftentimes ending with an unfortunate ear-tossing into the streets.

I read the inscription on the plaque again. And I was glad.

Miss Gavin peered through the door window and pressed the doorbell. The brass push was large and wide enough to fit not one but two of her skinny fingers into its debit. The low tone of the bell's gong echoed inside the mansion. Miss Gavin straightened herself, nodding for me to do the same.

No one answered. She rang the bell again. Still nothing.

"I don't understand why Mrs. Thompson hasn't responded," she said, giving the bell another push. She looked in the window for clues of life inside. She waited a moment, maybe three and then opened the door herself. We stepped inside the vestibule; the door clicking shut behind us.

The greeting area was nice sized, and its flooring helped ease my nervousness. I recognized a bit of home. Tiles set in geometric shapes of greens and reds, yellows and oranges were every bit as vivid and bright as Spring Green's one fancy housewares shop Nurse Price and I visited, 'just to see,' what was new when we went to town for supplies. It was the only shoppe with such flooring. For all others were planked with wood, worn and tired.

On the other side of the vestibule a set of double doors led into the mansion. They were shut tight.

"Shamus surely should have heard the bell as well as Mrs. Thompson," Miss Gavin said with certainty. "That's why I do find it very curious that she hasn't met us. She always greets the guests when they arrive. Shamus would have it no other way."

She opened the doors slowly. They creaked. She peered past the doorway and into the first room. It was just as silent inside the mansion as the outside.

"Mrs. Thompson...Mrs. Thompson..." Miss Gavin yelled into the quiet. "Shamus..."

She waited, then stepped into the main part of the room flagging her hand for me to join her.

"Razzle-Dazzle!" I whispered, holding my hat on top of my head as I looked about the place. "Razzle-Da-dazzle," I repeated.

Indeed. It was simply a wonderful, fine and true mansion. The sweet smell of wood burning in the fireplaces and savory beef roasting in the kitchen fingered our nostrils.

We seldom afforded such rousing meats as pot roast at Pine Brook except on holidays and special occasions, which were few and far between.

Miss Gavin motioned for me to sit on the warming bench across from a small fireplace situated on the left wall, an area large enough to be considered a vestibule all its own. I did as instructed, letting the heat of the hearth warm me. Unbuttoning my coat, I took notice of a stairway some feet down and to the right. A most elaborate stairway it was with rich mahogany wood and fancy rails carved to match the filigree on the doors outside. My eyes followed the steps leading up not one, not two, but three storied landings.

It was there in the ceiling that hung a most insanely beautiful chandelier. Though unlit, it was large enough to catch the light radiating from the gas lamp burning on the knowle on the very top landing. Its crystals glistened and sparkled giving enough brightness for me to see what I assumed was the hall were the servant's bedrooms were. And my heart sank, for though surrounded by the very finest living the year 1897 could offer, I was reminded of my position and why I was there.

"Mrs. Thompson must be upstairs preparing your room," Miss Gavin said, looking up at the lamp on the third floor knowle.

"M-my bedroom... w-w-way up there?"

"Oh, yes, of course. In the kitchen there's a back entrance to the floors upstairs," Miss Gavin said peering at herself in the gilded mirror above my head.

"You will use that back entrance along with Netsel," she said, primping this way and that, fidgeting with her hair.

"I just can't imagine why Mrs. Thompson hasn't come down." She took a final glance at her reflection, nodding for me to do the same. I faced the mirror and removed my poor old hat, now wilted as the day I found it. Like Miss Gavin, I gave my finger a quick lick and slicked down the wild strands of my own wandering hair, then wiped a smudge of soot off my cheek from the carriage lamp.

"This place certainly is large enough for us simple working folks to find it enchanting," Miss Gavin said, looking up to the third floor again. The gaslight on the knowle was still aglow.

"Perhaps a bit too large. Unfortunately, you'll find it does get twice as cold as a normal home this size, even though it has a total of nine fireplaces. It's built on top of a hillside, you know. The highest spot in Timber Town to be exact."

Miss Gavin looked past the archway of the vestibule and into the hall leading to the other half of the mansion.

"I just can't imagine why Mrs. Thompson hasn't come down.

"Camarilla," she said softly, "Shamus asked that I not say a word concerning, your, your, well... your overactive imagination. But I'm afraid I must. I hope it doesn't upset you. But as you can see, this home is certainly large enough with ample room for even the soundest of minds to conjure up a bit of fiction within its many shadows. I do hope you understand what I am saying to you."

No sooner had Miss Gavin said that when a slow, creak-creak-creaking could be heard making its way down the hall toward Miss Gavin and me. She straightened her blouse and skirt and looked at me to do the same.

"Perfect," she said twisting the gold band on her finger. "We are perfect, just as Shamus likes."

The creaking continued. With each rhythmic rotation of the wheels, his medicine chair became louder. "I-Is that him?" I asked, my voice shaking.

"Oh, come now," Miss Gavin scolded, a smile crossing her face. "Don't be so nervous. Before long the two of you will be old friends. You'll see. I've yet to be wrong about these things."

Taking hold of my shoulder she walked me to the middle of the vestibule. There were rooms to my left, and rooms to my right, and a few directly ahead lining each side of the wide hallway. Some doors were open, and some not. It was all very elaborate and filled with treasures begging to be discovered.

My stomach fluttered and tightened. Shamus was getting closer.

"Now, just remember what I taught you. Offer your hand limply to him first and let him take it. Then, without holding his fingers or hand, follow his handshake. Then say, 'thank you,' and give a slight curtsy. Let him lead the conversation, and us, into whatever room he chooses.

"Oh, you'll do fine, just fine," she said, squeezing my shoulder for reassurance just as Nurse Price had done to Little Margret Jean that very morning. "He's probably just as nervous as you are. Here he is now."

The eeking of his chair filled the vestibule then stopped. Miss Gavin, pushing me gently forward cleared her throat to remind me to express my manners.

Then ever so meekly, ever so shy, I looked up from the gray marbled floor and into the face of Shamus P. Fitzgerald. *Doctor* Shamus P. Fitzgerald. Miss Gavin standing straight and tall like the good servant she was, nodded for me to take Shamus' hand.

He looked straight at me, almost through me with his clear, ice-blue eyes. Grasping my fingers he moved them lightly up and down.

Though confined to his invalid chair, I could see he was a tall man of at least six foot-three. He was aged. But his hair and bearded face were perfectly groomed like freshly picked white soft cotton, framing his surprisingly handsome face. He didn't carry the scent associated with the elderly. The dull mothball odor mixed with one's personal unhygienic scent was nowhere detected. I was relieved.

I hadn't seen many men dressed in his manner, like that in the latest dapper apparel advertised in *The Courier*. His clothing was much too neat and tidy even for the finest business men coming and going up and down the main street of Spring Green. His shirt, day vest, and trousers were meticulous. Not one wrinkle or signs of thread worn shown. A black and red plaid lap-blanket covered his legs. The fringes dangling from its sides hung in perfect straight rows.

“Miss Gavin. I’m sorry,” he said in a rushed panic, dismissing me and my hand. “Please do forgive me. I am so very sorry.” The strength of his voice took me by surprise.

“What pray tell is ever the matter?” she asked.

Shamus shook his head, running his long fingers through his white cotton hair. The ticking of the grandfather’s clock in the parlor room to our left was the only sound to be heard as we waited for his answer.

“Come now,” Miss Gavin finally urged. “What possibly might have happened that we cannot fix?”

“It seems I’ve lost, err, misplaced Mrs. Thompson.”

Miss Gavin looked up at the third floor and groaned.

“I do hope she’s...feeling well, she is a bit older,” she whispered to me. “Perhaps I should check on her.”

“I heard that, Miss Gavin,” Shamus snapped. “I must say that I do not appreciate such comments. I am quite capable of taking care of myself, and Mrs. Thompson. I am a doctor, am I not? Besides, I already sent Patsy to inspect the situation. He assures me he found nothing. Not even Mrs. Thompson.”

“Of course,” Miss Gavin said. “I do beg your forgiveness. Now, why don’t you tell me what happened. From the beginning.”

‘*Patsy?*’ I thought. I wanted to ask who Patsy was but I dared not. Any further questioning would only agitate the already delicate situation. Besides, I knew I would find out soon enough.

“Oh, I don’t know where to begin,” Shamus said, his demeanor calming. “This is hardly the proper introduction I had planned. Please, can you forgive me?”

“Of course. There is nothing to forgive. Shamus, no one can misplace another person, especially a full-grown woman. Perhaps she went to fetch more wood for the fireplaces, or maybe she went to put more coal in the furnace.”

“No-no-no!” Shamus snapped, resting his head against his fisted hand. "Netsel had plenty in place, and then some. I tell you, Mrs. Thompson was here one moment, and the next she was, well, gone. Last I saw of her she was upstairs getting Little Mademoiselle's room readied. She never came down." Shamus gave a look of that of a child who had lost his puppy. "She'll be back," he whimpered. "She promised."

"Yes, I am sure she will." Miss Gavin said, nodding to me as if I too should reassure Shamus that indeed Mrs. Thompson was still there in the mansion. Somewhere. I wanted to tell him about Uncle Edward and how he would disappear from time to time. But I did not. It was too soon to discuss my own personal matters, especially disappearing family members, and especially at such a time as his Mrs. Thompson's own disappearance.

Shamus turned his blue eyes at me. They were a magnificent, clear blue. I no longer feared him but found him soft and fragile. I had the urge to console him.

Miss Gavin tapped the point of her shoe on my ankle encouraging me to take a step forward. I did and then curtsied.

"Yes, I-I-I am sure sh-sh-she will," I stuttered.

"Yes, yes... no doubt. I am confident she shall have no trouble finding her way back," Shamus said, wringing his hands. "Her brain might not be a high quality of intellectual matter, but her sense of determination and loyalty does make it highly probable that she shall return, and fully intact. But I am saddened to have to declare that her sudden departure leaves us all with quite a quandary, I'm afraid."

"Ye-yes sir," I said, stepping a bit closer to Shamus. "B-but if I may, wh-what exactly is the trouble?"

He said the next three words as if his heart was truly broken. "The pot roast."

'Jeepers-Creepers,' I thought. "The pot roast?"

He repeated the words. "Yes. The pot roast," he moaned, knotting his fist, thrusting it high above his head in exasperation. "Burnt, burnt to a crisp." His hand landed on his lap with a soft thud on his blanket. He looked away showing total disgust.

"The whole thing is charred...charred beyond any hope." Miss Gavin stifled her giggles.

"R-really?" I asked politely as possible. "M-may I see it, please?"

The clock in the parlor ticked and tocked as loud as Shamus' hesitation.

"Well," I said. "D-doctor B-Bruce always said, nothing and no-no-one is beyond hope."

Shamus sighed and turned the wheels on his chair. "I forgot to tell you," Miss Gavin whispered in my ear as we followed Shamus down the hall to the kitchen. "Shamus has a bit of a, well, shall we say he has a melodramatic side to him."

Shamus' chair stopped suddenly.

"Miss Gavin, why must I continue to inform you that it is my legs that do not work, and not my ears?"

"Yes, so sorry, dear. Please forgive me," she said a smile crossing her face.

Shamus huffed, grabbing the wheels with extra hard shoves, forcing the medicine chair forward.

I itched with curiosity, wanting to investigate each sitting room we passed as we made our way. The kitchen was no different. As we entered it, I gasped.

"Razzel-Dazzel," I said under my breath. "Razzel-Dazzel!"

It was quite large and doubled the size of Pine Brook's kitchen and with more modern accessories than I had ever imagined existed. I thought of Nurse Price and how she would especially enjoy such a wonderful work area with such ample space.

"So nice and clean, tidy, just like Mrs. Thompson," Miss Gavin said with high satisfaction.

"Not now, Miss Gavin," Shamus snapped. "We have a much more important task at hand."

Lifting a wobbly finger he pointed at the most ridiculously ornate cook stove I had ever seen. It was gorgeous, simply and purely gorgeous. And on top its burners sat a smoldering cast iron kettle.

"There," Shamus said, his voice shaky as his hand. "It's right there."

I looked past Miss Gavin and all the widgets and gadgets and made my way to the mess on the stove. I grabbed a cooking cloth from the table to protect my hands from the heat of the roasting kettle.

"Oh. I-I-see," I stammered, lifting its lid, peering inside. "I-I've had this happen plenty of t-times. Don't w-w-worry, all is not lost."

"Well, I don't know if that is a good thing or not," Shamus said, wilting in his chair. "If you have that happen as much as you say."

"Oh, i-it's a good thing, s-s-sir. N-nurse Price always encouraged me to make a-a-a-as many mistakes as p-p-possible. She said th-th-that way she could teach me what to do in m-m-most cases. Just like this one. There's a lot a person can do."

"Nurse? Did you say, a nurse? A nurse taught you?" "Y-yes sir. Nurse Price. Sh-she taught me lots of things." He put his hands out to me.

"Miss Gavin," he said. "Will you please do the honor of giving us a proper introduction?"

"Yes, of course," Miss Gavin said with a smile. "Of course."

That was one of the longest days in my life up to that point (besides when I lost my mother and father, and the day I received news of Huston's passing).

Despite how tired and nervous I was (and thanks to Nurse Price's enduring patience and Mrs. Thompson's well stocked shelves) I did manage to save that awful pot roast from certain disposal that night.

We sat down to a half dismal, but tasty meal. And I am happy to report, I heard no complaints. I served beef shavings in milk gravy with hot biscuits on the side. If anything, we did not go hungry, nor did we eat gruel. Not that night.

And as it turned out, it seemed Mrs. Thompson had gone the extra mile before her abrupt departure and seen to it that Miss Gavin was well cared for, and I made welcomed. Miss Gavin was given a most luxuriant guest room on the second floor and I, surprisingly, was very well suited on the third.

But by the next day, I was certain beyond any rationalization that Shamus would realize his mistake taking me in as his caregiver. Not due to my performance per se, for saving that miserable roast won him over, as did my being trained by a real nurse, but for the fact that I did indeed put up a slight protest concerning my strong distaste for

Shamus' close and special companion. A companion Miss Gavin seemed to have forgotten to mention. Patsy.

CHAPTER SIX

As I recall, that first morning serving Shamus I had woken when still dark, as was my habit. To my delight, the strong odor of rubbing alcohol and all such smells confined to places such as Pine Brook and other institutions, was absent. Instead, I woke to the scent of heavenly fresh, early morning air seeping from a crack in the window across my room. Along with the sweet smell came the long-lost sounds of nearly forgotten melodies. Hidden in the tree branches outside my window came the merry chirps and callings of the earliest of all morning birds. No windowless concrete walls held their mirthful songs at bay as at Pine Brook. To me it was all miraculous.

I would soon learn mornings at Shamus' were different from those of Pine Brook. No clanks, no bangs, no early morning screeches from Molly May Junction, or the strange sound of Mr. Hawthorn milling about the hallways. And unfortunately, no Little Margret Jean scampering barefooted into the bathroom before I had time to even open one sleepy eye.

The clock ticked on my nightstand. I stretched, my hands slapping the hardwood of the headboard of my new bed. It was huge, huge as Shamus and everything else in the manor.

I wholeheartedly declared my room was not at all what I had

expected. And I was delighted. More than delighted. I was ecstatic and so badly wished for Margret Jean to be at my side for us to enjoy it together. For it was nothing at all compared to the tales Nurse Price told and that of some of the poor, unfortunates passing through Pine Brook. They claimed their temporary madness was due to enduring wicked living and work conditions. Small, dreadful rooms with nothing but tiny, squat beds with just room enough to lay. And if by sheer chance a worker (male or female) came across an employer generous enough to provide a small dresser and chair, they were lucky, and the envy of the neighborhood. Some might even say blessed. Not I of course; for not being a praying woman I could never make such a claim.

Many testified no heat was provided except for what little seeped through the floorboards. "*Too costly*, the landowners claimed," Nurse Price stated more than once. "Besides, a luxury such as warmth encourages the employee to linger in one's room instead of providing service. All true thoughts for most British and other European countries," she'd tell me and Little Margret Jean. "But not the majority in America. America. Truly the land of the free."

I listened to the clock ticking on my nightstand as I sat on the edge of my bed. I fumbled for the box of matches Mrs. Thompson placed there for me. I struck one and lit the oil lamp. '*5:30 a.m.*' the hands on the clock showed.

My room was overly large, and comfortably empty except for the bed, dresser, vanity and a rocking chair all my own for after a long hard day of work. I had my own fireplace, which I was free to use at any time I wished. Wood, I found out, as well as coal for the basement furnace, would be provided and well stocked by none other than Netsel.

It sure will come in handy in the dead of winter, I thought, feeling the cold, smooth wooden floor under my bare feet as I shuffled over to my steamer chest. True to Miss Gavin's word, Netsel did indeed carry it up for me the previous night *after* he had attended to his horses. Like they, I was thankful for the bulk of his muscles for his age. For to deliver such a massive piece would have been a struggle even for a young man of regular stature.

So it was that first morning. And the first time I met the mansion's most peculiar resident. Shamus' friend. His best friend of all. The one Miss Gavin had forgotten to tell me about.

I opened the drawer to my new dresser and placed in the last handful of my undergarments (or as we referred to them in those days, under-linens). The night before, I was smart enough to adhere to Nurse Price's suggestions and hung the few waist-blouses and skirts I owned.

"It will help reduce the need to spend any more time than necessary to re-iron them," she tutored, during one of the tedious tasks I learned to master early on thanks to her. Ironing. *The most* tedious of all chores.

I wasn't sure if I was invited to use the indoor flushing toilet on the first floor next to Shamus' room as last night, or perhaps Miss Gavin's in the second-floor guest room. It was October so I knew there would be a heavy morning frost waiting for me, and Netsel in the outhouse. Just so there was no misunderstanding, I decided to use the fancy pedestal chamber pot hidden modestly in the far corner away from the rest of the room. Careful not to water stain the decorative tapestry woven on the lid, I covered it with a handkerchief I had tucked away in my dresser. I was especially quick so I could wash, dress and review the "Daily Maintenance Guide," Miss Gavin provided me.

It was typical. Much like the one at Pine Brook: Remove cold ashes from cook stove, set damper and add new kindling; wash the dishes, sweep and wash floors, carpet sweep or beat rugs as needed, wipe all gas-lamps; trim or replace wicks as needed; wash soot from windows...

Prepare meals: Promptly due at 7:00 am o'clock, 12:00 o'clock noon, Tea at 4:00 pm o'clock, supper 7:00 pm o'clock sharp-no exceptions...

I re-read Miss Gavin's roster concerning the meal schedule. '*Tea? Had I read that correctly? Tea at 4:00 pm?*'

We never had a Tea at Pine Brook, not in the formal sense anyway. Embarrassed or not, I was left with no alternative but to ask Miss Gavin how I should go about serving a Tea. Especially in *Shamus'* most perfect manner, of course.

I sat on my bed pondering how I might go about asking Miss Gavin such a thing without seeming ignorant of such class matters. And as I did, I fondled my new standard issue of dress. It was a lovely uniform without a shade, or stitch of Pine Brook gray anywhere. Which meant no more gravy and what-not stains on dull, faded gray and white. Instead, I would adorn a navy-blue uniform with a sturdy white bibbed apron with, *ruffles!* Real honest to goodness ruffles. I was so excited about those darn ruffles that I put it into my mind to tell Little Margret Jean and Nurse Price all about them as soon as possible. I would also have to tell Nurse Price how she was right all along. No matter the color, no matter how large or small, no matter how nice and neat they appeared, ruffles were not soft and light. For they truly were nothing more than overly starched, overly heavy, tethered pieces of cloth no matter how nice and neat they appeared.

"Yes, Nurse Price was right.," I sighed. "They are like cardboard as she claimed. Nevertheless, they were ruffles. And I refuse not to love them."

I picked up the shoebox from the nightstand and opening it I took out the few photographs I had of Huston and me, and my mother and father. We looked so young, and happy. Though it was not proper for one to smile during a formal session, the curve of Huston's lips did tug upward. He must have held that slight smirk for quite some time. Normally it took a photographer about five minutes to complete his task of picture taking.

That was my favorite photograph of all, the one with Huston's mischievous grin. Oh, how my heart yearned for him, and Mother and Father. I tried recalling their voices in my head. But alas, they were no longer there. I wondered. If not for the photographs would their faces have dissolved from my memory also?

I ran my finger against the tin plate, following the ribbon of hair the color of molasses that flowed past my shoulders. I was six years old, and my hair was long and dark, heavy with waves.

"I remember that dress," I said out loud. "It was one of my favorite dresses."

Though my dress was a magnificent shade as that of Shamus' sapphire blue eyes, the picture plate showed it as every possible shade of black and gray. Pleats ran down the front bodice, then round the side and to the very back; my shoes made from the same material had the prettiest little pink roses embroidered on the tops.

I looked down at my own shoes, black and so plain.

"Well, I-I don't have anywhere special to go," I chuckled, clicking them together. "Nope. Nowhere special."

I sighed, and putting the tin plate to my lips I kissed Huston, and then Mother and then Father. "We-we'll visit again," I told them placing them back into the shoebox. I glanced at the other pictures and picked up the one that held the image of the other family, the one that I did not know. They stood on a seaside, happy and gay, arms wrapped proudly around one another. The man wore a sea captain's cap, the others in finery suitable for a day at the beach.

All was content in their world for I imagined any worries that might had plagued the family were tossed into the ocean and carried off by the waves. A woman, a man and two older children, a brother and his sister. I talked to them as I did every time I held them in my hands.

"I do wish I knew who you all were, or perhaps still are. Mother and Father never said. Long lost cousins, I suppose. "One day I shall name each one of you. But not now. Another time. I shall visit you all another time. I promise."

I placed the lid on the box and finished dressing. I checked myself in the full-length mirror.

"Nice," I said, swishing my front side to back side. "Very, very nice." And so was my form.

My uniform was of good quality, heavy and a tad shorter than what I was accustomed to, coming clear up to the middle of my calves. My white stockings were wonderfully fashionable yet concealed my legs properly from the temptations of any improper glances. I pinned the little white cap onto my head, proudly calling it, "*my crowning glory.*"

And so, with oil lamp in hand, I stepped from my bedroom out into the hallway foyer. Mine was the very first room on the third floor, located directly across from the staircase leading down into the kitchen. Then came Nora's room, the one with the green door. Then

Netsel's. Across from our rooms were another row of doors. Six rooms total. None of which Miss Gavin had explained to me except my room, of course, and Netsel's, and in a dark tone she nervously rattled off a warning concerning Nora's room. Like all green doors, I was expected to stay away from it, "except if invited to enter."

Nora's room. I suppose I shouldn't tell too much concerning Nora's room. Not now anyway. For you shall discover the perils of her room soon enough. Just as I had since Miss Gavin was of no help concerning the issues beyond it. Even though I did inquire about it, just as nice and polite and mannerly as I could.

"Miss Gavin," I had said, "if I may, w-why does Miss Nora's private room have, The Green Door, and since it is a Green Door why is it on the th-th-third floor and not on the s-s-second floor or even the f-first floor as Green Doors n-n-n-normally are?

"A-a-and if I'm not imposing, might I also ask why is it a r-r-room, and not a hallway leading to the living area r-rooms?" That's what I asked her. All proper questions I assumed.

"Well, Camarilla," she replied, her tiny eyes popping open as wide as they could. I could tell she was relieved I had asked. Her sigh wasn't long and exhausted, but short and light.

"Shamus has no other door in this whole place painted green. This is the only one and he forbids anyone from entering. It was Nora's sewing room, her private hideaway. You must never enter it. That is why it is painted green."

Miss Gavin whispered so low and hushed I bent close to hear her. "This...this is Shamus' Green Door. Do you understand?"

I stared at the seriousness of her face. I swallowed and shook my head in agreement even though I had no more of an understanding than when I first asked.

I knew all manors with servants had a Green Door. And I knew no servants were allowed to open them to catch even a peek of what laid beyond, unless they were assigned to do so. And, even then, once on the other side of the door and into the household's living quarters, they were not permitted to come into contact with the residents of the home.

"They must never be seen or heard. They scamper quickly about to do their chores before their Masters and Mistresses are to enter. Poor devils. Lagging for a moment could cost them their jobs. Even when due not to their own hands. Poor devils." That's what Nurse Price told me every so often as we lollygagged about Pine Brook, keeping moderate pace with our mops and buckets of bleach water.

'Course them Green Doors are primarily in the upper crust homes in England and Britain and such. We have no worries of them here in the good old United States of America. Well, not unless the owners have an extra bone of snobbery borned inside them.'

Nurse Price's words, though spoken so long ago have never faded from my mind, nor did any of her lessons.

I held the lamplight up through the dimness of the hallway and looked at the door and studied it. It was just a door like all others but painted green.

Being on top of the staircase, the ceiling of the mansion was only ten feet above my head, and so hung the chandelier. Seeing it from that viewpoint was quite different then from the vestibule.

It was much larger than what it appeared to be, and even more magnificent. The light from the gaslamp blazed across its crystals causing them to reflect and sparkle against the ceiling like a ballet of tiny shards of frozen rainbows.

I peeked down the banister and recalled Nurse Price's instructions concerning such matters.

'Servants are forbidden to use the main staircase. The only time they are to be on them is to dust and clean them. That's how I was taught. However, here in the States, things are different. But to be safe, ask before you so much as step a toe on even one step. Promise to mind me.'

Keeping my promise to good old Nurse Price to do my best (and of course to Miss Gavin) I turned from the staircase and the chandeliers' delightful, glistening charms of display. I would use the same staircase Netsel and I used the night before.

I followed the steps downward to the kitchen, the curve and length between each stair gave just enough bounce to my step giving me a sense of regalness. I held the lamp high in the air, descending to the second floor, then the first.

The kitchen was empty and to my surprise was already warm. It being ever so quiet caused me to think of Nurse Price and Little Margret Jean and how I would miss our morning chatter.

I hastened to the ash box next to the stove, ready to clear out the ashes, now cold from the night before. It caused me no great alarm to do so for it had been one of my many assigned jobs back home at Pine Brook.

On a hook attached to the wall behind the stove's chimney was a cast iron cinder-scoop. Alongside it, the pot-mitt. I put it on and bent down and opened the ash gate and peered inside ready to scoop. But no ash was to be had for the ash box was clean. It was apparent while Doctor Fitzgerald, Miss Gavin, and I slept, Netsel had been busy with not only his own morning chores but mine as well.

The morning fire was set and ready for me to tend to breakfast. Again, I thought of Nurse Price and Little Margret and wondered how they were getting on. I tried putting them out of my mind and pulled Miss Gavin's menu from my apron pocket. I went into the pantry and began gathering all that I needed.

It was the basic everyday breakfast served at Pine Brook and one's personal homes, of fish, wheat cakes, and eggs, all washed down with steamy cups of hot cocoa. But Shamus, being Shamus, insisted a few more items be added: bacon, fruit pie, cornmeal mush, biscuits and gravy along with fried potatoes.

That would be the main breakfast I would prepare as long as I was with the doctor.

But alas, I would soon discover I would be preparing most of the meals for Netsel and myself. Not Shamus. He ate well, but unlike Doctor Bruce, Shamus was able to satisfy his appetite in meager portions of one or two limited selections.

It turned out Mrs. Thompson was a good housekeeper. Her ability to keep her pantry well stocked and organized helped cut the need for searching items and ingredients. I easily found the batter bowl and was just about done retrieving the last bit of ingredients when a certain movement caught my attention. It was studying me. And I was frightened. Glimpsing from the corner of my eye I knew it was not human. Out of fear I knew I dasen't look directly at it.

The creature appeared to be a foot and a half tall, no larger, and covered in what appeared to be black feathers. Then, just like that, it flashed out the kitchen disappearing into the hall. I opened my mouth to scream. That's when Netsel came in, arms full of wood.

“I bring more wood for you,” he said, rolling the splintered chunks into the wood box next to the stove.

I stayed in the pantry staring at the hall entrance.

“Miss? You okay, Miss? You want the lamps lit? It will be daylight soon. Maybe I light the ones in the hall for Mr. Shamus and Miss Gavins’.” He took off his hat and fumbled its rim, waiting for my reply. “You okay Miss?”

“Y-y-yes; th-thank you, Netsel,” I managed, not sure if I should tell him about the little black feathery thing hiding in the hall. “Netsel...”

“Yes Miss?” He continued mulling his hat.

“Do you know i-if, i-if, if Shamus prefers apricot preserves o-o-r th-the raspberry?”

“Either Miss. But I appreciate the raspberry myself,” he said giving me a hopeful look. He shuffled off to the hallway, hat in hand.

“Th-thank you, Netsel,” I called. *Hurry, run,* I shouted in my head wishing he would move quicker and not at the moderate pace he used wherever he went.

It is early, I told myself, grabbing a jar of raspberry preserves, hoping he might catch the black thing, if it were even real.

It could have been anything...a speck of ash or dust or soot floating past my eyes...maybe it was nothing more than my imagination.

I stepped from the pantry and laid out my cooking, all the while keeping my sight out for anything resembling a foot and a half tall black feathered creature.

By the time I loaded more kindling into the belly of the stove, Netsel returned. I waited expectantly for him to report that he too, saw the dubious feathered monster. But alas, he said nothing of the matter and went to the staircase leading to our rooms.

“I be ready for morning grub quick as a hot-footed mule runnin’ to his feedin’ trough, Miss,” he said placing one foot on the steps. “Mrs. Thompson and the doctor don’t mind me eating here in the kitchen long as I don’t be smellin’ like ol’ Mokey and Lucy.”

That was the most I heard Netsel speak (up to that point anyway). He took the steps two by two, his feet sounding like one of his horses making their way to pasture.

"Take your time, Netsel," I called after him. "Breakfast won't be done all too quickly." I looked at the cooking table and sighed. "Not this morning, anyway."

The task before me was overwhelming. I wished Nurse Price and Little Margret Jean were at my side. I recalled the advice Nurse Price gave me for such situations.

"When chores at hand seems much too large for you to handle on your own, break them down into several smaller tasks. Start with the biggest and most cumbersome first, then work your way down to the smallest and lightest."

I looked at the fruit pie. "The easiest for sure," I said setting it off to the side. Mrs. Thompson had several made.

"Bacon. The hardest, I think." I needed to slice several pieces from the slab of hog belly. I would start to fry it after I made the biscuits, then use the hot fat for the base of my gravy, setting aside a portion to fry the potatoes and eggs, and wheat cakes, adding more lard as needed. In between all the preparation, cornmeal mush would be mixed and set to steam.

"Quite simple, really," I reassured myself, thinking how we did it back home, at Pine Brook. Nurse Price truly was an excellent teacher.

By the time I had the bacon sliced, biscuits rising, and wheat cake batter ready to go, the sky had started its morning blush. I set the cake batter aside along with the eggs and cornmeal mush. While I waited for the biscuits to rise to perfection, I readied Shamus's bath. The previous night he informed me he insisted on taking full baths every other morning and a half bath the others.

"In the morning it will be my full bath day," he announced as I served the coffee that previous night. "Mrs. Thompson always prepares it right after she puts the biscuits in, and before she starts frying the bacon and her delicious wheat cakes with a side of eggs, over easy."

He deliberately added a firm sniff at the end of his instructions indicating he expected the very same service from me. And I had every intention of delivering such service, even better, but circumstances had other plans.

I wasn't surprised to find a running tap in Shamus' bathroom. A house as elegant as his wouldn't have anything less. It was a truly wonderful house that I feared would spoil me forever. How could it not, with a water pump installed at every sink in the house; and bathtubs in nearly every guest room, some even had showers.

But the biggest and best bath of all was in Shamus' private bathroom. I ran the bath water and began gathering his clothes for the day. From his wardrobe affixed to the wall that joined the study wall.

That's how I heard Miss Gavin chattering away. I tried ignoring it, but an eruption of laughter caught my ear pulling me from the wardrobe and into the hall for a listen.

I didn't recognize the voice answering Miss Gavin. It sounded human enough, but it was stiff and unnatural.

"Stranger danger, stranger danger..." it repeated.

"It's alright. You needn't be scared." Miss Gavin's voice was extra sweet and encouraging.

"That is Camarilla you saw, Shamus' new caregiver. Remember Shamus told you about her, and how she is going to help take care of him, and you. Come on now, who's the most handsomest one here? You can tell me."

"I am, I am," came the answer. "I am."

"Why, yes you are, you pretty boy, you!"

"Jeepers-Creepers!" I gasped a whisper under my breath.

"Take care of? No one said anything 'bout taking care of...Jeepers-Creepers!" I peeked around the corner hoping to catch a glimpse of who (or what) Miss Gavin was talking with.

"That's right, pretty baby," Miss Gavin prattled on.

"I am, I am."

It was the black thing I saw sprinting from the kitchen. It turned its enormous black feathery head and stared right at me. I gasped loud and clear, ducking back, hoping Miss Gavin did not see me. But it was too late.

"Oh, there you are," she chuckled, handing the 'thing' a stale hunk of last night's biscuit.

"I was hoping you would have a moment before the day starts. I want you to come meet someone very special." She flagged me to her side. I crept slow and uneasy into the room keeping a good distance between me and the black thing.

"Camarilla, I would like you to meet Shamus' very special friend, Patsy. Patsy, this is Camarilla, Shamus' new Caregiver."

My tongue stuck. I forced it free, stammering out, "I-is th-that a c-crow?" The *c* caught extra hard in my throat, almost choking me.

"Yes." Miss Gavin laughed. "Why yes, Patsy is a crow. They are quite intelligent, you know. And this little darling here has been with Shamus for almost ten years now and has been an excellent companion and helper. Haven't you, Patsy dear?" She said, gently patting its head.

"Patsy, can you say hello to Camarilla?"

The black thing cocked its head up and down, surveying me with its shiny, midnight-black eyes.

"Hello," the bird said reaching out its claw to me. "Hello-Hello." Instinctively I backed away refusing to take hold of its claw, a thick stick of what looked like, black scales.

"It's all right, Camarilla," Miss Gavin laughed. "You can take Patsy's hand, err, claw rather. He won't hurt you, see?"

She took hold of the beast's claw, ever so rough and encrusted looking as it was, into her own soft, pale hand and gave it a light bouncy shake.

"See? He loves it," she pressed her lips against the bird's enormous head.

"Patsy might not be the typical animal that one might expect as a companion such as a dog or a cat, and he might have feathers instead of fur, but I can assure you this old crow is just as good if not better than any of them, aren't you, pretty boy, hmm?"

It turned its head, ogling its black eyes at me, then splintered its beak as if to smile. It bared its tongue—long, brown, stiff and dry.

"Aw, look, Camarilla. He likes you already! Go ahead," Miss Gavin encouraged. "Take hold of Patsy's hand, err, claw rather."

The thing bobbed its huge head eagerly as if agreeing with Miss Gavin. I shuddered; yet the creature did hold an odd curiosity.

"I need to get back to my tasks," I said excusing myself, backing away. "I-I think I left Shamus's bath water r-running."

"Why, yes, of course," Miss Gavin said. "Silly me. I should have realized. I had that very same reaction the first time I met Patsy. I am so sorry, Camarilla. Please forgive me. You'll get used to him in your own time."

Stretching his neck to what I considered to be an abnormal length, the bird lifted his shiny black wings from his sides and gave them a good flap. They were surprisingly large and caused a breeze strong enough to stir strands of the gray hair sprouting from Miss Gavin's bun.

"Isn't it amazing how he can balance himself so well with all that commotion going on," she said, watching the bird lift one claw from its perch, placing it down, then lifting the other, while nipping his wings, preening them to perfection.

"I don't know what Shamus is going to do if Patsy, well, you know—" Miss Gavin checked her shoulder and turned her voice to a whisper, "takes that finale flight before Shamus does. And if Shamus outlives Patsy, who will take care of the dear old bird? I would, but with my beloved little Chi-Chi, well, it just couldn't work."

"Really, Miss Gavin." Shamus' voice answered back, giving us a startle. He had been listening and watching from the archway of the study. His clear blue eyes pierced both Miss Gavin and me.

"You needn't worry yourselves about such matters. I assure you," he boomed. "Both Patsy and I will be fine, just fine."

Miss Gavin's cheeks flushed. "Oh, I didn't mean—"

"No need for embarrassment, my dear Miss Gavin. You are like most people. Not truly knowing all there is to know about Patsy's species let alone the life expectancy of such a magnificent bird, as the crow. For that, my dear, dear Miss Gavin, I do take full responsibility. For the day I introduced the two of you I should had taken the time to educate you more precisely concerning such matters such as Patsy.

"You see, crows live seven to eight years in the wild, in captivity sometimes up to thirty years. So, I speculate our old friend here has another good twenty years left in him. And in that time, much can happen. Almost anything."

I will never forget the stern look on Shamus' face directed toward me as if I had done something so terribly wrong it was shameful. I looked helplessly at Miss Gavin. She in turn looked to Patsy, eagerly stroking the bird's glossy black head down to its tail feathers.

Maneuvering his wheelchair next to Patsy's perch, Shamus reached his arm out for the bird to scuttle up onto his shoulder.

"I-I-I'm s-s-sorry sir, but did I d-d-do s-s-something wrong?" I asked.

The silence was awkward as Shamus continued to stroke Patsy who sat on his shoulder. I wanted to run from the room in tears.

"Well," he finally turned to me, "We all have done something wrong."

"Don't worry, Camarilla, everything is fine. Just fine. Miss Gavin has done well. I am more than happy to have your company and service. But you must remember to turn off the bath tap before leaving the room, and all taps for that matter. You nearly flooded the whole house." Patsy shut his eyes, content as Shamus' long fingers continued to caress him.

"But there is one small detail that I do insist on. You must try forgoing those pondering looks of yours. They seem to plague your face.

"I can assure you, Little Mademoiselle, what disabilities I do have do not play any part in my ability to think, rationalize, or perform most, if not all intellectual tasks placed upon the average human. My disability has *not one thing* to do with my ability to think, and certainly not my ability to reason. My affliction has to do with my ability not being able to walk, and nothing more."

He wheeled his invalid chair across the study and back inside the foyer and down the hall into his bedroom. He slammed his door causing me to snap up straight. I looked at Miss Gavin who had taken her kerchief from her skirt pocket and put it to her nose. She sniffled, furrowing her brow as if Shamus made her cry.

"It happens now and then," she tucked away her hanky and took hold of my arm and walked me down the hall to his bedroom explaining how, "his behavior is due to a combination of age and circumstance. He'll get over it soon enough. Don't let him frighten you. He's a good man with a very good heart. And don't forget, he was one of the very best doctors in this area. He has much to teach you. You'll see. Now go ahead and assist him.

"By the way," she added, blushing deeper than a rose, reaching for the doorknob. "He is an extremely modest man, and proud, too. He prefers to stay covered until fully submerged in his bath water. He will call out to you letting you know he is decent. I know his modesty will help you feel a bit more comfortable also."

I stood waiting for Shamus to let me know all was well and that he was covered properly. The male form meant nothing to me. I was used to seeing it in its entirety. After all, Nurse Price and I had bathed and cared for many men during the course of my stay at Pine Brook.

I entered, giving Shamus as much privacy as possible, for his sake, not mine.

By the time he was bathed, dressed, and fed, he was back to himself. And surprisingly, I did find him to be quite pleasant, even entertaining. Plus, he had a whole new wealth of information that neither Nurse Price nor Doctor Bruce could ever give me.

Miss Gavin departed the next day leaving me alone with my new Charge. Netsel of course, had taken her home and wouldn't be back until the following day.

I watched them and the carriage travel down the road. My knees shook as the last clip-clop clip-clop of Lucy and Mokey's hooves echoed through the woods surrounding the mansion on its hill.

After all, I was only a young woman, and growing up in an institution, I always had someone at my side whether I wanted them there or not. And now for the very first time in my life I was alone. Very alone. And it was quiet. Too quiet. I would truly miss, Miss. Gavin.

Looking back, I was silly with naivete. What did I know about life and all that happens in it?

I might have stood there staring out the window of the mansions' door until sundown, maybe even into the next day if not for the list of chores in my apron pocket.

I unfolded the paper and read the writing (again): Wash dishes...disinfect counters...scrub floor. The chores went on. I sighed and fumbled with the ruffles on my apron.

"They sure are fancy," I said to myself. "But they can't help me, and without help it will take me all day and into the night to finish all this."

I turned and headed down the hall for the kitchen. First, I went to the sink. It was the most natural place to start.

"Thank you, Miss Gavin," I said aloud seeing she had rinsed and stacked the dishes, pots, and pans before leaving.

I took the kettles of hot boiling water she had prepped on the stove and filled the sink. Unlike Pine Brook's tepid water, the heat of Shamus' water instantly dissolved the soap flakes. Our stovetop never seemed to get or stay hot enough due to having to preserve our coal and wood supply. Nor did we have time to wait for good hot water. We were much too busy, and settled on what we could have. Nice lukewarm.

As I washed Miss Gavin's plate, I recalled the night before. There were a few matters that did not sit right with me. For instance, Mrs. Thompson's disappearance. Even though Miss Gavin did help Shamus remember what really happened to the woman (to which I will explain in just a bit), it seemed off that Mrs. Thompson, being head housekeeper, wouldn't wait for my arrival before departing from her station of caretaking Shamus, and to some degree, Netsel. And why did Shamus keep Nora's green door locked up tight? And why did the doctor keep a crow for a companion instead of a loyal old dog or a curious cat that would take long naps in his lap?

In the silence I continued with the dishes, and my wondering. *Just what did the future hold?*

Time would tell. After all, it always does.

CHAPTER SEVEN

Just as Nurse Price foretold, the rhythm of my days dawned and unfolded like the sheets I changed almost daily on Shamus' bed.

Her letters were an encouragement, along with Miss Gavin's once a month visits which helped guide me through that first winter, and a long one it had been at that. It turned out Mrs. Thompson never came back.

I was told her daughter lost her husband leaving the poor young thing and her new baby to fend for themselves in the world.

"Scandalous, simply scandalous," I overheard Miss Gavin remark to Shamus during one of her monthly visits. February to be exact. You see, the loss as it turned out was not due to natural death. According to Miss Gavin's whispers, the two never married. She claimed he was not only a piker, but also a masher who took to another's bed, hence leaving the young mother and child to their own demise.

'Things like that happen more than what we admit, even though everyone knows it,' Nurse Price wrote. 'Men are men after all. We mustn't expect much loyalty from them. And young women have their needs, too. Unfortunately, the world is not ready to accept any of that yet. But one day it will.'

Curious thoughts of one day having my own such personal

adventures in the bedroom chambers began filling my mind that year; and so did the washing, cleaning, meal preparation, and all matters tending to Shamus. In turn my natural yearnings and daily chores slowly began replacing thoughts of Mr. Hawthorn and Molly Mae Junction, and Pine Brook's other permanent residents. But not of Little Margret Jean, nor Nurse Price and her everlasting teachings, whose overly stern ways I once hated, now were proving to be useful. I gladly accepted their value, thanking her every time it came to cleaning Shamus' chamber pots, or making perfect stitches repairing his daywear and mine. Netsel insisted on doing his own tailoring and tending to his own chamber pot cleaning, of course.

Tea, I came to understand, was in keeping with Shamus' beloved Scottish tradition; and once I got a hold of its routine, it proved not as difficult as I had perceived. Since lunches were served on the lighter side after such a heavy breakfast, a good tea, I learned, was a way to fend off any hunger pangs until supper, which was served properly at seven o'clock in the evening. And, as with everything 'Shamus,' tea was to be just as timely:

'I find preparing the finger sandwiches while making lunch gives time enough for the dainty little morsels to chill to perfection by the time I serve Shamus his four o'clock tea.'

That's what I wrote in my letters to Nurse Price. But to Little Margret Jean I wrote differently:

'Patsy has become accustomed to me as I to him. The quick flashes of black captured in the corners of my eyes no longer startle me but is expectant, if not gladly anticipated. After all, what fun can I have here all by myself? Netsel is an old man and always busy, and Mrs. Thompson won't be coming back after all. And truth be told, Mr. Fitzgerald scares me at times. Most times, he is fine and peaceful and very kind and thoughtful. I suppose his moods swings are the typical for a person his age. But it is his forthright manner that intimidates me. I don't believe he means it to be on purpose but it is just in his nature.'

As I wrote my letters that first winter, I realized my work life was not so unlike that at Pine Brook, except I had no friends besides Shamus, Netsel, Miss Gavin when she came on her visits of inspection once a month, and of course, Patsy. But one late spring day I was to find out just what a different world I really was living in. Or, I should say, about to live in.

It was nearing the end of May, and the morning started no differently from any other morning except I hoped to please Shamus with an added breakfast surprise. I was to make him one of his very favorites: Berry Toast.

I will never forget standing in the pantry getting a pint of Mrs. Thompson's canned blueberries when what had become the typical fluff of black fluttered on my right side behind my shoulder.

"Hmm...I wonder where that Patsy is," I said grabbing the blueberries, sugar, and cornstarch for thickening. "I bet Patsy's hiding in the hallway."

His black wings rose, flapping with the click-click-click of his claws racing across the wooden kitchen floor. I giggled, peeking at him as he waddled frantically to the doorway and down the hall. "Well, he better run," I shouted. "Because I'm going to go look for him soon as I'm done here."

He bobbed his head three times (as was his usual) and then scampered down the hall into the study and on to the carpet where I couldn't hear his footsteps. That's how I knew he was racing to his favorite hiding place. He would wait there patiently for me while I finished preparing the berry sauce.

I measured the sugar and cornstarch, stirring in the berry juice, taking care to dissolve the lumps. I warmed it till it thickened, all the while stirring to keep it smooth. Setting it to the farthest side of the stove to cool, I was ready to find Patsy hiding in his small, tight spot behind the piano.

"Patsy! Now where is Patsy?" I said loudly. The pecking against the backside of the piano sounded like Mr. Hawthorn's fingers tapping out what he said was something called the Morse Code. Three short clicks and then three long dashes, tapping over and over again.

"What does it mean," I asked him each time he tapped it out.

"S. O. S." he always responded. "S.O.S. Save our souls, save our ship..."

Doctor Bruce said no such thing existed and that it was very creative for Mr. Hawthorn to express such a thing.

But Patsy's Morse Code spelled nothing, I was sure of it. No, *'Save Our Souls'*, or *'Save Our Ship'*, as Mr. Hawthorn's. Just a peck here and a peck there, teasing me with clues to his whereabouts. "Mmm, I know he's in here. I just know it," I said as I ran my fingers against the piano's keyboard, making an amateurish musical sound. Just as Shamus did, I raised my elbows to the ceiling. Hitting the last key (high C) three solid times, ending the commotion.

"So, you do like the piano after all?" Shamus' thunderous voice rolled across the room. I froze, not knowing if I should answer with a yes, or with a no.

"I-I'm not quite sure, sir," I said. "We had one at Pine Brook but I n-never really had time to learn it."

"Didn't have time, or didn't take time?" Shamus asked, wheeling himself up to me and the piano. He stared, at me with his sapphire-ice, blue eyes. I fidgeted. "There is a difference, you know. Not having time versus not taking time. The latter is a poor habit to get into."

"Yes, I-I'm sure that it is," I stammered clumsily. "I-I mean it is...a b-bad habit, not taking time. M-Mr. Hawthorn was going to t-teach me, but..."

"Aha, yes, just as I thought," Shamus interrupted. "You didn't take the time to learn. Another bad habit. Blaming another for one's own lack of responsibility for not taking the initiative for oneself." I knew he was right.

He pushed the piano bench to the side and rolled himself in its place. Positioned perfectly with the piano keys he called out, "Patsy...Johannes Brahms!"

Behind the piano the curtains ruffled and out came Patsy scuttling across the carpet, his mighty black wings lifted him to his perch.

"Arr-arr!" he cawed, and bobbed his head excitedly up and down.

Shamus oftentimes played that mighty instrument, the piano, making each concert extra special by playing as if for a full hall. As without the beginning of each performance he stopped suddenly, stretching his long fingers, then, ever so lightly, he touched the keys, elbows facing up. I stifled a giggle. He reminded me of an old, giant white-haired vulture.

But alas, his technique was so well orchestrated in such a loving manner for the music, that I have not heard or seen a performance like his since. So on that late day in May, seeping into the stale air of the study in that mansion on the hill a bit of magic began.

And it happened to commence with my mother's favorite: Brahms Hungarian Dance number five (for piano of course).

She often played the tender concerto while Huston and I sat on the floor engaging in childish games such as jacks or pick-up sticks, or scribbling on our slate boards. Huston, being older than I, played the games more or less to appease me.

And so it was on that bright morning in May as Shamus played in the comfort of his study that I happened to allow myself the luxury of letting memories of my past flow through me. And it was bittersweet.

Huston's giant smile warmed me in the cockles of my mind as he held up his board to show me the chalk drawings he'd made of flowers and dancing white and black birds on the dark slate.

"Just for you, my sister. Just for you."

I shut the vision from my mind. It was a mistake indulging in the past. My heart was finally healing (close to what was possible) and allowing such fond memories take over started breaking it all over again. I missed my brother and always would. After all, time really never does heal everything. Especially a lonely, broken heart. I decided to hang on to just enough of those memories so as not to forget, and let go of all the others so they wouldn't hurt.

I concentrated on Shamus. His shoulders and arms were not muscular like Netsel's, by any means, but firm from many hours, weeks, years spent at the piano and rolling himself around in his oversized invalid chair. For all I knew, he himself was Johannes Brahm's himself sitting at the piano. Same white hair, same white beard (except much better trimmed and groomed than Brahm's). I caught my imagination before it could totally run away from me. Oftentimes Doctor Bruce warned me of the possible madness people succumb to from venturing too far from reality.

Shamus, giving a final movement of his hands, flailed his arms this way and that in his most overly dramatic way. It was his way of signaling that the concert was done. And as always, I rose from the sofa giving a sincere applause.

"Why, thank you, Little Mademoiselle," he said as always. "And with any luck and lots of practice, you also will one day play as magnificently as I." The way he said it caused me to believe it was true.

He rolled himself from the study and into the entrance hall. "I will be waiting for breakfast," he yelled as he headed for the dining room.

Patsy, lulled by the music, napped contently on his perch. I looked at the piano. On the keys was an envelope that dear Shamus left for me. I picked it up and read the beautifully scripted writing on its face: *Mademoiselle Camarilla Berklemen.*

I eagerly opened it. And as I did, key fell onto the carpet. I bent down and picked it up and then read the note:

May 27th 1892

If it pleases Little Mademoiselle, I would like to request your presence at tea this very afternoon at four o'clock in the gazebo. If you accept, please dress appropriately. Hence the key. It will unlock the room next to yours. Nora's room. The one with the green door. In it, you will find a fine selection of dresses. You may help yourself but, please do be generous with gentleness.

With the greatest of sincerity,
Doctor Shamus P. Fitzgerald

Tea with Shamus? By that time I had definitely served plenty of teas but never had I sat down to one with the doctor. Naturally, I was nervous and so very unsure of myself, yet how could I refuse? After all, he was my employer, and I his caregiver. But the thought of dresses, yes, real dresses, helped take away the sting of any probable misfortunes of wrong manners that might occur. Besides, this was my chance to enter that room so forbidden. Nora's room, the one with the green door.

By the time I served the berry sauce and toast, my imagination ran rampant. My curiosity of Nora's room would finally be satisfied.

So, after breakfast I quickly finished my morning chores and set off for the third floor. And that's when it all truly began, my strange new life ahead.

I raced up the staircase, and as my foot caught hold of the last step. I found myself face down on the hardwood floor of the landing.

That's when I saw it for the first time—the movement of light under the door of Nora's room, The Green Door. And as I watched the something—or someone running to and fro behind it, a chill flowed through me so cold it felt like hot liquid.

I listened for any sounds behind the green door as I watched the bright slit of light move back and forth, flashing this way and that. The silence was ear-piercing, my thoughts stabbed me.

Had this phenomenon taken place before, I wondered. *Had I never noticed it until now? How would that be possible? Netsel! Perhaps it was Netsel...No, that was not possible...Netsel was tending to his chores. I saw him only an hour ago heading for the timber ridge...Should I run and get him? Should I yell for Shamus? No! No time to seek out Netsel, he could be anywhere on the property...Shamus, he's incapable of leaving his chair, he could never take on the task of climbing the stairs...*

I knew that I, and I alone, had to buck-up and take on the responsibility of finding out who, or what, was behind the green door. I had no choice.

I rose, and step by laggard step I forced myself forward not realizing what, or possibly who, I would encounter, nor the consequences thereof.

I placed my hands on the door, checking for any warmth that might be caused by a possible fire. Nothing. I checked for smoke and fumes seeping from the cracks of the doorway. Again nothing. Nothing existed except the white flashing light, and the stillness. The deafening stillness. Taking the key from my pocket I readied it to set in the keyhole and then stopped.

I have to get my wits about me, I thought backing away. *If it is not a what, it has to be a who.*

After all, the mansion was large enough to hide in without being detected. Patsy proved it time after time.

But who, who could it be? And why? Either a 'who' or a 'what,' how was I to confront it?

How long have they been in there, and how did they get in? Should I scare them? What good would that do? Sneak up on them and smack them in the head, and what if the who is a what...?

I needed to retrieve the heaviest article I could find. *The night lamp in my room. Yes, it's plenty heavy.*

I held the hem of my uniform to keep it from rustling in the silence as I tippy-toed past the door and into my room. Picking up the oil lamp, I headed back.

I took a deep breath, and tried to steady my hand and concentrated on inserting the key into the door lock. Then, ever so carefully, I slid the key in and slowly turned it. The clip inside the lock clicked. The door unlocked. I waited. Them, without a stir within the room, I turned the knob.

The wood of the door was dry and creaked with age as I opened it. And as I did, the light disappeared leaving behind darkness.

Peering through it I saw a double-sized bed to my left, and a large window with heavy drapes drawn closed as if to purposely block the daylight from exposing the contents of the room. I stood still and soundless as the walls surrounding me.

What...what caused the flashing light?

Holding tight onto my oil lamp, I quickly went to the window and pulled open the drapes. Afternoon rays of sunlight streamed across the room.

The bed obviously had not been slept in. Its floral coverlet was intact with not a crease. A few yards of navy-blue material as that of my uniform, lay draped over the foot of the bed; yards of white ruffles lay in a crumpled heap on the floor. I picked them up.

Nora's? Mrs. Thompson's? I wondered. *Left over...from when? Who?*

"J-Jeepers cr-cr-creeprs," I said out loud picking up the navy-blue fabric. It was the very same fabric as my uniform, and the white as my pinafore and ruffles.

That's when it occurred to me. How *had* my uniform been made to fit? I did not recall having measurements taken or being asked about them. Nurse Price surely would have 'tsked' and 'tasked' about such a thing, especially to me.

"It matters not what a person wears to get a job done. Fanciness will not make a person work any better. It's a person's hands and back that does the job, not what a person wears."

No, Nurse Price truly would have had something to say about the production of a fancy uniform for me.

And Little Margret Jean surely would have told me if she heard of such talk.

I felt the materials again. "Yes, they are the same. M-m-maybe it was Mrs. Thompson. M-maybe she made my uniform." I lay them back over the foot of the bed.

A kerosene lamp, long time dried, sat on the nightstand next to the head of the bed.

The room was of nice size and nothing was strange or odd about the place. It was, just another bedroom like any other (except desperate for a good dusting perhaps).

In the middle of the room, on a small round table, sat a tea set sat as if waiting for company to arrive. A pair of comfortable looking chairs covered in fine floral upholstery accompanied the setting. To the left of that, Nora's closet.

But there, between the table and the closet, was a sewing machine with a large, oval shaped floor mirror placed at its side. I walked over to the machine and sat my lamp on its wooden sleeve.

The machine was beautiful. I ran my fingers over the colorfully painted roses and morning-glories adorning its black metal body. I placed my foot on the pedal and pumped it up and down. It was in need of a good oiling, for the machine was stiff. It's slow, juddering jerks drew the needle up and down.

I touched the teapot and grabbed my oil lamp from the sleeve of the sewing machine.

"J-j-j-j-jeepers *cr-cr-cr-creepers,"* I gasped and readied myself to plunge it at the who, or what, was in that room. I touched the pot again. It was warm, and both cups had a spot of tea left inside.

Hugging my lamp, I looked about the room. There was no bright light, no movement of any kind. All remained silent and undisturbed.

Yet the table and its setting hadn't been forgotten or unused. "Wh-who could of...Netsel?" I said out loud. "Has to be! Wh-who else? I n-n-never really know where he's at, n-n-not really! And wh-when I ask Sh-Shamus, he s-says, *'he is where he is.'*

"He must've snuck in here for a tea of his own. H-he must had heard me and s-s-snuck out the w-w-window, onto the roof, closing the d-d-drapes after himself."

Images of him slinking in and out the room replaced my fear. It was settled. "Netsel it is," I sighed heavy with relief, reassuring myself. I headed for the closet and opened it.

Oh, how I "oohed and aahed" at my findings. As it turned out, Shamus was right. There was a very fine selection of dresses. Some full and long from times past, and some types of attire I had never seen before. Not even in *Harper's Bazar*. And yet in some peculiar way they all were familiar.

I pulled out a dress and examined it. It was bright yellow and made of very strange material, a netting but much lighter than what I knew of, and softer too. Patches of orange and pink patches in the shape of large daisies were embodied throughout. Glancing over the other outfits. I immediately recognized the seamstress used nothing but the finest of materials. Each appeared extremely well crafted, each designed in different colors, embellishments, and lengths and textures. And, just as strange as finding the teapot and cups still warm and used, it appeared as if the clothing inside the closet was tailored to personally fit me to a tee.

Had Nora been the same size as myself?

I searched for something usable for Shamus' tea. I was drawn to a purple velvet skirt and its matching jacket. The ensemble was perfectly consummated with a white faille blouse and its amazingly high collar adorned with the most delicate lace trim and a row of simple pearl buttons.

The jacket was extremely high class with its strip of luxurious black fur which accentuated the rich purple of the jacket and skirt, and white faille blouse with its pearl buttons. It was an outfit which I found odd to be within a closet from someone so long passed, as it was so up to date and so fashionable. It was extremely similar (if not identical) to one I had seen in the recent addition of *Harper's* that

Nurse Price had sent. If Mrs. Thompson had tailored the suit, it must had taken her a great deal of time. And if she had, *why hadn't Shamus or Miss Gavin mentioned her ability? And, how did she manage to style it so precisely and at a fit so tailored to myself?*

I ran my hand over the skirt. It was velvet, *real* velvet just like the jacket. I knew it for sure. For though having felt the material only twice in my whole life, I could never forget the way the short thick pile of fabric squished tenderly under the touch of my fingers, like the thick green moss Little Margret and I would peel from the rocks and tree bark back home in Pine Brook.

One of the two times I felt real velvet was when Nurse Price and the clerk in the fancy store in Spring Green were busy chatting and wasn't looking. I took the liberty of sitting in a rather unique chair upholstered with the very same velvety material. The other time I came across it was during our trip, in a very expensive shoppe in New York City. Mother and I crooned over the bolts of fabrics and tapestry lining the shelves of the famously world renowned, McCain's. That's when I found my love with the endless possibilities of fabrics.

My hands, now unrestricted to touching, trembled with excitement as I fetched the purple velvet suit from the closet. A chatelaine purse with a suede strap and silver clasp was attached to it. It was practical yet attractive.

All the ladies in *Harper's Bazar* carried one on their dresses and skirts. It was all the rage. Some plain and useful like the one fastened to my purple skirt, others accordingly to one's outfit, each outrageously fancy and decorative. Though I never had one, nor had the need for one, I knew what it was used for.

I loosened its strings and looked inside. It held nothing. Not a pencil or even a card for writing a quick invitation for a visit at a friend's house. Disappointed, I pulled the strings, shutting the bag.

I removed my uniform and stared at myself in the full-length oval dressing mirror which I also found to be odd as in the way it was turned and propped properly to my height.

Though appropriately clothed in my chemise, drawers, and decency-skirt, I still blushed, for under all those layers I could plainly see that I, Camarilla Rae Berkelman had grown into a full-fledged woman. And truth be told, Nurse Price had been right all along. Upon further observation of my anatomy (modest as the inspection was) I questioned my need for stiff, styes made of whalebone corsets to turn my body into a fashionable letter "S". Nor did I find the need for any cumbersome under-linings. For indeed, I wasn't what one could call Gibson Girl perfect by any means but being modestly plump in all the right spots I was rather well-formed, and to my surprise quite capable of filling any bodice in a natural way. This left little need for a bustle as my backside was very nicely rounded all on its own, and would serve well as a natural tournure, and quite capable of pushing up most bustles very nicely. But even at that, a horsehair bundle was on standby on a hanger if needed.

A swell of excitement grew inside me as I slipped the purple velvet skirt over all my underlings (proper as they were). The waist band was neither too big nor too snug and its length delighted me, crowning the top of my boots. I turned sideways and smiled as I recognized, my derrière truly was in no need of any extra help.

With eager hands, I reached for the white faille tailored blouse with its high lace collar and put it on. It was simple and perfect, snuggling close to my frame. Next, I took the waist jacket from its hanger and gently stroked its black fur trim. Watching my every movement in the mirror, I placed it over the white blouse.

The jacket was unlike my old one, big and loose. For this one was good and tight in all the correct places, sculpting my body to perfection. Carefully, I began latching each pearled button.

To top it off, sitting on the top shelf above the outfit was a hat perfectly matched. I fluffed the three peacock feathers and straightened the lavender and black ribbon bows and set it on my head. Every feminine nerve within me sprang to life. I felt gloriously beautiful.

I often question my memory concerning what exactly did happen next. More so I question if given the chance, would I repeat my actions? For it was either the fastening of the very last button on that purple velvet jacket that changed my entire life, or it was what came shortly after. To this very day I still wonder.

It was then, as I clasped the last waist jacket button in place, I felt almost instantly queer, warm, yet cold. Every part of me somehow was being pulled in all directions. The sensation was like a heated fever in the middle of the night but without the fear and discomfort such fevers bring. It didn't hurt by any means, nor did I feel the need for panic. For the stirring had begun flowing over me like a gentle river. And within a few moments everything felt quite comfortable, almost normal. Then as quickly as the sensation came, it left.

Without a second thought or hesitation, I turned and headed to the green door and to Shamus and the tea as if what had occurred was just as natural as breathing.

I reached for the door handle and took a last and finale look at myself in the mirror. That's when it happened. The journey beyond the green door. For if I had not seen myself, for myself, I surely could not, nor would not, believe what I am about to tell you. And to this day many questions if such a thing were possible. But I Camarilla Rae Berkelman do assure you, yes. Yes! Yes, it was indeed possible!

The light that had flickered and flashed inside Nora's room was again. It was so brilliant, and so bright it nearly blinded me. I chanced to glimpse through it, finding my reflection in looking back at me in the mirror. I watched the disbelief on my face as I began fading away, disappearing in some sort of a mist filling the room.

Within a few moments both the light and the mist lifted, leaving me in an abyss so dark, so black it very well could have gone on forever, and I am sure it did. Yet, as outlandish as it seems, I knew I was safe, and need not fear. Then, just like that, in the twinkling of an eye I was beyond The Green Door.

I had no fear of any kind, and felt quite comfortable as I took in my surroundings. And it was extraordinary.

I was in a tunnel of sorts, a vacuum tugging and pulling me as if gravity had fallen sideways. The sensation was incredible. Then, in a moments passage, the darkness began to glow. Slowly at first.

Thousands and thousands of different colors and hues and tints sparked and flashed everywhere filled the shaft. An endless brilliant shaft of colors set on fire. And it was warm. Nicely so. It was perfect. Outright perfect.

I stood still as I could. Yet the tunnel, as remarkable as it was, was began to twist and turn, spinning like a giant wheel not made of wood or metal but from the very same fibers of the clothing filling Nora's closet.

Each strand of thread held dazzling colors. Upon closer examination I found the tufts of fiber to be individual strands of a web, and each web was connected together making up the endless tunnel in which I stood.

The chamber rotated, and each string began shining with a different hue and tint, thus creating an enormous prism beyond every imaginable color.

Looking closer at the webbings, I discovered trillions of tiny flickering sparks of a golden fire. I leaned in, studying the tiny flashes. That's when I saw them. The numbers.

Upon further investigation I saw that the numbers were dates and times. And they were exceedingly precise.

Every date of every year since time began, glistened within its own golden fire.

The dates and hours and minutes, seconds, half seconds, micro-seconds, nanoseconds, picoseconds and beyond, they were all etched along the strings of fabric within the webbing.

And upon each date I saw a moving picture like that of a Nickel-odeon. I concentrated on one single moving picture.

I was astonished to find an event being played out in detail. Gold fires flared as the event occurring during the times and dates came and went. It was as if I truly were watching a Nickelodeon.

I followed the thread. To my surprise, other strands of time were also attached to that single thread. And I understood.

All moments of time, past, present and future are grouped as one. Yet, every second, every minute, every hour, day, month, year, decade, all work independently from the other, yet all are connected to each other, one thread at a time.

"Razzel-Dazzle," I whispered as the chamber continued to turn. "Razzel-Dazzle."

A hum rose, echoing throughout the shaft. I looked down the tunnel as far as I could see hoping to find where it came from. A very large and extremely bright mechanism turned at the very far end of the tunnel. It held all the strings together. As it turned, the thread loomed together. And as it did, all sounds of every type of life sang, and cried, and laughed together as one. From the most meager amoeba to the most intelligent and complex.

The hum rose and eddied low and steady resonating in harmony in as many octaves as the colors filling the shaft.

I recognized the light of the loom to be the light that flooded
Nora's room. The light of time.

Digesting all that surrounded me, I took a heavy breath. Then, with my curiosity overwhelmed, I once again bent over and looked close as l could at the glittering dates. And I touched one.

March 26th, 1953.

CHAPTER EIGHT

The tunnel slowed, and with it, time. for but a moment then dissipated, leaving me in sunshine. Real The webs lifted, returning sunshine. Just as real as the sun I left behind in 1892. The sun was the only thing I recognized besides the ground beneath me which proved firm and hard, and solid. Unlike the tunnel, my surroundings frightened me.

March 1953. It was loud (much too loud) with unrecognizable rumbles and roars and screeches: and the air, it stunk. I covered my nose with one hand, and with the other I tried to block at least one my ears from the excruciating sounds around me. I was in a city, or to say the very least, a much larger town that I left behind known as Mill Town.

Church and school bells rang loud and clear. Horns blaring from strange and wonderful horseless carriages fleeted past me at a pace faster than I could comprehend. The autos were the very kind Mr. Hawthorn talked about many times, and they traveled on a street of the solid pavement he also swore existed, but no one believed to be true. Not even Little Margret Jean.

From what Mr. Hawthorn had described, I stood on what I assumed to be a sidewalk. It was unlike the wooden-walks, and walkways made of dirt and gravel that I was accustomed to. For under my feet was the same material as what the autos rode, a solid gray road.

Very few passersby took notice of me standing in the midst of all the confusion and mayhem, and those who did eyed me up and down as curiously, as I did them. It was if they wanted to tell me something but didn't dare take the time. They ran past me among the tall brick and mortar buildings lining the street, hooting and hollering, excitedly shouting, "a cure, a cure! They found a cure!"

Behind me was a thick glass door. I stepped back into its large, long doorway. On the inside hung a giant picture drawing, an advertisement of a red headed young boy with freckles, proudly holding his hips. He was dressed in what I assumed was supposed to depict some sort of Robin Hood outfit, including a cap with a feather. Under him was a group of men and women, some children, and a burly dog, and a pirate, all of which were dressed in colorful costumes. Under it all was a cheerful sign that read, Peter Pan showing at-7:00 p.m.-all seats 60¢

It must be a nickelodeon...a huge nickelodeon like a New York City Broadway theater...

I realized the world which I was seeing was not anything I had ever, nor even could imagine, even when in one of my very finest fits of Absorption Psychosis.

I looked out at the street and those passing by. The clothing and hairstyles of both men and women were simply, and most clearly, outrageous.

For there was not one trace of manliness on the men's well shaven faces. Gone were the men's beards, mustaches, and long, full sideburns. Their skin was given to that of soft, well-kept babies' behinds.

*Jeepers-Creepers...dandies...*I thought. *A world chockfull of goldang dandies!*

A few fellows did sport a sprout of upper lip hair. But even that I found silly even if their fine, thin mustaches appeared to be well groomed and oiled. But I do admit, the hair on their heads, worn short and greased in a neat and trim style, did look rather nice (dandies or not).

And their daywear was just as absurd and strange to the eye as their hairless faces. For gone was the pride of wearing collars up, large, tall, and stiff. Instead, these men found satisfaction wearing their collar's folded *down*, and thinner, as were their ties, skinny and skimpy. Not at all full enough to fill the open gap of their three-piece attire (which also had been replaced with nothing more than a simple white shirt and a dull, gray suit jacket).

Gone were the men's everyday sack coats, worn heavy and tight fitting with matching waistcoats. Absent were the tastefully colored contrasting checkered and striped trousers. Nay! These men ran about in some sort of, lightweight, simply tailored, loose fitting suits. To my eye they were truly unsophisticated and dull. All the men looked alike in their solid monotones of matching gray, brown, or black. And no top hat, or walking cane in hand could I see.

In shock, I drew in my breath and then gasped. I blushed in shame for the women. For they were appalling and most indecent. Although finding their fashion artless and dishonorably scanty, I did (upon closer consideration) conclude they were quite smart for their clothing choice after all. For their attire (unlike mine) seemed to be cool, carefree, and far less cumbersome compared to my overly large balloon sleeves, hidden under my tight suit jacket. My blouse held heat within the elephantine puffs leading from high shoulder to elbow, then trimmed tight down to my wrists. Winter months found them wonderful, but summer served us women miserably with its hot, humid air trapped within.

I touched the pearl buttons cinching my collar that strangled my neck. Yes, indeed. The women's blouses, skirts, and dresses were quite the opposite of mine. Under their floppy opened coats, I could see bare necks and arms. Their legs (God forbid) were exposed yet covered in a very strange stocking that looked like a silky second layer of skin.

Their shoes were not the fashionable and sensible black button-ups, but were small, barely covering the foot at all. Some had thick sticks on the heels of their shoes; others were flat with barely enough substance to keep the feet warm, yet others had a sort of galosh-boot that in my opinion (despite being a boot) would indeed keep one's toe dry, but certainly not warm. Yet, they all came in a very nice variety of colors matching the lady's coats and jackets. Very few wore the proper standard color of black or gray.

But their hair, how splendid was their hair! Easy short waves sculptured to perfection, and some styled longer and curled under.

Their faces had color too, some with colored lips red like cranberries and apples.

Certainly not all can be Painted Ladies, I thought taking in everything I was seeing and hearing and smelling.

Horseless carriages drove by casting trails of putrid air. It had a tinge to it, as did the whole air of 1953.

It was not the refreshing, crisp, clean air of May that one smells on such a spring day, but a smell emanating a foul odor of rotten eggs. It caused me an upset stomach making me cough. Again, I covered my nose with my arm trying to block the aroma.

I was somewhat aware of these horseless carriages and the unclean scent they expelled. I knew of women whose 'businesses' required them to paint themselves a bit more than considered proper and who hid in the dark corners of the streets. I knew of the dandies who walked tight and quick from one shop to the next, bundles of secret frills held possessively hidden under their arm. I had seen all these from time to time when traveling in Spring Green with Nurse Price. But here in the new Spring Green of 1953, all was in view, unhindered and in a great bounty.

Babylon, I thought, *Had Babylon risen?*

"They found a cure!" a woman shouted out at me, running past faster than an alley cat after a city mouse. The sticks on the heels of her shoes clicked and clicked on the hard surface of the sidewalk. I wondered how she balanced herself so well without turning an ankle.

Nurse Price surely would never approve of such footwear.

"A cure!" she shouted again to the next person. "Save the children! They found a cure!"

I backed-up deep inside the doorway of the theater where I stood. Across the street I took notice of a line of thick pines and maples. They were much like the ones surrounding the mansion in Timber Town. Except these trees were much larger and taller and happened to line a knoll of green grass that spread before what appeared to be a park. Yes, I truly was standing somewhere in a different time, but not a different place, for surely indeed, lurching above the tips of the tree tops of the park, I spotted the roof of Shamus' mansion.

"Jeepers-Creepers!" I gasped frantically stroking the soft fur on my jacket. "Jeepers-Creepers!"

I tapped my foot on the pavement for reassurance that the sidewalk and this new world truly was real. I stepped off the walkway and headed for the park hoping the trees would lead me back to Shamus and Patsy and Netsel, and Miss Gavin.

I jumped off the walkway. Horns honked viciously at me as I raced between the road machines. I dodged them fairly square on, except one. I misjudged my space and speed, and caught the tail end of a hunk of metal. The auto traveled on leaving me to deal with my own injuries in my own manner while curious onlookers within their horseless slowed. They pointed at me with spooked faces as if they had seen a ghost. They sped-up, hurrying off in a blur to places I could only imagine an automobile takes its passengers.

Despite my hobble I made it to the park in one piece. To my luck, my misjudgment caused me nothing more than a bruise.

The ground, wet and soggy from the melted snow of the early spring, was every bit as solid and green as I recalled ground in 1897.

Rushing to the farthest end of the park, I hid between the thick and sturdy tree trunks. Sounds of the city waved through the barrier of great maples and pines; a chill in the air filled me with gratitude for the extra length and thickness of my clothing. I pulled my tight jacket even tighter.

The realization that everything around me was real turned my stomach ill. Fear took over in full force and I started to cry. Silently at first for fear of being discovered by someone or something, perhaps a wild animal or wild person that might hurt me worse than the autos, and dandies, and painted ladies roaming the streets. Amazingly, not a creature, or human, bothered to discover me leaving me to sob out loud. I wanted to go back; back to the mansion and Shamus, back home to Pine Brook and Nurse Price, Little Margret Jean, and Dr. Bruce and all the others.

Through my tears I quickly searched the grounds for a path leading to the mansion. I spotted one and began my journey hoping each of my passing footprints would bring me back in time. My time. Back to 1892.

That's when I noticed a rather odd contraption standing a good three hundred feet in front of me. It was a set of steel tripods painted in stripes of red and white like giant candy canes. They stood fifteen feet tall at least and a bar composed as the same sat on top the structure. From there, on the top bar, a set of heavy chains dangled nearly down to the ground. Attached to the chains was a seat made from a wood plank. There were two swinging seats total.

And on each of the planked seats sat a youngster, swinging back and forth like pendulums. Their lightheartedness told me the rumblings and commotions beyond the park were no more a concern to them than the foul smell of the air.

Amused, I watched the children stretch their legs, flying up, and down, each time they flew even further up and back again, much like Little Margret Jean and I had swung on the rope hanging behind the feed barn at Pine Brook. And as I watched the children, I caught a glimpse of the path cutting between the trees bordering the park leading to the mansion left behind from so long ago. I studied it, and that's when I witnessed the time lapse. A snap in time.

It was Netsel, and he was traveling down that very path in the woods with Mokey and Lucy. With them was a small foal, well protected between Mokey and Lucy, and of course, Netsel.

"Razzle-Dazzle! The strings of time must have crossed," as I reasoned watched them fade away into the air like ghosts.

The laughter of the children brought me back to my own dilemma. The distance between me and the path leading to the mansion was great. Too great for me to just run out to it in plain sight. I held my ground hoping the children would not notice me. But I was mistaken.

They slipped off their swinging chairs and, huddled together, they stared at me as if they were afraid of me as I was of them. Then, raising the quick arm of youth, one pointed to me.

At first, I believed them to be two boys for each wore Levis. But it mattered not. Boys-girls, they did see me and were making their way toward me.

"Look! The ghost of Jenny! She's here!" I heard one say. *What? Who? Me? Me, a-a-ghost?*

"Razzle-Dazzle! Run!" I heard myself say out loud. "Run!"

I ran like a mad dog being chased by a pack of wolves. Except I couldn't breathe. Fear and foul air filtered through my nostrils causing me to cough and spit the taste of repellent in my mouth; yet I had to keep moving and moving fast.

"The mansion! Oh, I must get to the mansion!" Picking up the bottom of my purple velvet skirt, I headed for the path Netsel and his horses had taken. I was correct. It led into the woods of the timber ridge surrounding the mansion.

Would...Shamus and Patsy be there? Could they be there? Would I see Netsel and Mokey and Lucy and their baby along the way?

I forced myself to run, hoping the end of the path would be the end of my adventure, and I would truly be home, proving all the day had just been a bad dream, like my episodes at Pine Brook.

Absorption Psychosis... Gotta be," I heaved, keeping pace. "Absorption Psychosis..."

But nay. The children were close behind and catching up. I could hear them plain and clear. I dared not look back to see how close they had gotten for it would slow me down. Though I was young, they were younger and could catch me if I made one slip of a mistake.

Though many years had passed causing the forest to grow, I knew it well and ran through the first bramble of trees, becoming more grateful the further I got. As the woods thickened and became more clustered, the cries of excitement from the children began to fade. My legs slowed a bit as I came into a clearing. The mansion was straightaway.

"Thank goodness," I panted, keeping the bottom of my skirt in hand, looking back at the children. They seemed long gone.

I turned my head and I plunged into something so hard and so solid it knocked me down. The ground was wet, and my hands dove into a puddle of thick, wet mud. Fearing my suit was ruined, I began to rise finding myself looking up at a tall man holding a shovel. A fine line of sweat formed on his brow. A handsome brow.

"Uncle, Uncle," the children called, making their way through the thicket of gnarled brush and low, twisted tree branches.

"We saw her! We saw her! We saw the Ghost of Jenny! We did, we really did!"

"The ghost of Jenny, huh?" The man said, smiling down at me.

His voice was full and deep, his hair and eyes, dark as the spring dirt he toiled.

It appeared I had stumbled into Shamus's beloved rose garden. And although much older (years and years older) it was well kept and flourishing as I never dreamed possible. And there, some feet away was the mansion, Shamus's mansion. My mansion.

The sight of it filled me with another fear. The fear of knowing that too much time had passed away and logically Shamus nor Patsy were alive and well, waiting for me to come home. I looked at the man hoping he and his world would disappear and that mine would come back.

"You jokers," he scolded, laughing at the children.

I looked away from the mansion and turned my attention back to the man. Oh, he was a handsome man. Though a stranger, somehow I knew him. He was fading. Yet I could hear and see him as plain as day.

"Ghosts don't bump into a person and get knocked over; and they are not so beautiful that they take your breath away," he said putting his hand out for me to take. It was a big hand capable of handling any labor given to it. Yet it radiated a gentleman's gentleness. I stared at his hand trying to determine where I had encountered it before. For I knew him. Somehow, indeed, I knew the man.

"Come on, 'Ghost of Jenny,' I'll help you to your feet."

I did not hesitate. I so badly wanted to take his hand, and yet by the same token, I wanted to go home to Shamus.

I reached for the man and as I did, I once again turned both warm and cold at the same time just as I had in Nora's room. My head spun. I knew what was happening; I was being drawn back, back into the tunnel. But yet I wanted to fight it. I was compelled to reach through the haze for the man before the mist overtook me as it had when I first traveled through the threads of time.

The hum of the tunnel rose. I fought the tug of its vacuum pulling me back in; it was of no use, the web of time surrounded me. A look of peril was replaced the man's cheerful smile. I was sure our fingers touched through the mist, and equally sure a part of him was with me as the darkness of time laying between us grew.

And so it was that I left the man's world behind, taking with me a fragment of him and a bit of the wonders of his time.

The threads spun quickly, radiating the brightness of time. I tried to ignore the brilliant colors and images each year brought, and concentrated very hard keeping watch for May 27th, 1892.

Blazing reds, and every shade of orange and yellow, cannons and fireworks, men captured and tortured overlapping scenes of those happy and content filled the cavern and danced with glorious hues of blues and greens and every color and hue imaginable. Only a few seconds passed, but it was long enough for me to miss my chance to touch May...27...1892. And I panicked. I watched the years fly by; my mind raced with them. The hum was no longer tranquil and soothing.

It careened with my rising fear.

1878...1872...The dates traveled on, turning my panic into horror.

I was frozen. 1865...1858... 1847...1843...

I prayed to the God (in whose existence I did not believe) to stop the threads from turning and twisting. I ended the prayer with that I learned as a child, "In your name. Amen." And as I did, I was drawn to the strings above my head.

I stood on tiptoe lurching high as possible to see the threads dangling from the tunnel's ceiling. 1882! The year sparkled and for a brief moment so did I. For 1882 was the last year I had seen my father and mother. And there, right there before my very eyes, tangled within the other strings were they. My heart and soul leapt. And so did the hum, nearly piercing my ears.

My parents were tiny and small, yet I could still see them plain and clear as if they were standing in full flesh in front of me.

"Mother, Father!" I shouted. "Mother, Father..."

My voice blended with the hum, echoing pass them. I stood even taller, forcing myself upward to my very limits.

"If only I can touch them, touch the date... Mother, Father..." I called out again. I watched as they looked at each other, showing each other the hair standing on their arms. They laughed, and patted down the strands.

"Mother! Father!" I screamed again. Tears flooded from my eyes. Again, they patted their arms. It was no use.

My heart ached as I watched them slowly slip away, turning away with time. Again, man's God had tormented me. And again, I reaffirmed my vow to disengage any thoughts that might entertain the possibility of His existence. I turned from the dates coming and going along the ceiling of the tunnel and put forth all efforts to find the time to which I belonged. I followed the strands.

"1776".

The date spun slightly above my head, catching my eye. The thread, to my amazement, carried the moving images of a large group of rather expressively dressed men. White wigs, fancy ones, adorned some heads I had seen in one of my school books at Pine Brook. Their clothing was equally important looking.

Hunched over a table, each man took his turn signing some sort a document, then took his place in line congratulating the next to sign. Just as the last person bent to autograph the paperwork, a tall man, as the one in Shamus' rose garden in 1953, fled from the scene and scurried up the thread of time, disappearing into the date of 1783.

"Why, that's when the Declaration of Independence was signed, and the other years are when the American Revolution took place!

How can this be? And who in God's name was, err...is the man running along the timeline?"

I looked closer into 1783 and then stopped myself. There were so many dates, and too many people, and too many events folding and unfolding on each and every strand. It made my head swell with confusion. And so did the hum. I feared being woven in alongside the man. Hence, I needed to clear my thoughts.

One wrong move, one brush of my finger, my hand, or the hem of my skirt would send me hurling again to a wrong place and time and into worlds which I knew nothing about. For I knew what ever date I touched would pull me to that exact date, the exact moment, hour, minute, second. I wanted to go home to 1892. But where was 1892?

"My own life in the thread of time. I must find my own Life Thread... my own Life Thread..." The thought intrigued me.

'*What if...What if...*'

"If I have if I were to find my own life in the Threads of Time would I then be able to go back to Mother and Father again and..." The very thought almost brought my heart almost to a stop.

"And Huston, I shall see Huston! I'll make sure of it!" I was determined to follow through with my plan.

Thoughts of my life and how I had the power to change all the wrongs within it filled my mind. I eagerly searched over the threads.

There were so many. The beautiful bedlam of perplexing array of colors and hues, spun, weaving, turning and unweaving. I thought of Pine Brook and the hum inside the tunnel started to race. A spark blasted down beside my left ankle and black boot. I thought of Little Margret Jean. Another spark shot out from the same spot. I bent to investigate.

The hum in the tunnel jumped with my excitement as I squinted at the timeline. I gasped. For the spark was a warm glow of golden yellow, and on it was none other than My Little Margret Jean. I reached for her, then stopped.

"If this is Little Margret Jean's timeline, then mine must be connected to hers somewhere."

I took further investigation, following the line. Backwards. That's when I saw her and wished I hadn't. For she was being born.

A woman pulled her from her mother's body and quickly cut the cord connecting them. Without so much as a wince of remorse the woman dumped Little Margret Jean into a bucket, and then roughly tossed a rag at the mother, she laid in her own birth pool of blood. The woman left the room, leaving Little Margret Jean and her mother to their own demise.

"Oh, My Margret," I cried, tears streaming down my cheeks. "My poor, poor Little Margret Jean!"

I was overcome with despair as I watched her mother move no more. A spark connected directly to Little Margret Jean's timeline suddenly appeared. It was a radiant crystal fire that I perceived as the start of some sort of sacred thread. For unlike most fires of life, this one traveled opposite of all the others. Instead of going to the Light, this one came from the Light and merged on the ones ending.

The string fizzled making its way from the rotating spoke which continued to draw all but a handful of dulled golden sparks into its wonderful, brilliant light. All the while, the hum in the tunnel turned from high to low, and then a sweet tone sounded, lasting but a moment, just long enough for the mothers Thread of Life to burn low as it traveled along its thread, and made its way to the wheel of light. Her residue, left behind, sagged the Line and rested nicely atop Little Margret Jean's. The two, I knew, would not be separated forever, but be a part of each other until the end of Little Margret Jean's own time of life.

I watched further. And as I did, I witnessed a young man enter the room with rags, a mop and two buckets of water. His attention turned from cleaning up the mother and her mess to the bucket where Little Margret Jean laid, crumpled and cold. Gently the man reached to pick up my Little Margret Jean. He held her close, carrying her to the table of her dead mother and swaddled her dearly. His Life Line glimmered along Little Margret Jean's. Upon another look closer at the man, a smile spread across my face. And as it did, the hum of the tunnel rose to a glorious, peaceful pitch. For the young man was no one other than, my beloved, Doctor Bruce Bayshore.

I took a few steps away from the birth of Little Margret Jean, and counting a few strands of thread upward, I was able to narrow down an approximation of where my Timeline might be. Hence, I refused to give into any further temptations of glimpsing into any other fragments of time other than to find June 3rd, 1892.

It was a quick discovery as I forcefully tore myself from the distractions which tried to capture me. I took a deep breath and hoped my calculations were correct. With a snap of a prayer to the God of my parents, I touched the single fiber of thread that read precisely: 3:05 p.m. and 30 seconds (the time I guessed my departure between Nora's room, and arrival into 1953 took place).

The tunnel and all its threads of fiber moaned softly, weaving and unweaving its massive collection of dates, and times, seconds, and colors, all filled with images too numerous to make out. And somewhere in all that, I found myself back in Nora's sewing room, looking in the full-length mirror.

I touched my face and arms and ran my hands down my velvet, purple jacket and its black fur, then over the purple skirt. Everything was solid. *I* was solid. I tapped the floor with my foot. It too, was solid. Solid as the ground of 1953.

How long had I been gone? Was I in the right time? The right place? Was Shamus and Patsy still alive and well?

I raced out the room, down the stairs and into the kitchen. To my delight, I found Patsy sitting quietly on his perch, his head tucked sleepily under his wing. I sighed with great relief and looked at the clock. It was as if I never left. For just enough time had passed for me to properly dress and arrive in a timely manner to arrange the tea for Shamus and myself.

In disbelief, as to what happened, my hands shook and my knees wobbled as I checked the wood in the kitchen stove, and put the kettle on to boil.

Lord knows I wanted to rush out and find Netsel and Shamus to tell them where I'd been and what I'd seen. As I raced to the back door, my senses came back to me.

"No, I mustn't," I spat in a whisper. "I must not tell a soul. Not a one, for they will think me mad; mad as a hatter and send me back to Pine Brook. *Absorption Psychosis.* That's what they will claim, absorption psychosis. An overactive imagination."

I straightened myself and headed back into the kitchen. This time with a limp.

CHAPTER NINE

A bsorption psychosis. It has to be, Patsy. It just has to be. How else can it be explained," I poured steaming water into Nora's silver teapot. I tried to push away the pictures that formed and reformed in my mind of that afternoon.

"*Time travel!* Such a thing is not real. It can't be. If it were so, then scientists all over the world would know about it. And if they know about it, then they would be traveling all over different parts of history, making bad things good. No Patsy, I'm telling you. I was not traveling in time. I just had a bout of, absorption psychosis. That's all. Another bout. Nothing more."

Patsy pulled his head from his wing and wobbled to the other side of his perch and stared at me.

"I'm sorry, Pats, I really am." I cooed at him and rubbed my thigh. "Listen to me going on and on about such foolishness. But you see, if I say anything about what happened Shamus will tell Miss Gavin, and she'll tell Doctor Bruce. And if that happens, they'll send me back t-t-t-to Pine Brook.

"Not that I would mind so much... I sure do miss Little Margret Jean... and Nurse Price and... well, everyone. But I like it here, too. I really like it. I have grown fond of you and Shamus and Netsel, and Miss Gavin, of course.

"Cream," I sighed, making sure there was enough in the silver charger. "Shamus does like his cream. I prefer lemon myself."

Patsy curiously watched my hand shake as I took a small yellow citrus from the side-counter and placed it in the waste bowl. "Back at Pine Brook such fruits are unheard of. So are a lot of things. Except when a person learns about them in books. Or, when someone coming through talks about such odd and marvelous things." I ran my fingers lightly along the rim of the tea pot.

'...a gift from Nora's grandfather given to us on our wedding day,' I recalled Shamus proudly discussing the tea set. *'He had it forged specifically for us. Do notice the fine etching along each individual piece. The shamrocks signify her Irish family side, and the Scottish thistles convey my national heritage. It was to be handed down to the next generation, Nora's offspring, and mine. Of course, we never could conceive. My fault, not hers. That's obvious.'*

Everything in that mansion was Nora's except the mansion itself. That was Shamus'. And that was obvious.

"She sure must have loved him, Patsy. Nora, that is." Patsy bobbed his head in agreement.

I checked the silver service. Butter knife, silver sandwich plates, the necessary silver tool kit Shamus insisted I include each and every time, the silver cream and sugar bowls, and of course, Nora's special monogrammed napkins made just for afternoon teas, finished in none other than real silver threading. It was all there.

Placing the serving tray on the tea cart before anything else was a trick I quickly learned. Once the tray was loaded with everything needed for a proper tea, it would become much too heavy and cumbersome to lift. That I learned by trial and error and some from scolding's from Shamus (and of course, Patsy).

"*Absorption psychosis,*" I mumbled, taking the silver plate filled with my fine quartered cucumber and water chestnut sandwiches from the ice box. I placed them on the cart. "That's all it was, just like Doctor Bruce said, absorption psychosis."

I checked the tea and myself for the last time before heading onto the back porch and out the door to the garden gazebo. Everything was fine, just fine, and in place.

It was late spring and not quite summer. And so, the air still cool, had a chill to it. It smelled sweet and fresh just as I knew it ought to. I made my way down the path leading to Shamus. My thigh throbbed. Thoughts of 1953 and the man and the two children followed. I tried shaking them from my mind like the foliage along the path trying to shed the last bit of late spring snow from its awaking world.

The rose buds, larkspur, and lavender, though eager to bloom, still had plenty of time to rest for the long summer ahead. But the daffodils and tulips were wide-awake. I delighted in them as the clump-clump-clumping of the tea cart in front of me chased away the chipmunks and squirrels nibbling on the tender spring foliage. I watched them scamper off to other parts of the garden to hide from human eyes, and Patsy's. The gazebo was straight ahead.

I could see Shamus through its wide, windowless frame. He sat patiently, picking at nonexistent fuzz and loose threads on his day-wear. It was a habit he and Mr. Hawthorn and a few of the older gentlemen at Pine Brook shared (besides looking lonely and bored). He stopped his nit picking, and sighed, and turned to the Edison Phonograph at his side. The one he had Netsel deliver to the gazebo earlier that spring. It would remain in the gazebo all summer, until once again, as every fall, Netsel would haul it back into the mansion. Shamus cranked the handle and sat back. Mozart broke the silence. I followed.

"Hello," I rested with the tea cart at the end of the ramp leading up into the gazebo. "Can you use s-some company?" Shamus sighed.

"Yes, I suppose," he sounded exhausted from waiting. I pushed the tea cart up the ramp and parked it between Shamus and his favorite white lattice table. The matching white chair next to it I assumed was meant for me.

"N-nice afternoon, isn't it?"

Again, he sighed. This time what seemed intentionally longer and harder. "Yes, I suppose." This time he didn't bother to gaze over the tea service, inspecting it as he usually did. Instead, he twirled his finger for me to rotate and inspected me from head to toe.

"Why, you look lovely Camarilla, simply lovely. The color serves you well." He eyed me suspiciously. "But how did you come to have mud splattered across your backside?"

Patsy flitted on the open window sill and bobbed his head.

"Y-y-yes, sir." Curiosity flared in Shamus' eyes. "I um, I um, ww-well..." I was scared. Frightened. Stunned. I had left 1892.

"It matters not," Shamus' long fingers gracefully wrapped around the teapot. He let out a satisfied, "ahh... Nice and hot. And I see you included the proper sandwiches. I trust they are also at the correct temperature?"

"Yes, I-I-I believe so." I nervously patted the few wrinkles in my skirt, fighting the urge to twist it to check the mud I brought back with me.

"Oh, please, do forgive me," Shamus wheeled himself to my side. "Little Mademoiselle, will you please do me the honor and join me?" He took my hand and led me to my chair.

As I had seen Miss Gavin do numerous times, I sat pertly on the edge of the chair. Then, gracefully as possible, I opened my napkin and placed it across my lap and ran my finger anxiously up and down the monogram on my napkin, S.P. F. & N. R. F.

"Is something troubling you, my dear?" Shamus asked, grabbing a lemon. He rolled it between the palms of his hands. "It helps break down the meat of the fruit. It gives more juice this way."

He placed the lemon on the cutting board, and picked up the cutter. The knife sliced through the yellow ball of fruit. *'Shhunk,'* the knife sounded hitting the wood board, *'Shhunk, shhunk.'*

"She knows," Patsy screeched, flying off the sill and onto the perch kept for him inside the gazebo. "She knows." Shamus stopped slicing.

I stared at my napkin and retraced the loops and curls of Nora's monogram swirling before my eyes. Patsy flapped his wings.

"Is there something you would like to tell me?" Shamus placed the lemon wedge alongside my cup on the saucer sitting on the table. My finger froze on a loop.

It was no use telling him any sort of tales. Lies and misgivings would only hurt my situation and raise the risk of being sent back to Pine Brook. Evidence of 1953 mud on my skirt and bruise on my thigh or not, I decided to be honest and throw myself on the mercy of his knowledge and understanding of my so called physiological condition.

"W-w-well sir," I flipped over the napkin, then flipped it again. "I-I don't know exactly how to p-put this. But something strange happened t-t-to me. I believe I had an e-e-episode, a-a-a severe e-e-episode, of well, m-my absorption psycho-psycho-psychosis. That or I am t-t-truly loose in the head," I chuckled, hoping to ease the sensitivity of the situation.

He stopped pouring the hot water into the teapot and wheeled himself to the ledge of the gazebo, "No, my dear," he finally sighed and stared out at his rose garden.

"Your symptom, this, absorption psychosis, it occurred when you put on that suit, didn't it—" His tone was calm. "I assure you Little Mademoiselle, you are not a lunatic. I am. I am the lunatic."

He continued to gaze at his rose garden. His wonderful rose garden that just began to bring forth life. His next words turned his voice heavy. And my very being in a delirium to near hysteria.

"I assure you, what you experienced was not a bout of psychosis absorption because you never had such the thing called absorption psychosis. Time travel, Camarilla, that is what has been causing your spins all this time...the effects from time travel. And your so-called psychological, and physical abnormalities, your absorption psychosis, your overactive imagination, even your... stuttering...all of it. They are *all* effects from time travel!

"Your abnormalities were used to your advantage as a ploy, a cover-up, to keep you safe from your own self which gave good reason to place you under the care of Doctor Bayshore in that dreaded monstrosity that he and the State refer to as a certified mental hospital. No, Camarilla, I do assure you that you are not loose in the head, as you put it. Not by any means. What you *did* experience is, as you, yourself put it, the result of your, *Green Door Project*."

I was stunned speechless. So much so that all I could manage was to watch Shamus wheel himself back to our tea. It was madness. All of it, pure madness. Mozart's sweet music playing on the Edison added to the folly.

The water inside the kettle was, "hot enough," Shamus decided, feeling the pot. He poured us each a fresh cup. Mine with lemon, his with the thick, heavy cream he loved so much. He took a sip then carefully placed his teacup and saucer on the small white lattice table between us. I dared not lift my cup, for my hands trembled too greatly. Shamus turned to the Edison machine, both beast and savior. He turned the handle.

I stared at the garden. The very garden which that same day I'd been chased in, fallen in, and looked into the faces of strangers in. But looking at it with Shamus that afternoon in that late May of 1892, the garden was not as full and lush as in 1953, but small and just beginning to grow. And the clear, clean air and smells and sounds were free of that time long yet to be.

I watched the wax cylinder of the phonograph go round, and round as Shamus cranked the Edison's handle. Mozart filled the sweet clean air once again.

"You do not realize there was a time when you knew how to service a tea quite well," he reached for his tea cup, his eyebrow flinched as he took a sip from his tea. "You have not lost your touch, my dear Little Mademoiselle." He took another taste, his ice-blue eyes looked at me with compassion that turned to anger.

"You are braver than you ever thought possible. Truly. Otherwise, I would not have allowed you to come back. I would have left you safe and sound at Pine Brook. And, I certainly would not have invited you to this special tea; nor allowed you to try on the dresses. Those damned dresses," he cursed.

"Of Course, I understand you have no idea as to what I am talking of. And so it is that we have stuck to our plan to a tee. Besides, it was you, yourself, that made me promise to arrange all this despite the demands of the others. That is why I am the one insane. Insane to had allowed you to talk me into this in the first place. And for that, all blame will fall on me."

I was dizzy with Shamus' lunacy. For what he was saying was absurd. All of it. As well as what I had experienced.

I sat my teacup and saucer on the table and rose from my chair. I was scared and wanted to leave.

"You must sit. You are as white as, well, white as a ghost, as some might see you. I understand how you feel. How well I do understand. I felt the very same way when you came to me with all this the first time. Those suits, those dresses, those damn dresses and such. I should never, *never* have allowed you to..."

Shamus' blue eyes gazed tight on me. My stomach churned. "Th-th-the first t-t-time? The first time I c-c-came t-t-to you?"

"Oh, it is quite the story," he said, turning again to the phonograph.

He removed the wax cylinder. "The best place to start any story is at the beginning, as they say."

What he was about to tell me was so unreal, so unbelievable, I never would, never could, believe it to be true had I not experienced it myself. But if you recall I did warn you from the very start of this story that Shamus had his own plan for my servitude. And so not to prove me a liar, did I not express my disdain prior of a machine I considered the serpent's finger, and another an irresistible monster? And as before, I do guarantee you, every last word put forth is true.

I flagged away the fresh cup of tea Shamus handed me.

"Please, do sip your tea. It will help settle your stomach, and nerves." I hesitated then took the cup, my hands trembled. He leaned into the Edison and opened its doors.

"Shall we begin?" he reached into the cabinet and tugged on the shelving door. It opened, exposing a small row of secret wax cylinders. "It's quite simple actually," he said plucking up the first one, and sat it on his lap.

"You see, Camarilla, everything surrounding us, everything in existence, such as teacups and saucers...even Edison's talking cylinders, is held in place by gravity, even things we cannot see, like the trees on the other side of the woods. Correct?"

"Of course," my voice shook, barely audible.

"Now, would you also agree that we can weigh and measure those same trees on the other side of the woods, that we cannot see? And what about this tea? Can we say the same for this tea?"

I nodded in agreement. Shamus took my tea and poured it onto the wood floor of the gazebo.

"What about now? Does the tea still exist? Of course it does. It is still tea? Absolutely. It has only changed form, from wet soon to be dry. Either way it is still tea and it is still in existence so, hence, we can still measure it. See how simple it is?

"Now, once again, gravity holds it all together. Correct?

"What if I told you time works in the very same way? And like everything in existence, time is also held together by gravity. Time is like the trees on the other side of the woods, it is like the tea in the floor. We can't see it, but it is still there.

"We measure time even though we cannot hold it in our hands. Time cannot be held or seen in a bottle. Unless a person can capture it and hold it as you, yourself, have managed to do. But yet, we do. "We measure it in seconds, minutes, hours, days, weeks, years...memories. Fascinating, isn't it?

"We see it taking hold in everything surrounding us...people, material goods, food, and...even gardens. Yet very few humans believe it is possible to manipulate time as we do tea in tea cups and lemons on saucers. And now, Little Mademoiselle, we must add to this." Shamus carefully picked up his teacup.

"Everything is connected. Everything! You have proven this to be true.

"No matter how large or small, far or near, young or old. It all has substance. And that substance is little particles of neutrons. Millions and millions and trillions of the little buggers. And those itty-bitty little neutrons are pockets of energy. Energy, Camarilla. Energy that you captured and have proven how everything is composed of energy. The more pockets of energy, the warmer the item becomes.

"And now, we shall take it all even further.

"Little Mademoiselle, you and I are connected to the tea I spilled on the floor."

Shamus sat back. He bit the tip of his thumb; his blue eyes shined with excitement as he waited for my reaction. I looked down and focused on the splat of brown liquid.

It didn't touch us at all. It was far from both Shamus and myself. He was so positive that the half-dried splat of brown touched us, despite it being some inches away from either of us. I had to decide how to answer.

"Yes," I said softly.

"Are you positive? Truly positive?"

"Um, y-y-yes sir, I am," my stomach tumbled.

"Sure enough to stake your own life on it? Sure enough to stake *other* people's life's on your belief."

I stared at the tea. It was gone, absorbed into the wood floor of the gazebo. Only its stain remained. I bent over, looking at it even closer.

"W-w-well sir, it seems to me that although I c-c-can't see it, doesn't mean it's not there. It just changed form is all. From wet to dry."

"Correct!" He shouted nearly jumping from his chair. "Correct!

"Now, if you will, Little Mademoiselle, take your finger and draw a line from the evaporated tea, along the floor boards, to my foot, up my leg, around my shoulder and head, back down my other side and again onto the floor board."

I did as asked. I ran my finger everywhere Shamus requested. When I traced my finger around and around him and down to his shoe, he said, "now, without lifting your finger, run it along the floor to your boot, around your own self and back to the spot of tea." Again, I did as told.

"Now tell me, at any time did your finger disconnect anything in its path, or did everything in the path stay connected?"

I thought about it for a moment. "Well s-s-sir," I said. "I do believe looking at it that way, I must say everything in the path is connected."

"Connect-amaltrie," he said delighted. "Yes indeed! Connect-amaltrie!

"We, and everything in the universe, no matter where it is located, are connected! Including time. Since it is measurable, it has substance. And substance makes up those pockets of energy that holds gravity together.

"Now, the problem is, since the protons heat up due to the activity of energy, how does one get from one point in time to the next without the substance of time becoming overheated, which in turn would melt the time substance, which then naturally will damage and destroy the timeline. It would cause horrific distortions, you know.

"Hence, as you came to discover, weaving keeps it moving so as to cool it and yet doing so keeps it close so not to distort it.

"But there is another problem, my dear Camarilla. Since time is also substance but just in a different form, it therefore can be manipulated in the same manner as the tea, can it not?"

I had grown tired and confused. Not wanting to exacerbate the situation I simply nodded, hoping to calm Shamus, and myself.

"Time, like everything else," he went on, "never ends and is forever touching, connecting. It does well on its own. But when fools such as you and I try touching it, manipulating it in hopes of constructing better lives for ourselves, it loses its shape due to the extra heating of protons caused from the extra energy activity. Hence Camarilla, we cause ripples in the timeline, which then naturally causes snags, which of course calls for distortions to occur.

"Our meddling, *your* meddling, shifts time, causing terrible shifts...destructive distortions...all due to the foolishness of us mere mortals trying to create for ourselves a life of perfection. Like the one for freeing me out of this confounded medicine chair.

"Unfortunately, a few have managed to actually rip through the thread of gravity of time itself, causing true ripples. The effects were hideous. Parts of our history is proof.

"But only one person has ever come close to accomplishing a ripple with only a few fluctuations. Yet, unfortunately, those fluctuations were enough to have consequences. Consequences that you, yourself, insisted be repaired.

"For it is you, Little Mademoiselle, yes you, you yourself that managed to break through the gravity field that holds time. And so, it is upon your very own request that I have brought you back here to weave time back to what was once normal."

"You are mad!" I gasped rising from chair. "A lunatic!"

Nora's beloved teacup and saucer fell from my hands and onto the ground with a crash. Patsy flew from his perch and onto Shamus' shoulder.

"Why, you...you are mad...mad as a hatter!" I screamed. I headed for the entrance of the gazebo. Nora's china crushed under my boots.

"Oh? Am I?" Shamus said. "If I am the one who is mad as a hatter, as you claim, then you, you Camarilla are equally, if not more so, the queen of hatters..."

He turned to the Edison, and carefully unwrapped the wax cylinder sitting on his lap.

"I assure you Little Mademoiselle, what you are about to hear is as important to you as your very own breaths of life."

Patsy buried his head under his wing as Shamus attached the roll to the phonograph. And as he did so, somehow, somewhere in the back of my mind all that Shamus had explained was becoming clearer and clearer.

"Behold!" he thundered. "Behold"

I can still hear the needle grinding into the hard brown wax, slowly scratching its way across the cylinder. Then came the voice that forced me down into my chair. I froze. For the words held me there. For what I heard was impossible. Or was it? I nearly fainted as the words befell forth.

"Hello Camarilla. Due to the length of time available on this recording I must unfortunately make this message short. I have so much to tell you. But as you will soon find out, I cannot. I have left much of it in Shamus' hands.

"I assume you, err, I am in the gazebo sitting at a tea with dear

Shamus; whom I assume is now old, yet still very handsome. And Patsy I assume is nearby. And of course, I, you, Camarilla, are nevertheless in shock.

"But you must trust what you are hearing, and what Shamus tells you. You have a mission, a responsibility not to *do*, but undo. You are a Caregiver, a Caregiver not for dear Shamus, but a Caregiver of time. Remember that and use it well. And please, give Patsy an extra petting and an extra muffin with an extra spread of butter that he is so inclined to enjoy. Be strong, Camarilla. Be strong.

"And not to forget one last thing...we all will see you beyond The Green Door."

The words were gone. And the needle scratched on.

"Enough," I said, holding my hands to Shamus. "Enough!"

I was beyond stunned. Beyond shock. Beyond horror-stricken. For the voice I just listened to was none other than my very own.

CHAPTER TEN

Supper that evening was quiet, not heavy with the usual chatter between Shamus and me. Fortunately, dear Netsel had decided to supper with us that night and not alone in the stable with his horses as he usually did. As it turned out, he and Shamus made the proud announcement that Netsel's mare, Lucy, was having a foal. The foal I had seen in the time lapse in the garden that day in 1953.

I so wanted to tell poor old Netsel all about it in order to comfort him, seeing he was nervous as a new father-to-be always is. I opened my mouth to begin when Shamus let out a hoot just as he dropped his hot bowl of beef soup on his lap. Between that commotion and Netsel expressing his concerns with anxious talk as to his plans for the new addition, along with an occasional compliment on our meal, gave little chance of conversation to fill any gaps of empty air that remained.

So, with that, it wasn't hard excusing myself to retire earlier than usual. Truth told, I believed Shamus was grateful for the distraction of Netsel's need to receive assurance that all would be well with his Lucy and Mokey and their yet to be, newborn. And I am very sure Netsel found the time alone with Shamus a treasure in his time of need.

Therefore, without much ado, I finished cleaning up what Shamus considered necessary, and wished them a well goodnight.

It would take a great deal of digesting concerning what I learned that afternoon and where better to do so then in my private chambers.

The fizzle of the gaslight on my nightstand kept me company, as did Patsy who slept soundly on his perch next to my bed. I laid awake thinking about all Shamus had told me and what I'd told myself—and what I hadn't.

Yes, time travel was possible. After all, I did hear myself for myself, from myself. And as Shamus claims I told him, "time travel is very much possible if one knows how to break through the law of gravity and weave the threads of time so as to keep them from heating and burning up in a sizzle."

"Time," I said with an unsettled chuckle and sigh. "How did I, Camarilla Rae Berkelman, manage to turn theory, and more, into fact and not recall such a thing."

I reasoned what I had done, or I had already done. And having to understand all the nips and tucks of it required needing no more in-depth knowledge of it than needing to know what is an empirical formula and molecular formula in order to create a cake.

I turned on my side and watched Patsy sleep. Was I going to try again? Was I going to attempt to fix the tangled disasters I left behind from the other times, despite causing even more turmoil? What possibly caused me to undergo such an adventure in the first place? I thought of Shamus. Why were he and I so close that I put myself to such a heavy task for him in the first place?

Overwhelmed or not, I wasn't so foolish not to have asked Shamus those very questions that afternoon. He claimed the answers to those questions would have to wait. It was, "imperative that I not be told." That is what he claimed I had told him.

"You did not know what was intended to be, and by you meddling with what was meant to be, caused a chain reaction on the thread of time. Thinking you knew what should and should not be, and trying to untangle those threads of time in order to force them to your liking is what caused the problem in the first place." That's what Shamus said he was to tell me, *"Trying to untangle those threads now might cause even more entanglements, making things even more worse."*

"Or make them better," I told Patsy who continued to sleep soundly on his perch next to my bed. I, on the other hand, only yawned. For Shamus' lecture would not leave my mind.

"At first, I laughed thinking you were out of your wits, and yes, a lunatic, a true lunatic by all standards.

"Why, I sat pinned in this blasted medicine-chair day after day watching you put together outfits, *'very special outfits,'* you claimed. Then one day you claimed you had discovered, *The Golden Threads of Time* and was about to enmesh them into your outfits. Those threads, those miserable threads, you claimed would bring you instantly to any time you chose. I laughed, calling you mad. Yes, Camarilla, I first called *you* mad as a hatter.

"But one day as I sat watching you slip into one of those wretched skirts, and put on one of your bizarre jackets, and pair of godawful shoes... it happened. I was helpless, unable to move in order to stop what was about to happen. Then poof! Just like that, I watched you... disappear.

"Thank God you returned within just seconds. But you, you claimed to have lived almost a whole lifetime. *'There, over there. I grabbed it, Shamus, I actually grabbed it.'* Those were your own words. You, *'grabbed it.'*

"Your face, your hands, the very skin covering you was younger.

Taut. Youthful. You brought back a true and real thread of time. That is when I realized you were telling the truth.

"But one day you never came back, and I sat here in this bloody mansion, in this bloody chair, waiting! Waiting with these wheels for legs...legs infected with this damn polio you promised you would find a cure for, "in the future," you said. But you didn't, did you?

"Instead, you got mixed up with a few innocent people and managed to make a horrible mess of their lives and, in turn, infected perhaps thousands more."

Shamus' words bit me. Breaking into a sweat, I sat up in bed. Patsy stirred nervously on his perch.

"You know more about all this than what you're letting on, don't you, old boy?" He looked at me, his black eyes now wide awake. "This isn't the first time we met, is it?" He bobbed his head.

I knew what I had to do. I rose and hastened to Nora's room. Patsy followed.

I stood at the green door and hesitated for just a moment. Then, with heavy heart, I turned the door knob. Patsy bobbed his head, and flapped his wings. Again, I opened the Green Door.

I Placed my gaslight on the table and sat down at the sewing machine and stared at it.

It was a beautiful machine. Shiny black with contrasting-colored flowers painted on its metal body. I found it somehow well oiled, and with the needle threaded with a fine, gold silk, as if it had just been used. And the cloth. The cloth I had draped over the bed with the white ruffles lay on the sewing machine's arm. I reached out to the tea pot and touched it. It was warm, but barely. The cups empty but for a few left over drops of tea.

I pet Patsy as I thought. The things I had put out of my mind when I first came to the mansion was becoming clear to me. The light on the knoll when I first arrived with Miss Gavin, Mrs. Thompson's sudden disappearance, the way Patsy reacted to me when we first met.

And the two recent odd occurrences; the brilliant flash of light under the door that occurred that very afternoon, and finding that wasn't Netsel wasn't a stow away after all, using the tea service on the table beside me.

"'Be strong, Camarilla. Be strong. And not to forget one last thing... we will all see you beyond The Green Door.'"

I stroked Patsy's soft, black feathers, and looked at the closet. The door was closed. In my rush to get downstairs that afternoon, I had left it open. I knew I had.

"I really am not alone in all this, am I, Patsy? But who are they? The ones I told would be there waiting."

"Awe" Patsy squawked. "Awe-Awe."

And so it was that night, through the dim glow of the gaslight that I again opened the closet door. I looked over the outfits I made for me and pulled out the one I was already familiar with. The purple velvet.

With troubled hands I fretfully undressed from my nightclothes, and again I donned myself with the purple velvet suit that brought me to 1953. This time I hoped to be within a time frame acceptable to the attire.

Fastening the last pearl button on the high lace blouse, I slipped on the jacket. The black fur trim rested against my breasts, forming perfectly with them. My black dress boots shined nicely, and my hat, adorning my head was handsome as any other I had seen in Harper's Bazar. I tied the lavender and black straps of ribbon neatly into a bow tucked under the side of my chin. As if by instinct, I fluffed the three peacock feathers fastened straight up on the rim.

Turning to the mirror, I saw I looked modest, and superbly perfect in fashion. "The only thing missing is a parasol," I said straightening myself. "But I guess my chatelaine and purse will do."

I checked to make sure they were both attached to my skirt and jacket. I picked up Patsy and nuzzled him close to me.

"You know what's going t-t-to happen, don't you, old b-b-boy." He snuggled closer.

"I-I-I'm s-s-sorry, Sh-Sh-Shamus, r-r-really I am. B-b-but I have to, j-j-just one more time. I-I-I'm sorry. I just have to."

And just as before, the gentle river of time flowed through me. The same fever of warmth and cold took its hold, and again the brilliant light came into existence. Before me, the mist formed, and I watched myself and Patsy fade into the abyss of time.

It was blinding at first, but my eyes soon adjusted as they had before, and I was able to see the huge sprocket spinning and twisting and weaving, casting dates along the timeline and then retrieving them.

And as it had been before, the sound of time was a comforting sound. I no longer feared it, nor the threads of life feeding through the wheel of light. I watched the threads glow. Pictures of people and dates forming along the strings glistened and glowed, sparking golden fires of the breaths of life.

I watched the breaths of life darken as they came to their end of existence on Earth; then, with one last brilliant glow, they entered the light; then came a final blackness.

With Patsy tucked tightly under my arm, I stooped over and studied the people on the timeline. I knew many of them, some from another place and time. Those were the faces of the forgotten. My forgotten.

Some faces were strong, some tender, others tired. Most disturbing was those expressing naked fear that I somehow had caused.

"My God, What, wh-what have I done?" I cried. "What have I done?" Shamus' spiteful voice came to my mind.

You got mixed up with a few innocent people and managed to make a horrible mess of their lives and, in turn, perhaps thousands more...

I looked at Patsy. "I see them now," I said softly as if my voice might once again disturb them. "I need to go back and help them,"

"B-B-But wh-wh-where do I s-s-start?" I stammered looking at a thread. Then another, and again another.

I studied the golden glints and their movements and realized that in order to fix the past, we would need to go forward to the future.

"Don't you see, Patsy? It's so simple, really. By first sewing the farthest tear in future Time, Time will stop but for a nanosecond. Which will cause a fluctuation at that exact time and location on the Time Line. The fluctuation will then cause time to swell, which in turn will cause a natural swelling, a tidal wave if you will, just as a tidal wave of water happens in the ocean, but in this case, it is Time that will be affected, not water. It will cause a Time wave.

"Once the new time is corrected, it will flow backwards, just like water in a wave does, due to the swell of fluctuation. It will then refill and reconstruct the past as to what it should had been in the very first place. See? Easy!"

Patsy squawked and hid his head in the crook of my elbow.

I leaned close to the wall of the tunnel careful not to allow myself or my clothing to touch any fibers.

"Razzle-Dazzle," I spat reading dates, years and days, minutes and seconds speeding past my eyes. That's when I saw *him*.

"*It's him*," I gasped with excitement. Instead of being inside Shamus' Garden, the man was deep within the threads. He was younger. Much younger. Yet I still recognized him as the man from 1953.

"Who are you?" I asked. "*Why* are you?"

He was near a boat. Not just an ordinary lake boat or even an ocean boat, but the biggest boat I ever saw.

"A steamer, Patsy, I believe he's on a steamer ship...a liner...an ocean liner, but much, much larger!"

I strained closer. The date in which the man stood was: April 11th, 1912.

"I just might be mad as a h-hatter, Patsy, I j-just might be. Let's hope this outfit is m-meant for the year 1912."

As the dates spun quickly past, I watched closely for the year, 1912 —month, April—day, number eleven. It arrived and I touched it.

I could only guess at how long I would be gone.

CHAPTER ELEVEN

There was a tug. We slowed to a stop. A few seconds longer and we began moving again, this time forward, forward into time. The hum inside the tunnel slowly ceased leaving the sound of silence to surround us.

"Well, old boy," I said apprehensively, holding Patsy tight in the crook of my arm. "I do believe we have arrived."

Of course I was anxious. After all, we were in the future, and being so, I realized I was unprepared for the everyday social graces, and taboos and activities I would be embarking upon. It meant I would need to find a few good newspapers and chronicles to study from in order to help me acclimate to twentieth century life and its economic structure, for in my time, the condition of both were yet to be determined, and upon conversating with those, I wished not to appear ignorant or simple.

I also had concern of any new inventions that Pasty and I might come up against. For, if and when that too were to occur in front with the others, how could I explain my ignorance on all of the said such matters?

Despite my best efforts to keep Patsy safe, we tumbled out the tunnel and onto what appeared to be a hard concrete surface. He toppled from my arms landing a few feet away as I was startled for but a moment then quickly rose and snatched him up and out of the way of the feet of the people stampeding past us. I held him tight under my arm and looked to see where we were.

And to my true and utter astonishment, we were standing unexpectedly on a very long, very wide, very busy and very noisy pier at a seaport. But which ocean, and seaport I did not know.

Despite our unusual whereabouts, I did find the people (and smells) to be more of what I was accustomed compared to our trip to 1953. Here in 1912, I did not find the clothing so to strangely absurd, but much more so like my own (with a few variations of course). I was sure I would blend in well enough.

I knew right off Nurse Price certainly would appreciate such a fashion era. For it appeared the tight fitting *what-nots* of our fashionable under dressing had been discarded, yet both men and women's daywear remained highly appropriate, unlike the showing of bare calves and faces, such as it was, or is, back (and forward) in '53.

I found the air wonderfully odd and ridiculously refreshing, tinged with the scent of what I first thought was possibly frogs and swamp such as in the back fields of Pine Brook. But after a moment or two I realized the weighty smell was not that of frog or swamp but an off odor of fish and sultry water that I heard Mr. Hawthorn describe as, "good ole' salty sea air, the best air any man can breathe." And on the breeze rose a sound in the distance that I recognized to be of a fog horn from a tugboat crying out its warnings to, "clear the way," for the large ship it was towing into the harbor. "Razzle-Dazzle!" I said under my breath in a-near whisper.

"Razzle...Dazzle...Patsy...Look!"

At least a good mile and a half away from the dock on which Patsy and I stood was a sight I had never seen before and never would ever see again. It remains burned in my memory forever (and Patsy's as well).

Under what appeared to be the late morning sky, laid a ship resting on the waves of the ocean. Even at that distance, its girth was so grossly huge it was unmeasurable. Alas, I knew at once it was our destination; for it was the very vessel I had seen sewn in the threads of time.

But how Patsy and I were to board the beast, and where its destination lay, was as much a quandary to me as to where Patsy and I stood.

Tucking the old bird close to me, I focused on the situation at hand. The boardwalk was bursting with not only people, but horse-less carriages as well. The iron and steel monsters motoring past us, were unlike those both back home in 1894, and in 1953. These were supported on tall, thin wheels with horns that blared loud and strong like giant geese as they passed us by. They frightened poor old Patsy so that he tried climbing out my arms ready to attack the next one passing us. I jumped to the side and out of its way just in the nick of time.

"Jeepers-creepers! I-I I'm just as scared as you are Patsy, but I don't think either one of us c-c-can stop those machines no matter how hard we try." I forced my tears and fear down into my gut, for I had no time for such.

Patsy settled down and nestled in my arms while I tried to gain perspective to our whereabouts and hopefully our mission.

And as I did, I noticed a couple that stood behind us. I listened intently to their conversation. Their speech was rather unorthodox as well as that of those persons scurrying by. And so by tuning my ear to their babble, I was able to put together clips of recognizable words, thus enabling me to at least piece together our bearings.

"And over there next to the White Star Ship office is Queens Hotel...snuggled in right tight here inside Corks Harbor. 'Tis said it's so tight in them rooms that if you reach your hand out your rooms' window you might touch a liner or two passing to and fro."

Adhering to the woman's chatter, I looked over my shoulder and to the right. A hotel sat on the street abutting the pier on which we stood.

"The Cobh Pier," the woman called it. I repeated the name under my breath pronouncing it as she. "Cove."

I studied the buildings behind us to which the woman referred, the White Star Ship office and Queen's hotel.

They were painted mustard yellow, which the sea air had crackled, making their structures and paint look like giant, dried salted kippers in mustard sauce.

"Well, if that don't beat all, cousin," the man said.

He was older, and though he did carry an accent, he pronounced his words more adequately than the woman. No dropping of consonants, nor rounded vowels plopping about as if his mouth were filled with mashed potatoes. He spoke what we Americans claimed as English. Maybe not good, pure, clean English. But English nevertheless.

"Aye," the woman continued in her thick brogue. "You be looken' at the Cork Harbor, cousin. Second largest harbor in the whole entire world. The first being in Australia." The tone of Irish pride trilled in her voice.

"I haven't been here for some time, so seeing you off was a splendid way for me to see the ship that all of Queenstown and all the world is yapping about. Aye, see there? She is anchored off the point of Roche. 'Bout good mile and halfway, she is. From what I can see of her, she looks seaworthy enough I'd say. Looks the same as her sister ship, the Olympic. This one be mere three inches longer, but mind you, she does outweigh the Olympic by a good 1,000 tons."

"Aye, cousin," the man answered lightheartedly. "Even at a mile and a half off, a body can see that she's good and sturdy. They say she's even more luxurious than a person can imagine. Course me traveling third class I doubt I will experience any of the fancy trappings she holds in her. Second class might give me a taste of it. But third class?

I think not. Though some say her third class is that of second class, and her second class that of first. As far as ship travel goes. I suppose either is fine as long as I am not traveling with the usual livestock and dysentery. Course there be times telling is hard between the man next to you and the cattle. Sometimes I prefer cattle." The man chuckled.

"Now what might that building out there on that island be?"

The man's finger pointed to an island in the distance sitting before the vessel. That's when I noticed the poor fellow had but one arm. The sleeve of his plain gray shirt was tucked and pinned ever so neatly up close to his shoulder; his beard trimmed in typical style hid most of his simple, plain face. I felt my own chin, wondering if I were a man, would I sport a beard? And if so, would I be capable of keeping it so pin-neat even with two arms?

I heard her swallow as she pushed out her words Her tone darkened. "Aye," the woman said, "That chop of land!"

"That, my dear cousin is Spike Island. I haven't laid eyes on it since me and the family moved to England. You know...after we got word." There was a heavy pause.

"Looks dismal," the man finally replied.

"Aye. That she is, lovey, that she is. She was once a monastery, you know. Now it's a prison holding those waiting on transportation to their next prison. Once a body is in, there is no escaping other than their transport. And if not that, they wait their death. They say some men have been in her belly since their youth, long forgotten now, dead of old age for sure and desperation. Or rats.

"Rats," she repeated. "Most prisoners in ol' Spike eats rats for a main meal; it's all them poor Limeys gots' to fill their guts." The two cousins fell silent. They dared not look at the other.

Spike Island, I thought. *Spike Island... Rats.* The name fit. I clutched Patsy hoping the warmth of his body would catch the sudden chill that ran through me.

The two cousins wistfully watched the ocean waves washing against the heavy wooden legs of the dock.

"Did you know him?" the one-armed man asked.

"Aye," the woman answered. "Quite well. 'Twas always a kind soul to me and me loved ones. Hard times has a way of hurtn' all of us, on the outside and in. I'm afraid he just got caught trying to fix his hurtn', is all.

"Rats," she said again. This time she spat on the ground in disgust. "Those damned rats ate ol' Paulie but good, before he could get to—" Her voice trailed off sounding out the word every person lives for, "*Freedom*. He got it all right. Just not the way he intended, is all.

"Daniel," the lady said composing herself. "It sure was fine seeing you and what the New World has done for our families. Look at you. A fine caretaker of a big, fine mansion."

Daniel. His name was Daniel. I watched him hang his head. He shook it and laughed.

"I'm afraid America hasn't done much for me. I think England was a might brighter in some ways."

He moved his shoulder up and down, flapping the empty sleeve of his shirt as if his cousin hadn't noticed the stub protruding from his shoulder.

"Down to selling bloody popcorn and peanuts to whoever will eat the bloody stuff. Oh, I make a good living at it, I suppose. What with being a groundskeeper I have no real living expenses as most folks do However, truth told, that big, fancy mansion does not keep me warm enough, especially if I venture out my little room and away from my hearth. But it's the kindness of the folks back in Timber Town that keeps me warm, in here."

I watched the man tap his chest with his good arm. The woman touched his face with the affection which one long lost cousin touches another.

Timber Town? The mansion? I held my breath hoping the loud pounding of my heart would fill not my making me lose one word of the conversation.

Could that be the mansion? Shamus's mansion? It has to be, it just has to be!

"Life here hasn't been any more kind to us either," the woman said staring at Spike Island. She was as simple looking as her cousin.

"Aye. I will give the rest of the clan your love," she said, dabbing tears from her small green eyes. "The luck of the Irish...Baugh! 'Tis more the curse of us Irish."

Together they looked at the ship anchored the mile and a half away at Roche's Point.

"Looks as though the tenders are ready to ferry," the man Daniel said, his voice lowering.

"Maybe we should go forward to the pier. I take it you will be riding the 'America' out to Roche's Point?"

"No. Seeing the mail and extra provisions will be taking the America, I'll be riding the Ireland out to Roche's Point, to the ship." In a splendid Irish twist of the tongue, he repeated, "Roche's Point." His trill made me giggle. I also tried rolling my tongue in the same splendid roll. It didn't work.

The shrill of whistles sounding from the White Star ship office signaled that the departure of the tenders heading for the ship was upon them. The two cousins pulled each other into one another's arms.

"Patsy, if my geography lessons serve me correctly, Queenstown and Cork Harbor are in Ireland! Is that even possible? Are we actually in Ireland in the year of 1912?"

I looked out at the steamliner and then at the people rushing about, all giddy and spry. The horseless carriages, honking and rattling, prattling past the Queens Hotel and White Star Boat Building ticket office were making their way onto the tenders that would transfer them aboard the monstrous ship.

I checked the man standing next to me and trusting my words would sound smooth and fair, I cleared my throat.

"America?" I said to him. "Do they say the ship is going to America, or do they say it is leaving America?"

"Now see here," the man snapped rudely, stepping away from me. "Have you no clue as to what ship this is?"

"Why, n-n-no sir, I do not."

"You look like a fine young lady, not the kind that takes to drink especially in this early hour. It is just past noon, no later.

"Leaving for America!" he snarled, snapping his cane at me. "Did you hear me? *Leaving* for America.

"Why, I have heard of simpletons but never came across one, especially an American simpleton. And mingled with a crow no less. Disgusting." He sniffed at me and walked away. I sniffed back.

"I assure you sir, I am not a s-s-simpleton! And besides, you, you t-t-talk funny!" And he did. I turned my attention back to Daniel. If he indeed was from Shamus' mansion, I needed to stay close to his side for he was the one I had traveled so far for. I was sure of it.

"Aye love...time to go," the woman was saying. She hugged Daniel. "Tight enough to last 'til you get yourself back home all safe and sound." She reluctantly let go.

With his good arm Daniel took up his baggage and walked away. "America!" The woman yelled after him.

"Daniel Coxon, next time it be my turn to come see you in America, aye?" Daniel turned. A smile crossed his face.

"Yes! America! Aye?" Patsy and I followed him.

"Yes, America," I said under my breath. "America! 1912!"

CHAPTER TWELVE

As it turned out, the White Star office was the ticket office for the ships belonging to the largest ship manufacturing company in the world (up to that point in time, anyway). It was there that Patsy and I stood, watching the people (one hundred and twenty-three) walk in, and then out the doors of the ship office.

Men and women hugging one another, patting children's heads, flagging their tickets excitedly in front of themselves as if the sheets of paper declared the holder the ultimate winner to one of the most sacred places a human could ever arrive—their freedom.

Patsy and I planned to be passenger one hundred and twenty-three, and passenger one hundred and twenty-four and a half. Since Patsy did not qualify as a full-scale passenger, half would do. And that's when it occurred to me.

"How, Patsy, h-how are we going to get on board? We haven't a ticket nor the money to purchase one," I said, staring at the tender boats at the end of the pier, Cobh.

Travelers were already milling about the small wooden bridges leading to the decks of the tugs. Two of the three tugs were to ferry us across the one mile of the cold, murky, rough April waters of the Atlantic, pass Roches Point, and deliver us to the ocean liner.

The steamer. It was so enormous that even from where we stood, so far away, I could see rows of windows dotting the enormous hull of the vessel. They were perfectly aligned just waiting to light up the blackness of the ship's hull like stars set in the night sky. "Lots and lots of them. Kazillions maybe, Patsy! Look, look at them all!"

Patsy blinked several times cawing in agreement. "Caw. Caw-Caw."

The vessel's splendor and girth were amazing. I counted four upper top decks, stark white and brilliant as the snows of Wisconsin laying in a farmer's field. Guardrails, thick and sturdy, stood ready to fence in and protect its travelers. The idea of boarding such a vast man-made structure sent me a thither.

How could I, or anyone trust such a vessel? I thought taking a deep breath.

I spotted Daniel managing his way to the planks leading to the ferries. I thought for a moment, but a good moment it was. For an idea occurred to me.

If my plan went correctly, within an hour or so we would be aboard that ship waiting to course thousands of miles over and through crashing ocean waves, back to America.

I held Patsy close. "I need you need to take flight," I whispered. "But keep your eyes on me so we don't lose sight of each other. We'll catch up in just a bit when I get aboard. You'll see."

I dodged cleverly between a pair of horseless carriages, and then sprinted past a sweetheart'ed couple and, tripping on my own skirt, sprang behind poor Daniel as if I were a giant wild cat let loose from the zoo to capture its prey. I 'accidentally' shoved him into the woman in front of him.

"Excuse me...excuse me," he muttered politely grappling his baggage with his one good arm as the cases banged the woman's skirt and legs. The woman gave a trifle scream.

"Sorry," he apologized again, turning to the woman. I had made my chance and I took it.

Before Daniel and the lady had the chance to turn and face me, Patsy bobbed his head and flew from my arms and into the shadows of the tree branches behind the White Star Office. He was safe. Safer than me. For I could not speak the truth as to who I was, where I was from, and certainly I could not tell why I had come from so far away. To try and explain would cause concern as to the wellbeing of my sanity with no Doctor Bruce to help.

After all, who I was, where I came from, how I arrived and why, was ludicrous. Therefore, I did the only thing I could. I took a deep breath, swallowed, and then I lied. And loudly.

"Cousin Lexington, here, take my arm. You mustn't be so mean and nasty to this fine man. I assure you he means you no harm."

I turned to Daniel. He was older than I thought, rather rough and yes, uncomplicated looking. A sad sort of tired gentleness in his dark eyes caused me to pause for a moment and wonder what sort of man Daniel was.

"Please sir, do excuse Cousin Lexington," I offered. "She has a bit of a hearing problem along with poor eyesight. Despite the fact she tends forget who she and her beloved family members are, and though she does pose the rather disturbing conduct of getting into other people's way, she truly is a very nice and decent person, as you yourself are, I am sure. She might be a bit feisty perhaps, but, all and all, she is decent." I forced my arm to her hand. "Here Cousin, let me help you. Do take my arm."

"Now see here!" the woman scorned, pulling herself away. "Who do you think you are talking to? Why, I have never been so mishandled in all my years, and by a stranger!"

"Oh, now Cousin Lexington. Don't fret. Papa is just ahead waiting on the tender for us."

"I beg your pardon!" The woman scowled, stepping away from me and Daniel. Daniel looked confused.

I noticed her clothing was not so much in style as other women's.

Nor was my new cousin's coat bright and fancy but the dull gray I was more accustomed to seeing Nurse Price wear. And when I caught the tail of her coat in my hand, holding tight and hard, I noticed the hemming was worn and tattered. A patch sewn on the backside told me she would not be traveling first class.

She let out quite the unruly squawk trying to break free from my grip.

"Cousins," I said, struggling to hold on, "they are a blessing and yet they can also be, well... must I say more?"

I forced a chuckle, smiling my best smile hoping to convince Daniel that the woman indeed was my beloved older cousin, Lexington, 'memory' loss or not.

"Now, now, cousin," I said in a most cheerful manner, grinning away the panic rising inside me.

The woman turned and gave me a push, forcing my hold from her. I fell against Daniel.

"How dare you!" She shrieked, grabbing up her baggage. "How bloody dare you!"

"Here, here now," Daniel exclaimed, catching me with the nub of his shoulder. I watched my *cousin* escape into the crowd.

"You're mad!" she yelled glancing back at me, "Simply mad!"

"B-b-but Cousin Lexington!" I called after her. "No Cousin, you mustn't...come back! Papa...Papa is going to be very angry that I lost you...again! Please, please come back!"

I continued shouting phony reassurances that I had indeed 'again' lost my difficult and somewhat 'psychologically disabled', yet much loved cousin, Cousin Lexington.

"Oh dear," I pretended to sob. "Now what shall I do? Papa surely is going to disown me. He did once. It took months for him to reconcile. Months I say. I could never endure such a punishment again. Ever. I would rather die..."

I cupped my hand around my mouth calling out to my very own and very new, Cousin Lexington.

"I-I I am so sorry," I said turning my teary eyes to Daniel. "But, she-she has our tickets! We have to hurry and catch her!"

"Me?" Daniel answered. "Oh no, missy. You have the wrong man for that job, I'm afraid."

"But-but you just have to help me," I begged. "I can't manage to find her all on my own, not amongst all these people. Oh Please? Please?" I begged. "Oh, pretty-pretty please?"

I knew Daniel couldn't refuse for I did sound so pathetic that, I myself, found it hard to resist me. For extra assurance I forced a few more tears from my eyes, and parted my lips giving them a slow, slick smooth lick as I saw the painted ladies do to the men passing on the streets.

The way Daniel looked at me I knew my mouth glistened in the early afternoon sun. He swallowed slow and hard like the men always did before leaving with the ladies when *they* did such things.

I played it through, puckering my lips outward, all pouty, making them look fuller and rounder than they actually were.

"Oh, all right then," Daniel said with a heavy sigh. "But just till we spot her then."

My heart thumped inside my chest as Daniel and I made our way to the gangway leading to the tender, Ireland.

I looked up at the tender and its hordes of people on it, all shouting their goodbyes and farewells to those watching from Pier Cohb. I knew what I had to do. I surveyed what I could from where we stood, knowing my next move had to be my best performance if Patsy and I were to go on board with the others.

"Oh th-th-there, there Daniel, th-th-there's my Papa, that tall man with the mustache and beard and hat. Yes, the man with the hat...Fa-father!" I yelled, my arms flying in the air. "Here F-Father, here!

Cousin Lexington, she..." I took hold of Daniel's good arm and held on tight. I felt him stiffen up.

"Oh dear..." I started to cry. "Look...Papa, he c-c-can't hear us. But he sees us. See? He's w-w-waving at us. Wave back, Daniel, wave back."

I waved all right. I waved at the hundred waving men with mustaches and beards and hats. But Daniel did not. He stared at me with his rich, dark eyes.

"Us? Daniel? How is it that you know my name?" he questioned.

"And why do you include me as, 'us'?"

My stomach flopped not once, not thrice, but four times. My head turned light causing me to feel dizzy. That's when I did the only thing any respectable young woman could do in such a circumstance. I fainted. Or at least pretended to.

Daniel dropped his luggage, again catching me the best he could, this time with his one good arm. I was grateful he was able to break my fall. I held in my breath as he lowered me roughly to the ground.

"What happened?" I heard a man's voice ask above me, loud and clear. I dared not move.

"I, I don't know," Daniel answered, confusion filling his voice. "One moment we were standing here, she was waving to her father up there on the Ireland, and the next, well, you can see for yourself."

'Oh's' and 'ah's' of every sort floated above me from every direction. The clopping of shoes and boots, and ruffling of dresses and men's trousers shuffled next to my ears.

"Oh, the poor child," a woman's voice rang out. "So much excitement is not good for a young woman, you know."

"Her father, you say? Where, which one?"

"The one with the hat, and beard and—"

I slit an eye just enough to see the man and Daniel take in the possibility as to which man aboard the tender could be my father. The man scratched his head while Daniel looked up sheepishly, showing just how foolish he felt realizing he didn't know which man was who. "Practically all the men up there look like that," the man said.

"Perhaps he can't see down here from the tender's deck. We best get her aboard and let them take a look at her."

It worked. I was going aboard the tender Ireland.

I hadn't believed myself to be such a heavy toad, but I must had been. It took five men to carry me aboard the Ireland. I lay limp as they placed me on a bench on its deck. Patsy's caw blended with the calls of the seagulls swarming above us. I flipped my foot just enough letting him know that all was well.

A man's hand smelling of snuff and brandy came close to my face. His finger lifted one of my eyelids. I was sure he felt it fight to close against his prying fingers and the glare of sunlight. I concentrated on the smell on his fingers and let my eyeball roll to the back of my head.

"Strange," he said adding a heavy, 'humph'.

"Her reflexes are good. Sharp. Watch."

I felt a prick on my forehead. I fought, resisting a terrible urge to crinkle my brow. I so desperately wanted to swat his hand away and whatever it was he was using to ruin my free ticket aboard the ship.

"See, she twitches." I knew my guise was up. I had to do something. And quick.

I recalled Nurse Price attending Doctor Bruce in what was one of the worst sights I had ever seen at Pine Brook. Some poor woman had what was called, The Convulsion Sweats.

So, with the heat of the direct afternoon sun beating overhead, along with my full-length skirt and all that was under it, along with my tight-fitting jacket (and nervousness) I was already providing the sweat. Now all I had to do was reenact what would scare any normal human away. I began with a short jerk of my leg. Then the other.

"See, see here! What scam is this?" The man asked, no longer poking and prodding me. I jerked again. This time, both legs. Then an arm, and then the other.

"Good Scott!" The snuff and brandy smelling man gasped. Others followed as I gave myself over to what I had witnessed that day at Pine Brook.

I simply shook, and I shook, and I shook some more. Tossing myself hither and thither, rolling off the bench and onto the deck of the Ireland. The men, including the stinky doctor, scattered away leaving poor Daniel with his "monster," as they referred to me.

They left and I opened an eye ever so slightly. Through the narrow slit I saw the horror on poor Daniel's face. I closed my lid. His silence was brutal, forcing me to react. And I did. With a moan.

"Ohhh," I agonized.

"Ohhh...D-da-Daddy. D-Daddy...Cousin L-Lexington..." I waited to see (or listened, rather) for Daniel's reaction.

"Whoever you are, are you alright?" he asked. Fear had taken over his voice rather than concern.

"May, may I please have a glass of cold water? Would you mind?" I asked weakly, knowing such a request was expected. Besides, having a few moments alone would give me time to come up with my next move in order to get me on the big ship.

Daniel looked at his luggage then at me. I flagged my hand.

"No, don't worry. I won't touch it."

I spoke so soft and sweet I even convinced myself I was too delicate to raise a finger, let alone run off with a heavy bag of luggage.

"If you see my D-Daddy, please...Please let him know I h-h-had another...s-s-spell...If you could...If you see him." Daniel turned pale.

"Sp-spell?" He asked. "What-what sorta' spell?"

"Oh, my lovely Daniel, I will explain once I find the strength. Water, water please."

It worked. I watched him walk away with the truest of urgency in his every step. He looked over his shoulder twice before slipping in among the other passengers just as Cousin Lexington had. Seeing the coast was clear, I rose my arm for Patsy to join me at my side.

"We're almost good as gold," I whispered, giving his big black head a reassuring pat. "Now go up in that crow's nest and stay there and keep close. We're going to transfer onto that big new ship out there, but first I have to figure out how to get us from here to there."

Patsy flew to the tall mast looming toward the sky from the middle of the Ireland. I sat up and began formulating our next move.

That's when I spotted Cousin Lexington. She had what appeared to be some sort of constable with her. She pointed a finger at me and I panicked. Quickly rising from the bench, I grabbed Daniel's luggage, and I too slipped into the crowd. My newly found cousin and her officer followed.

CHAPTER THIRTEEN

The Ireland rested in the port waiting to depart. Beneath me the slow, rhythmic clank -clank, clank-clank of the tug's steam engine resonated. And somewhere on the deck peculiar music sounded drawing me to my feet. With Daniel's baggage in hand, I followed the music, the liveliest I ever heard.

Daniel's luggage was extremely heavy which surprised me since he carried it effortlessly with one hand, his only hand. Whereas I struggled with it two-handed, making my way past the herd of passengers standing and listening, others dancing powerful jigs; some with partners, some without. I put down Daniel's baggage. My arms thanked me.

There in front of me and the others, in the middle of the ferry, stood a man tall and broad with hair red as the embers of burning coal on a cold and dismal October's night. And he was holding the most peculiar instrument I had ever seen. A giant flute of sorts attached to two leather bags.

The fellow took a few showman bows, showing his appreciation for the hoots and whistles and splattering of applause of those listening to him.

Then, sitting himself down on the bench along the railing of the tender, he rested the odd instrument on his lap. For a few moments the sights and the excitement in the air caused me to forget poor old Daniel who was in search of my non-existent father. And also, Cousin Lexington with her police officer in search of me, her non-existent cousin. I, along with the other passengers, stood about curiously watching the man ready his giant flute with its two attached bags.

He situated the leather bags under each of his arms, then wedged the long black stick attached to the middle of sacks between his knees. I expected him to put his lips onto the stick and begin to blow. But nay, he did not. Instead, he pulled one arm up slightly off one bag and then pressed it down upon the same sack again. The movement caused the opposite bag (under his opposite arm) to fill slightly with air. He repeated this folly, working his arms smoothly and rhythmically up and down until the one bag was full of air. Then tapping his fingers over the various holes of the giant flute stick, what I heard next I shall never forget.

The music turned slow and mellow as it came out of that contraption. Haunting, yet vibrant. I listened quietly and contently. But no sooner had I memorized the melody when my serenity (and that of those around me) changed. For the tempo picked up and so did the reactions of the passengers.

They flew off their seats, once again dancing jigs and schottisches that were equally foreign to me as the accents and brogues they shared.

Heels kicked and clicked, skirts and trousers flared this way and that. The turns and swirls made me dizzy just watching. Then, as the oldest couple aboard hit the floor to join in, the low hollow sound of the tender's whistle blew from the smokestack above my head. A puff of steam escaped upward into the blue sky of Ireland. And the music stopped. It all stopped. All the laughter and all the dancing. Conversations about arriving in the New World in style, *"thanks to the White Star Ship Company,"* all stopped. I looked about for Daniel. He was nowhere in sight, and I panicked.

Another man, lean and equally tall as the red haired music man, rose from his seat next to the music man and removed his cap and bowed his head in prayer. Those who believed in such things did the same while the very few of us who thought otherwise looked upward with respects, and watched the seagulls circle our vessel. Their cries along with the steady clank-clank, clank-clank of the rolling metal and iron of the tender's steam engine filled the silence in our hearts while prayers of the others filled theirs.

We felt a forward jerk pulling us away from the pier. The whistle blew one last long and lonely time. That's when the music man rose with his odd instrument, and so did the voice of the man next to him.

"Please join us in showing grace and respect to our dear motherland. For many of us, this will be the last we see of our dear, dear country, and that of our most beloved families, friends, neighbors. Ladies and fellow countrymen, raise your voices and hearts as one as we give our respects to our country with our national song, 'A Nation Again.'"

His smooth brogue mixed words so sweet and powerful with such sincerity it made me wish that I, too, were one of them, with a belief so strong that no man or woman could tear it asunder from my heart or soul. But nay, I was merely an observer, watching as one by one, all joined together:

"When boyhood's fire was in my blood I read of ancient free-men. For Greece and Rome, who bravely stood Three hundred men and three men. And then I prayed I yet might see our fetters rent in twain. And Ireland, long a province, be a Nation once again..."

Though I did not understand the meaning of the words, I did understand what the tears rolling down the passengers' cheeks stood for as they sang and the music man lovingly played on. For ready or not, we were on our way, heading for Roches Point and to the biggest ship to ever float upon the ocean sea.

By this time Daniel arrived and was in sight, heading for me as those around me dabbed their eyes and blew their noses in their already tear stained handkerchiefs. For we were slipping past Roches Point leaving behind mothers and fathers, sisters and brothers, countrymen and country.

Yes, surely this was the last remaining chance to glimpse and hold forever in one's mind the splendors and wonders of the colorful villages dotting the rugged, salted white cliffs and emerald green hillsides of Queenstown and all of Ireland. And yea, tucked away and kept in that special place where all Irish stories are born, both young and old, men and women, and grandparents too, brought with them tales of personal sightings of leprechauns and elves, unicorns and rainbows, all of which were found among the magic belonging only to the hills and forests of Ireland.

"I spotted your, *cousin*," Daniel said rustling next to me, a disgusted look on his face. "I will be delivering you to her, and your *father*."

I looked down at Daniel's baggage and kicked it gently with my foot. My face burned not from sun and wind, nor the salt air, but my lies. I had the urge to run. But where? A jump in the Atlantic? I backed away, slow at first, then picking up speed one foot at a time. But before I could turn the corner, Daniel stopped chasing me. And I stopped running. All the while the music man continued piping his tunes creating songs and melodies I had never heard before, and would never forget.

The vibration beneath our feet from the dancers no longer existed. Everyone aboard that tender stood side by side, staring up at a wall of the rising black before us, halfway to the sky. It appeared we had reached our destination. Together, Daniel and I also looked up past the deck rail of the tug.

And if everything went correctly, I soon would discover the true enormity of the vessel before us. For truly I do declare that what I saw before us on that tender that mid-April afternoon was outrageous, simply outrageous. And well-deserving of its name boasting on its side. I looked up at Patsy wishing he was at my side.

CHAPTER FOURTEEN

We all remained standing in stunned silence. We had to. For talking was impossible. Even the music man put his ulliam to rest. And the seagulls circling overhead begging the ships to spew their waste so they could feast, also went silent. For the vessel before us was beyond gargantuan.

It blocked the path of the early afternoon sun, which drew the salty, April sea air even colder.

I found it very odd that although the tenders were as ducklings bobbing alongside a whale, their rumblings fairly outweighed that of the monstrous ocean steamer.

As the gulls regained their endless begging, and us our gawking, I thought of possible reasons why such a deal should be.

Perhaps due to the ocean-liner's engines being so far down past the waterline. I bet sixty feet, maybe more.

After all, the tugs had one steam paddle each with 1,100 horsepower, while the monster had three steam engines, and two propellers with three blades, measuring twenty-three feet and six inches each, and 50,000 horsepower. So I heard.

Now, I do not like bogging anyone down (or myself) with monotonous and overwhelming facts especially having to do with widths and heights and anything measurable, but this is one time I must. And I do so sadly; not due to the burden of putting forth such dry subject matter, but for lack of my human ability to properly describe and bring to life the girth of that wonderful beast of a vessel and all within it, though it sets still in my mind.

To say her size was vulgar is understandable. For she was nothing-less than an immense, floating palace made of steel. Her girth was a width of ninety-two feet, and a length of eight-hundred and eighty-two feet (plus a good eight inches to boot).

She stood tall, sixty-two feet high not including its four funnels (which only three worked.) Adding the funnels brought the total height to a monstrous one hundred seventy-five feet. Yet above all that, aerial wires were strung, set and ready for what I would learn was called her, '*wireless radio*'.

She held ten decks, and weighed fifty-two thousand, three-hundred and ten tons (to be exact). And the windows Patsy and I saw from Cohb Pier numbered, two-thousand (give or take a dozen here, and perhaps half a dozen there.)

Our tug rounded the ship to her other side, the left side, and everyone began chattering again, running about catching a look at her name. I later learned when properly done, all boats board on the left side, called 'port side' (the right is known as: starboard).

Finally, someone dared to shout out the steam-liner's name boasting on its side in the largest black lettering I ever saw. A name that could not ring any truer; nor was it a name I or the world would ever forget.

"Titanic. RMS. Royal Mail Ship."

The distraction brought my chance to call Patsy down from the tender's crow's nest. I left Daniel in the mad rush and positioned myself in a vacant corner of the tug. I put my arm up, flagging Patsy to come to me. He was swift, and I quickly stuffed him down into my jacket and told him what a good and loyal boy he was. He snuggled his head against my chest, giving me reassurance that he, too, was glad to be at my side. Laying down deep in the bottom tucks of my jacket he caused me to look as if I were with child. Three months and two weeks' worth, to be exact.

"You be a good boy," I told him, patting him on his head. "So you know, it might be awhile. Just pretend we're playing hide and seek. I'll let you out as soon as I can. I promise." I stepped out from the corner.

"'Tis the largest and most elegant ship the world is ever to know," a man commented leaning over the tug's railing, staring at the mighty Titanic with his friend. "A shame not more came to see her off in Southhampton. We had more here to see her."

"It's understandable," his friend said, puffing gently on his pipe. "Most of those interested in such things as ships already viewed the Olympic. Cost them each fifty cents to do so. After all, the Olympic is the very first of the massive ocean liners coming into existence. And everyone knows the two are close to identical so one would have to consider the worthiness of one's time and money to see it twice. The Titanic here is only three inches longer, and a little over a ton more than Olympic. No real difference really."

"True, true," the man agreed. "What do they figure, a few hundred people showed up to tour Titanic here, and a few thousand stood in line to view Olympic?"

"Ah-huh. I'd say so. At least somewhere along them lines in Southhampton." He took several quick, deep draws from his pipe. Its smoke lingered like a small gray fog in the air. "Bloody nice the money collected on Olympic went to the Seamen's Charities."

"Yes. Bloody well nice indeed. Seeing they say this one here be cursed."

"Yes, cursed indeed. Some say she's unsinkable and that God himself can't make her go down. That'd be the making of a curse if I ever heard one."

"Ah-huh. Yes. True. True. Some even demanded their goods and belongings be pulled from her. Them smart ones know God will not be mocked."

While the two stood conversing about such matters of widows' pensions for husbands lost or killed at sea, and cursed ships, I wondered how something of such magnitude could possibly travel the ocean with such ease and grace? Truly such a feat goes well beyond normal understanding.

And, like all the ship's passengers, I was small and insignificant next to the Titanic. We were like tiny water-bugs floating along in the Prairie River back home in Timber Town.

Timber Town. I shut out my yearnings for it, and Shamus from my mind. I had to. I had to complete my mission, and if I allowed myself to think of him and Netsel, Miss Gavin and the mansion, and those back at Pine Brook, I feared I'd be overcome with homesickness and return to 1892 defeated.

We were getting closer to the Titanic, and the Ireland's passengers began scuttling about, gathering their belongings. Their excitement and dismay were salty as the air, and many went to crying again. I watched with pity as a good many ladies turned their faces from the beast, burying their heads deep into the coats of their loved ones so dear. This time their tears turning to sobs.

"Maybe we ought not go."

That was the main theme for showing their fear and second thoughts. I patted Patsy and reminded him he ought not move about or cause a squawk.

"Caw," came his muffled answer. "Caw-Caw." I knew he understood.

I looked for Daniel. He was moving to the other side of the tender. I followed.

"Daniel...please, don't-don't discard me," I shouted at him, holding onto Patsy, making sure he would not fall out.

I caught up to him. He stopped and leaned away from me, against the railing.

"Listen, missy, I have no time for these foolings of yours. I don't know what game you are playing, but you are not playing it with me," he said looking at my belly. I saw his confusion. "You didn't, you weren't...Ugh! You'll need to find the man who did you that. Not me! Now please, leave me be."

"Oh no, Daniel, I-I-I'm not...Oh dear, no!" I patted Patsy.

"I-I mean, yes, yes I-I am...I-I I am in a predicament. And I-I don't blame you for being so s-s-skeptical. I would be, too. But I beg you. P-p-please, please take me with you. I have to get on that ship. I have to, I have to, find...him...you know," I said rubbing my belly (full of Patsy).

No sooner had I gotten the words out when a man, much taller than Daniel, and much younger with a much stronger build, stepped up behind us.

"We had a deal," the man said. "A deal I ain't gonna' see go wrong either."

"Listen," Daniel said, trying to sound calm, pulling himself from the railing. "This isn't the place to discuss this sort of business. We should do our business there, on the Titanic, not here for god sake."

"Lookie here, I ain't taking no risks that this plan is going to work. So just in case it don't, you're paying for that ticket along with the rest of my expenditures, right here 'n right now, or you'll be finding yourself overboard before ya' set foot on that liner. Now hand it over. All of it!"

Daniel slowly dropped his suitcase and looked over the ledge of the boat. The waves, high and choppy and quick, eagerly licked the sides of the tug. Just the mere sight of the water sent a shiver down my spine.

"My circumstances have changed, Michael," Daniel said. "Do with me what you will. But remember, if I don't show up, the others will be suspicious. And if they become suspicious..."

The man grinned and put his hand in his coat pocket. "I ain't worried 'bout that," he said.

Daniel turned and stared at me. His dark, brown eyes begged for help. Before the man could pull his hand from his pocket, I did the only thing I could. I shouted loud and clear. Very clear. And very loud.

"Cousin Lexington! Oh Cousin Lexington, here I am, here I am." I clutched Patsy and watched my dear old cousin Lexington and the constable dash to me and Daniel.

"Oh, thank heavens I found you, my love," I said holding my stomach. "The baby, I think I felt our baby move..." I smiled sweetly at Cousin Lexington and her constable. "Can you feel him?" I asked, taking Daniel's hand to my 'swollen' belly.

"Aye, there now," said the constable. He stood with Cousin Lexington between the man and Daniel. "What is all this?"

Daniel pulled his hand from my stomach. I immediately covered up his lack of words.

"Yes, see," I said. "See? Daniel does feel his son. Don't you, Daniel?"

The constable looked me and Daniel over good. "This little lass belongs to you?" he asked Daniel.

"If not him, then who?" I sighed, as if I were truly forever, pathetically and hopelessly in love with Daniel.

"I would rather jump into that cold dark ocean than belong to another."

I put my head on Daniel's chest. "I am so sorry for giving you all such a stir. You see, I have a condition that rose due to my pregnancy. It's hereditary. My own momma had it when she carried me. It's called...it's called... 'Pregnolancy Hanallusion'." I looked mournfully at Cousin Lexington then cast my glance downward in womanly shame.

"I am so sorry to have caused such a stir. I meant no harm. Truly, no harm. It's a terrible condition I assure you. And my dear, dear husband loves me in spite of it all."

I squeezed Daniel around the waist. He gave a startled jerk.

"I am so sorry, dear," Cousin Lexington said. "If I would have known...pregnancy is hard enough for us women to endure, let alone with complications added on. It's enough to make a woman go mad. As you well did. All is forgiven."

"Thank you," I interrupted before anyone (especially Michael) could ask another question. "Officer, this man here is pursuing us." I pointed at Michael. "He stole my ticket to try and gain passage on to the Titanic. My name is...is...Michael, so the ticket will work for him." The officer looked at me in disbelief. (So did Daniel, of course).

I giggled nervously.

"Yes, I know, it is rather strange, and I do not blame you one iota for thinking me a liar. Please allow me to explain. You see, my father was, well...shamefully half in the wind when I was born, if you understand my meaning. And due to his, inebriation he signed my name on my birth certificate as Michael by mistake instead of Michelle. Mother, unfortunately being in the worst way, was unable to make the correction. No one noticed and all was forgotten until I was almost grown and since I had made it that far without any problems, my parents never bothered to correct it.

"Can you please place this man under arrest before he hurts someone? And my ticket. I need my ticket!"

I started to cry, forcing my face deep into Daniel's chest. I shook my shoulders with the same grace and elegance I had seen many women do when distressed.

"Aye now, missy, now don't you worry your pretty head none," the officer said as he reached for the man Daniel called Michael. "We will take care of it."

Daniel and I, along with Cousin Lexington and a few onlookers, watched the officer poke and prod the man. He pulled a ticket from inside the man's vest and before the constable had a chance to look it over, handed it to me. I wiped a tear from my cheek as if I were receiving my very own, 'flag of freedom.'

"Thank you, officer. Oh, thank you so, so much," I sniffled, grinning up at Daniel's confused face. "My true love thanks you also." I gnarled my brows for Daniel to give the appropriate response.

"Yea, I mean yes, thanks. Thank you—"

"And, if you need anything, anything at all," Cousin Lexington interrupted, "you just come to me. I'll make sure you get the help you need. Poor little lamb," she muttered.

I reassuringly patted Patsy while thanking my cousin with all the gratitude a person can give on such an occasion. Then, taking hold of Daniel's good arm, I picked up his suitcase and with a grunt and an encouraging nudge, we strolled onto the walking plank leading inside the Titanic.

CHAPTER FIFTEEN

I had been learning some very important lessons concerning life's adventures (up to that point in my life). And like all young ladies, I had plenty more lessons to learn. One being that some of the very best adventures can start anytime and anywhere a person decides to plant their feet and commences to walk. And some simply start when meeting someone new. Or, as in my case, *being* someone new.

It's not often a person of the female gender accidentally (or otherwise) obtains a male name such as Michael, along with the identity behind it.

And seeing it was 1912 (referred to as the Gilded Age) to be male meant having a male occupation. And unless one was well educated, or came from a family where finances were not an issue, a laborious occupation would have to do. And from what I could tell, Michael Braxton (Michael L. Braxton to be exact) had neither employment nor money. Which left me with only one conclusion. I, Camarilla Rae Berkelman had unknowingly became a crook.

And being the crook Michael Braxton was, I was sure he had compiled a way to confiscate what he felt my Daniel owed him.

See, the way I figured it, Crook Braxton never did have intentions of boarding any ship, least of all one voyaging 3,630 miles to America. But, if need be, he would do so without incurring any further debt out of his own pocket by passing the expense onto the White Star Ship Builders (and Daniel, of course).

How? you ask. In the same manner I, or anyone else without sufficient funds, would. By providing physical labor on the Titanic in lieu of the price of the ticket and traveling expense. Michael planned to add the aches and pains that occurred while doing such assiduous labor during those eight days onboard onto Daniel's bill.

Hence, if Braxton could recoup Daniel's debt prior to boarding, all the better. If not, the aforementioned would be set in motion. It was a good solid plan if it hadn't been for me and Patsy, and yes, Cousin Lexington who, by the way, was standing in line in front of me and Daniel, waiting to board the Titanic.

And so there we were, anxiously holding onto the guardian ropes of the wooden plank bridge leading from the Ireland onto the biggest ship in the world.

"I sure do not like these wooden bridges," Cousin Lexington said not daring to turn her head to me and Daniel. A breeze carrying the ocean's spring air rushed up our backs, wrapping its salty chill around our shoulders and necks.

"Well, I d-d-don't care for them much myself," I answered, trying not to look down, and over the edge of the ropes. Instead, I focused on the back of Cousin Lexington's hat as it sat neatly on the back of her head. It was nowhere near what the other ladies were sporting. For hers was a bonnet. A simple, gray bonnet matching her dreary gray coat. It reminded me of the outerwear Nurse Price wore.

I pushed the thoughts from my mind. For I had to inquire of Daniel if what I had collated concerning Michael Braxton was correct. "Th-that baggage is awfully heavy, D-Daniel," I said putting down his luggage, rubbing my arm. "What do you have in it, m-metal b-balls?

Daniel, I was th-thinking. Michael Braxton, h-h-h-he's a crook, isn't h-he? And I bet—"

"Isn't none of your business. None of it," he said, quickly jerking up his baggage. "Please. Do us both a favor and leave me alone."

He pushed his way past Cousin Lexington, and the couple in front of her and the next in front of them. His need for me and more of my shenanigans had obviously worn away. Any more of my interference and I was sure he would gladly jump ship.

The Ticketmaster and Registration Officer stood guard at the entrance doors of the ship leading off the tender's plank. One took each passenger's ticket, eyeing its content as quickly and efficiently as possible, then gave it to the other who, confirming the person's name, wrote it on the sheet of paper attached to his clipboard.

"They're searching for scalawags that might be trying to board the ship illegally," someone behind me whispered.

A scalawag like me, I thought, reaching into my coat, patting Patsy. "Try to be extra good. We're almost there," I whispered.

"Oh, honey," Cousin Lexington said sympathetically, turning to me. "I am so sorry. But being good won't help. I had me a husband just like that once. Took everything I and the good Lord could do to hold him long enough for me to birth my Robert B. He was a big baby, a real whopper. Darn near tore me in two. The doctor said he didn't know who to feel most sorry for, me or Robert B.

"Poor baby boy, huffing and puffing his way into this world. His body much too large for those little lungs of his. And me! Lord had His merciful hand on me that day, I tell you! Both me and the good doctor thought for sure I was going to either lose me mind or all me blood in me body—"

"Next," the Ticketmaster called.

I watched Daniel nod his head to the two men. The three laughed as he said something while handing the Ticketmaster his ticket.

Cleared, Daniel walked from the plank into the ship. I panicked, knowing I was on my own and might not be able to find him again.

"Next."

The couple in front of me and Cousin Lexington clung to each other as they hobbled to the Ticketmasters. They were old and still very much in love and obviously very much dependent upon the other.

"Tickets."

The old man slipped his hand inside his coat and fumbled for the tickets tucked in his breast pocket. The woman reached in and helped him.

"Sorry sir," she said handing the master their passes. "His sight and hearing isn't any longer that of his youth."

"What's that you say, Elsie?"

She looked at the men as if they might turn them away from the voyage.

"Nothing, Leif," she said pulling his coat collar up, blocking the chill of the wind. "Just talking 'bout the weather is all." The Ticketmaster nodded for them to continue to board.

Arm in arm they huddled, walking inside the ship.

"Next."

"Where you might be from?" Cousin Lexington asked, taking a step forward. "Seems I seen that pretty face of yours somewhere. Seems I knows you."

"We said, next!" the Ticketmaster shouted. "Come on now. We haven't the time for diddling about. Besides, it's a bit chilly. Hurry on now"

I pointed for Cousin Lexington to move forward.

"Name?"

"Miss Ruby Drake, sir."

Ruby Drake. I repeated the name in my mind., *Ruby Drake*. The name suited her well.

"You been through the medical exam and lice check?"

"Of course I have!" She snapped. "It's checked off right there, can't you see?"

"Baggage to declare."

"In holding, sir. Now, may I please get aboard? This walking plank makes me nervous. Lord, just look at those hungry waves. Licking about, just waiting for one for us to fall in. Lord knows there ain't much between us and them."

"If'n you wouldn'ta 'been yapping so much, you could of been off'n here three minutes ago.

"Say now, your ticket says here, you're domestic help. Kitchen crew. Third class." He paused, eyeing her up and down. "Steerage," he concluded.

"I know bloody well what the ticket says I am," Cousin Lexington snapped, plucking her ticket from his fingers. "And if'n you and your partner here want to take issues concerning my station, I will be more than happy to help you do so."

The two fellows looked at one other.

"Pass," they said, in unison.

Picking up the bottom of her dress, she huffed passed the two men.

I watched the patch on the back of her worn coat make its way from the narrow walking plank and through the doors of the ship. I was next and my heart pounded and my stomach stirred with a queasiness as I took a step forward, wishing either Daniel or Cousin Lexington was at my side.

"You been through the medical exam and lice check?" The Ticketmaster began, taking his turn at eyeing me up and down. My knees shook as I handed him Michael Braxton's ticket.

"Y-yes sir," I lied, hoping his ticket was stamped claiming I had. Patsy tried to stand to rearrange himself. I held my hand on top of my coat letting him know he oughtn't move, not even a flinch. The Ticketmaster looked suspiciously at my belly.

"I'm with child," I said shyly, blinking my eyelashes at him. I looked down hoping he'd see my blush indicating he should end discussing such a delicate subject. He cleared his throat and looked at my ticket.

"Michael?" He asked. "Who is Michael?"

"Michelle, the name is Michelle." My voice cracked.

"But the name on this ticket says Michael." He touched each letter giving it a jab with his crusty old finger. "M I C H A E L. Michael."

"Well, err, y-yes it does s-sir but it was s-supposed to read, M I C H E L L E. For M-M-Michelle. You see, my d-d-daddy, he was a-a d-d-drunkard, and the night I was b-born he was even more so th-th-than usual. And what h-happened was, you-you see, what happened w-w-was, well, the w-w-whiskey got his eyes and mind pretty blurry and w-weak, and instead of p-p-p-putting down M-Michelle upon my birth r-r-record, the way he was s-s-supposed to, well, he w-w-went and put down, M-M-M I C H A E L. M-M-Michael, like his b-b-brother who passed not too long b-b-before my birth. He-he passed, he passed from...from...cholera. Y-yea, that's what it was, c-c-cholera...my uncle, he passed from c-c-cholera. So you see...it's not m-m-my fault my ticket says M-M-Michael instead of M-M-Michelle. You can ask the constable if you'd l-l-like."

I smiled so wide at both of them I thought for sure my whole face was about to crack in half. Why, I couldn't even feel my lips!

"And it says here you are a domestic. Third class, steerage. Madame. I'm not sure of the first part of what you are telling me to be true, but being a domestic and, well..."

He eyed me up and down, stopping at my belly.

"In the family way," the registration officer chirped in softly.

The person behind me gave me a shove. "Hurry on now," he said, "before they draw up the plank and we find ourselves in the ocean." I felt Patsy tumble as I jolted forward.

"Oh, my b-b-baby, my baby..." I cried, holding my stomach,

stopping Patsy from falling out. "P-please sir, D-d-don't hurt m-me and my b-b-baby! Besides, I'm with her." I pointed at the door toward Cousin Lexington.

The Ticketmaster puffed his checks. "Michelle it is," he said letting out a huge huff of breath. "Pass!"

Hence, I stepped off the gangway and entered the Titanic.

The door was small for such a large ship, only four- and one-half feet wide, and six feet tall. And it was white. As everything on the Titanic. Titanic white. The tall, eight-foot ceilings, the twenty-foot wide hall. Everything.

"Deck C," a man called out. "This is Deck C. All third-class women, children and families, please line up in front of me. Any single men must, I repeat, *must* line up to your right per White Star rules, no single gentlemen allowed with the lady's and families. You shall be escorted to your own lodging and berth area."

I glanced over the other passengers hoping to catch sight of Daniel amongst the confusion.

"Every time we board a boat of any sorts we're the first ones on and the last ones off," a woman complained with the group of other women, who all looked anxious and weary, chattering loud as magpies, "and always an official on hand to see to it we keep on our way. An escort they likes to call 'em."

"An escort with a constable stick," another said. "Not our fault we were born into an unfair lot in life."

Their self-inflicted criticism was harsh and unjustified for they were dressed just fine and even a bit more fashionable than what they were accustom. I could tell the latter due to their constant primping and safeguarding of any soilage that might spoil their clothing.

"You know well as I that having us boarding first gives the upper crust the right to their certain 'tasteful' social rank privileges," the woman next to her said.

To my surprise it was Cousin Lexington. She stood next to the group with a dignified grace that separated her from the rest.

"It's tradition, you understand. This way they're safe to bring aboard last-minute visitors without us *scoundrels* underfoot. Besides it lessens the chance of stowaways. Considering the latter, perhaps such a way of boarding is correct after all." She gave a light laugh, tugging up her ruffled collar. "We are third class after all. And a dignified third class at that," she sniffed. The women around her giggled.

"Yes, that we are," one agreed with a chuckle, cinching her own collar.

We moved forward, following the young steward who was to escort us to our private deck and what would be our living quarters for the next fourteen days. I patted Patsy and reassured him everything would be just fine. Then I patted myself.

I held to the back of the group seeking out Daniel in the men's line marching behind us down the hall to the next stairwell. The chirpy chatter of a young couple within our group allowed me to weave my way closer to Daniel's line, whilst keeping Cousin Lexington in sight as we traveled down the magnificent ship's gilded hallways.

Gasps and squeals of delight escaped us as we passed fancy eating rooms and gathering rooms, stopping only briefly enough to peer inside them to capture their wonder. For only a few of us had the privilege of being a part of such a world. And that was due to nothing more than our domesticated employment. After all, we were the lowest class of all passengers. Third class.

As the steward lead us to the stairwell, he explained how each room held a different style from a different era. He pointed out how one room, the smoking room (men only, of course) had mother of pearl inlaid in its mahogany paneled walls. I took an extra moment and looked deep inside the room. Though not a soul was inside, I could smell the lingering, heavy molded aroma of cigars. And it being empty, I imagined the tinkling of glass snifters of fine, expensive whiskey, brandy, and sherry. The room's panels of glass windows enchanted me. Etched within them were many of the world's ports of call. Their function, besides being amusingly decorative and informative, was to separate the private portions within the room. And they did it well. For it was truly a splendor of art.

We came to a stairwell with its doors open wide.

"Deck D," the steward shouted. "Deck D."

Our clanking and clambering and chattering filled the stairwell as we obediently followed him. The further down we went, the more uneasy we all became. I reassuringly stuck my hand inside my coat, resting it on Patsy. He nudged against me, his feathers soft and warm.

"I know you're hungry, old boy. Just a while longer and we will be home free. It won't be long. I promise."

I was squeezed and pushed and shoved down the narrow third-class stairwell. Thankfully I found the bottom step just in time, preventing me from tumbling face forward on top of Patsy and anyone else below me.

"Stay together, stay close," the steward ordered, rushing us past tea rooms and dining rooms, and lounges, so massive and with decor so rich, some thought perhaps we were glancing prematurely into Heaven itself. Truly, the Titanic was a palace floating proudly on the sea. For the true enormity of the vessel itself was enough to declare it outrageous. Remarkably outrageous. And beautiful. Truly beautiful.

Our quick tour was coming to its end, and our group paused. Those of us who could read, read the sign above the staircase.

"Here we are now, Deck E, Scotland Road, final call," the steward announced.

"Deck E," I repeated softly out loud.

I stared down past the steps and at the heavy red metal door. Thick, incased windows and bolts held it tight and secure to the ship's white, steel walls. Our cabins laid just beyond it.

"Aye," Cousin Lexington repeated softly. "Deck E, it is. Scotland

Road. The deck designated just for us, the third class." She raised her voice, filling it with hope and pride. "Take hold now brothers and sisters. Here we go now."

The passengers looked concerned at one another and followed suit, taking hands for assurance. One by one and two by twos, we started below, down to deck E. There was to be seven-hundred and eight of us *steerage* in the belly of that great ship, the belly of the Titanic.

I took in the last of the ship's magnificence and followed. And as I did, I listened to the orchestra on the top deck perfecting its venue which would be played again and again, welcoming the privileged on-board. The splendor of such cultured music captured my ears, but it was the purity of the spirit of the music man and his uilleann pipes that stirred my heart.

And so, we went forth making our descent down the cement staircase.

As the cellos and harps and violins of the orchestra began to fade away, I began to panic. Holding tight as I could onto the railing, I allowed Patsy to perk his head out my jacket to look about for a moment, and so that I could feel the comfort of his soft feathers with my fingers.

"I assure you, once we find our cabin I will let you out. Please Patsy, stay good for just awhile longer."

People rushed by, ignoring me, pushing me and Patsy away from Cousin Lexington and her group. Daniel. Daniel was somewhere behind us with the other single men. I stopped and grabbed the banister and held tight to it, letting the frenzy of confusion pass over me.

Stampeding of boots and shoes, human voices, shouts and laughter, cries of frightened children and adults within the crowd was so loud, so immense, it became one very large, single squall of sound.

A man, large and round with a woman half his size, and at least six children (if not more), shoved me causing my hands to lose grip of the metal banister leading down the stairwell. Another couple thrusting past caught my shoulder. I stumbled down the last three stairs and fell to the floor.

"Daniel!" I yelled through the scores of feet, trousers, and skirts tramping past us. "Help! Help me!"

The heel of a shoe crushed my hand. A black feather floated past my eyes. I screamed, then cried. And so did Patsy as he waddled in a confused circle next to me.

"Awe-awe," he squawked. "Awe-awe."

Immediately I forgot my own pain and quickly grabbed him, putting him inside the safety of my coat jacket. I tried standing. It was no use. There were too many people scurrying and dashing about.

It was obvious I couldn't fight the stampede surrounding us. Horrorstruck, I crawled between men's black and gray slacks and women's rustling skirts, all whose hems had been dampened and discolored from the salty sea water collected on the dock, foot bridges, and tugs. I managed to crawl to the wall and railing and hung on tightly. Frantic that I might soon be a casualty, I called out, "Daniel...

"Daniel," I called out again. "Daniel..." A set of hands grabbed my shoulders, pulling me to my feet. "Oh, thank goodness you came back for us," I said, turning about.

The face was familiar but it did not belong to Daniel. Still, it was familiar, and I was grateful. Very grateful.

"My lord! My dear, you are just a baggage of trouble, aren't you?"

"Cousin Lexington..." I wept, this time with real tears. So unnerved was I, my *thank you* was barely audible. "How, how did—"

"Never mind all that," she said brushing me off. "Hurry now, before it's too late and we both find ourselves put to rest at sea before we even get started."

I wrapped my hands around the outside of my jacket, holding Patsy safe and tight inside. Cousin Lexington looked at my bulging stomach.

"Dear God in heaven. Now where is that miserable husband of

yours?" She shook her head. "Leaving you like this to fend for yourself. Shame on him! 'Tis the evil serpent's doing for sure! Abandoning a lovely little wife, and his child to be. 'Tis the evil serpent's doing!"

"Oh, please don't be too harsh on him. I can explain. I, er, you see..."

I felt my face turn a rose-colored blush. Patsy's claws dug into my blouse as he repositioned himself. Frantic due to his movements, I had no choice but to accidentally fall into Cousin Lexington, pushing her ever so gently backward and into the arms of the woman with six (possibly more) children.

The woman's husband took quick notice and eagerly began reprimanding dear old Cousin Lexington with such foolhardy accusations of her trying to pickpocket. I could not, nor would not, stand idly by and allow it.

"Sir!" I snapped, pulling my coat sleeves up to my elbows in the same fighting manner as he. "I demand you release my cousin immediately or I shall have you arrested and thrown off this ship for false accusations, and for manhandling a woman. Trying to lift your money bag! Why, I'm inclined to think perhaps it is *you* who is trying to lift *our* money bags!"

I stared him down and waited. A sweat broke across his tough, thick forehead. Yet he stood his ground, and I also was beginning to sweat. Patsy too was overheating. He tossed himself around and tried to lift his wings. The man narrowed his eyes at my belly and snarled.

"What do you have in that jacket?" He leaned toward me. Cousin Lexington stepped between us.

"Now see here," she said, her hands on her hips. "If I have to take a whop at you myself, God forbid, I will, then we shall see what the constable has to say."

"Drew," said the woman standing beside him. She looked tiny and frail next to him. Hardly the robust figure one would think it takes to birth such a clan as theirs.

"Drew! 'Twasn't her fault. 'Twas mine. 'Twas all mine fault. I tripped and tumbled, and if it not be for her, you might have to call for a scraper to get me off the floor. Drew, please..."

She took hold of his coat sleeve and gently tugged his arm downward to his side.

"Drew..." she said.

Her tone, sweet and scolding, affected him in such a way as to cause him to appear to be that of an overgrown child freshly caught doing something mischievous.

"Drew..."

"Tilly, are ya sure 'twas ya and not her? Are ya really sure?" Tilly patted his arm, soothing him. She managed a quick smile, hidden but from me and Cousin Lexington; she reassured him.

"Yes...yes, Drew. 'Twas me, not her."

Drew grunted. "Mmph," he said, his long, heavy fingers scratching his head. "I have no choice but to believe ya, dear Tilly." He twitched his eyes at me and Cousin Lexington. "Let's go find our cabin and berths and get ourselves settled. But if I find these two come near you again..."

Tilly bowed her head to him. "Yes, Drew," she said taking hold of his big, tough arm, following his lead down the hall. The children paced behind them.

As for Miss Tilly, she didn't look back, and she didn't look forward, she simply followed. And as for myself, it was looking as though I had not a husband, nor Daniel to follow. But I did have my dear old cousin, Cousin Lexington.

CHAPTER SIXTEEN

The Steward's directions added to the confusion, but though hard and unclear as they were, we did manage to find our way. "Scotland Road, men to port, women and children and families aft."

"Port?" I asked Cousin Lexington. "Aft? What does that mean?"

"Aft, my dear, means after, behind you. Port is opposite, meaning forward, in front of you. But don't you worry 'bout any of that now. I gots' me my instincts that the Good Lord gave me, and that's plenty enough for me."

Cousin Lexington saw that I was completely muddled by her and the whole situation at hand because she grabbed my arm, demanding I follow her.

"Oh, just come on now, and don't you fret," she said pulling me close to her.

She did not smell of old perspiration mixed with new, which surprised me. *Why didn't she?* I thought. For I myself had the odor of a well-worn traveler, as did everyone else aboard the ship. The hallway reeked of it. Rather, she had the scent of clean soap and linen. It struck me as very odd.

The flooring on Deck E was no longer posh but turned into the same hard concrete as its stairwell. If not for the passengers absorbing most of their sound, the echoes would have been quite miserable, bouncing every word and sound down one end of the long hallway to the other. For the lavished first-class accommodations of Titanic could not be found.

The quiet hallways with their soft padded carpeting and well-lit halls with encased lights shining from both ceiling and walls, were far behind us.

Cousin Lexington and I steadied ourselves against the wall catching our breaths and gathering our wits. There was no handrail to help guide us down the hall. For it too was gone with all the other first (and second) class frills.

"By that time, we third class passengers' turns came about, very little funds was left to cushion our passageways," Cousin Lexington explained, ducking her head inside every third cabin or so. "Although from what I can see, our accommodations are not bad after all. If not for this being the great and wonderful Titanic, we truly would be traveling third class," she went on as we continued down the hallway with the others.

"Why, I remember one time during a voyage I actually sat next to a pig," Cousin Lexington boasted. "Yes, a real live oinking pig. It wasn't half bad, I must admit. I have sat next to worse humans, you know.

"No, that particular pig belonged to some fancy sort of people and it was born and raised to, well, it was to add a better bloodline to its owner's stock and because of its mission in life, it became a pet to the family's child as well, and I must say the young lad did keep his prize very clean and tidy. Better than most dogs."

"Y-y-yes ma'am," I stammered, trying to keep up with her pace.

There were so many people. Each time a body nicked my shoulder, I was tugged away from Cousin Lexington. And each time I was grateful to manage to make it back to her side.

"What cabin are you and that rascal you call a husband in?" she asked, charging forward, refusing to excuse herself to those she pushed aside.

I dug into the pocket of my jacket and pulled out my 'golden' ticket. "It says here, Cabin number 69, berth F, E deck."

Cousin Lexington furrowed her brow. "Now that's a might odd. I believe this ticket is for the men's side, the *single* men's side."

She squeezed the ticket in her hands. I could see they were hard working hands and aged, as Nurse Price's hands. She closed her eyes and sighed, ever so slightly shaking her head in disappointment.

"I take it your scoundrel has your luggage." "Yes. Yes, he does," I lied.

"Well, that's a fine arrangement. Too bad he can't keep track of you as well as his fine luggage. Poor darling."

We looked for our cabin numbers on the doors as we walked. I let her do most of the talking for I did not want to have to recall what I told her (and what I did not). She was a sharp cookie. And future questions would certainly lead to unwanted suspicions if I were to answer incorrectly.

"Well, me dear. I do believe this to be my home for a few days," she said, sighing as she looked at her pass one more time comparing its numbers on the cabin door.

"You be off now, my love. I'm sure we shall run into each other again."

I watched her unlock the small, white metal door. And as she did, another woman's voice screamed from within.

"Have the bloody decency to knock. It's tight enough in here with no room for a fool," Cousin Lexington's roommate shouted as if both were deaf.

Cousin Lexington immediately began making her own demands more than perfectly clear. And so, I began my travels down Deck E, Scotland Road alone. And it was a long road at that.

I had no baggage to carry and no hand to hold onto as I traveled down that very long, very narrow, very noisy corridor. But I did have my Patsy. I opened my coat for him to peek out at his surroundings for he was as curious as I.

"You are such a good boy, Patsy. And as soon as I get food, you shall feast like a king. I promise. We must almost be to our cabin."

Scads of people rushed by yet not one took notice of the dear old bird peeking out from my coat. And for that I was grateful, for without dear old Cousin Lexington at my side, he was the only security I had. And though I was confused as to where I was going, I did manage to keep my eye out for Daniel. I figured since he was also traveling third class he would have to be nearby, single man or not.

I checked my ticket periodically as if perhaps the cabin numbers might magically change and appear on one of the doors in front me. On my tenth attempt at reading the cabin numbers, I mustered up the courage to seek advice as to which way I ought to go. Up the corridor or down. After all, a smart woman knows when to ask for assistance.

So, I did just that. I asked a steward.

"Naw," he grunted, keeping his pace. "You be going aft now. Go port. You going aft now. Go up," he repeated. I looked at him dumfounded.

Tsking, he tried again. "You know, port? Up? Go port. You going aft. No aft, no down, but go port, up."

Well, that I understood loud and clear. I had to turn around and head the other way. Port I was told, so port I did.

The excitement of the voyage was contagiously giddy and floated everywhere in the narrow hall of Scotland Road. I couldn't help but envy all those aboard that grand new ship. Wonderful conversations of new lives bursting with hope filled the hallway from, port to aft. It seemed everyone was sailing away from something in order to gain something, something like a much brighter life.

Phrases like, "our new beginnings," and, "our chance for a whole new life," ricocheted off one person's lips and onto another's.

I puzzled over Scotland Road. Its concrete flooring seemed to go on for a mile. As did all of Titanic. And it had an ever so slight descent to it which would not have been noticeable if not for a few metal marbles rolling their way down the hall past me. Patsy, like the marbles, drew no attention as we graciously accepted warm, and friendly, "excuse us," and, "so sorry, beg your pardon's." of passersby bumping against us as they scurried up and down the hallway.

I read the numbers on the cabin doors, slowing as I came upon number 65. I looked about realizing very few females were to be found in that particular vicinity. And the ones who were, slowly drew themselves away from their lovers, leaving behind a white glove or some other token as a reminder of their passion and desire.

I, on the other hand, hadn't spotted Daniel. I knew he was there somewhere among the 709 third class passengers, but where?

I was pondering that very thought when a man's voice came behind me.

"May I help ya,' missy," he asked so close the warmth of his breath fluttered across the back of my neck. The stench of sweat and urine was overwhelming. I froze, giving Patsy's head a soft pat to tuck himself away in my coat. I turned to the man.

He was ugly and greasy, not from work, horrific manners and but poor hygiene. He smiled wide. The aroma of old, soured snuff mixed with the dull rot of tooth decay escaped his mouth. I backed away instantly.

"'Ay now missy. None of that," he said showing off the few teeth he had. Bits of black tar sat primed between gnarled fragments of yellow bone protruding from his gumline. "I'm just tryin' to help a poor little lass as yourself, is all.

"Say now, what's we got here?" he asked eyeing up my purse dangling from its chatelaine attached to my skirt.

He grabbed it and eagerly looked inside. "Aye now, what's we got in here? What's you got for your mister?" He turned the purse over, giving it a shake.

I pulled it away. He held tight. I grunted, sounding hysterical.

"C-c-bin-bin," I stammered, my hands frantically flailing this way and that, tugging the chatelaine. "C-c-bin, C-c-bin."

I frightened the man as much as he frightened me. He unlatched his grubby hands from my purse and stepped away. Backwards.

"C-c-bin-bin," I grunted again. "C-c-bin-bin, C-c-bin-bin."

"Say now, you be one of 'em deaf mutes?" he asked staring at my belly, taking yet another step back. "I'll have no thing done with no deaf mute. And a pregnant one at that!"

He turned, hobbling up the hall, taking his rancid smells with him. Shaking, I sighed with relief checking to make sure the chatelaine and purse was still attracted to my skirt. I continued my search.

Cabin 69. I stood outside the room and watched what would've been, four of my five roommates unpack their possessions. I had laundered plenty of men's belongings and was quite comfortable doing so, yet these men were young and vibrant, as were their johnnies and such which, to my surprise, caused me to blush and turn away.

They chuckled and carried on conversations, excited that their cabin was far better than any free faring ship hands ever were assigned before.

Cabin 69. It was a simple but adequate cabin made of all male kitchen helpers. From what I could see, it contained six bare bunk beds (referred to as berths). One berth assigned to each man. They were to share the two wash basins sitting side by side, each with its own taps. And surprisingly a flushing toilet was off to the side in a closet all its own.

From their worn duffle bags the men pulled bed sheets, blankets and pillows. I guessed bringing one's own sleeping gear was expected. Perhaps not of all passengers but primarily the 3rd class. I later found my assumption was correct. It was not only for sanitary reasons as one would reason, but 3rd class would use their bedding in their new homes in their new country, for such things would be much too costly to replace.

I dared not go into the cabin. It was forbidden, me being a girl. Besides, I needed to think. How was I to address myself and my situation, and to whom? I had no bed sheets, no blankets, or even a pillow; not one stitch of clothing other than what I was wearing. And how in blazes could I explain Patsy? A dog or nice kitty would have no call for explanation and could be kenneled, but a bird? And a big black crow at that.

Patsy slipped his head out from my coat and took in the fresh air.

The poor ol' dear. The loud cackles of the men enjoying good-hearted teasings, their hands playfully slapping each others' backs, and the passengers bustling about with jovial chatter and laughter was overwhelming.

He slid back down into the security of my jacket. I rested my hand on top of him reassuring him we were safe and that everything would be alright (even if I did not particularly believe it myself).

Roommate number five arrived. I was hardly noticeable to him as he shoved past my backside with not a word of excusing himself for jolting me practically off my feet. He was louder than the others and carried far less packages. Only one. He plopped it on the far upper right cot. Berth F. *My* berth.

"Well, roomies. Looks like we're going to have ourselves a whale of a time. Yes, we are. With old Oscar here, nobody will go without entertainment. I can assure you all that much."

I hated him. Right then and there, I hated him. Even though *'Old Oscar'* was as American as I. He was obnoxiously loud, with an air of overconfidence that superbly defines self-centeredness and conceit. And he was excessively good looking. The way he smoothed the waves in his well-oiled, blonde hair on the spot without even so much as passing a glance in the mirror proved to me that he knew it all too well to be true.

I stood in the hall watching him stroke his square jawline. All the while smiling at those around him. They smiled back.

I suppose it was the years spent at Pine Brook that taught me to oppose such behavior. Or maybe it was Nurse Price and her guidance.

"The most important characteristics humans can possess are free, and not bought, or found in a fine tailor or in what society considers a face pleasant to look at. No, the most important characteristics we humans can hold are the same found in old loyal dogs."

'Old' Oscar glanced across the room. He caught me watching him. His lips turned upward in a devilish yet boyish smile. A deep dimple showed in both his checks. His eyes startled me. They were not a comfortable dull gray but an alarmingly bright and full of life silver color.

Yes, he was beyond good looking. He was beyond handsome. Ridiculously so. And to make matters worse, he was oddly familiar. Not in the comfortable way like when meeting someone such as Netsel, but in a resigned and mournful way. And it made me abhor him even more.

He nodded at me then looked back at what was supposed to be my cot and continued unpacking his gear.

"Yes sir-ree," he said. "We are in for a whale of a time. A true adventure. I can feel it in my bones."

Something tapped against the bottom of my boot distracting me from obnoxious Oscar and the other men. I bent in the doorway and picked up the object. It was another metal marble, and it was curiously warm. I put it in my pocket and scanned the hallway floor for any others. Another sat a few yards aft. I snatched it up, and it too was warm.

How odd, I thought searching for more. A few doors down I noticed yet two others and made my way to them through the crowd of men. I eagerly gathered the small balls of steel into my hand. They were warmer than the others, much warmer, bordering on hot. I looked at the door to the nearest cabin. It was slightly open. Taking a few steps forward, I crouched low by the doorway and peered inside.

A man stood next to a berth, his suitcase fully opened. I gasped not because who the man was, but what he'd been carrying in his suitcase. But the true question was, why?

It was Daniel. And he was glaring at me.

In front of him on the lower bunk, hidden in his suitcases were marbles. Hundreds of small shiny steel marbles. He stepped toward me, slamming the door in my face.

I tapped on the door. Nothing. I tried again, this time nudging it just enough for me to watch him without his noticing.

He looked worried. His lips mumbled words that I could not make out. I strained to listen, hoping to hear something that would make sense of him and his hoard. But not a word could I understand.

While I stood contemplating my predicament (and Daniel's) a finger tapped my shoulder. I didn't turn right off for fear of exposing Patsy who had grown impatient and was at this point hanging out of my jacket.

"Oscar here, Miss. Oscar to the rescue..."

Oscar, my heart pounded. I kept my sights straight forward on Daniel.

"This man annoying you?" he asked, nodding at Daniel through the crack in the door. "I couldn't help notice the antics he's been causing you all along."

"Antics, what antics?" I answered back. "When? Daniel, he isn't, h-h-he hasn't caused me any *antics,*" I injected quickly, knowing not to say more.

"I wouldn't be too sure about that," Oscar said, ignoring the tightness in my voice. "A body never knows who their true friends are, especially during a new adventure."

"I beg your pardon!" I raised my eyes to his and looked deep inside hoping I would prove my resolve to be stronger than his. His pupils were large, oversized nuggets of black, adding to the brilliant silver pupils surrounding them.

"I do not s-s-see where any of t-this is your c-c-concern," I squirmed, turning to the cabin door, trying to shield Patsy. Oscar laughed.

"Well, now, what, or who pray tell, might I ask, is this?" He chuckled and reached out patting Patsy's head. Patsy nudged against Oscar's hand.

"Or perhaps I need to ask, who might this be?"

"That also is n-n-none of your concern," I said pulling my Patsy from him.

"Fair enough," Oscar said, tightening his jaw. "Fair enough. But do keep in mind when you are troubled you can always come to me, Oscar. And mark my words. There will be a time when you are troubled."

His words angered me. He angered me. Everything about him angered me. I watched him meander like a true gentleman down the corridor to his cabin. Our cabin. He (as well as myself) was out of place amongst those stationed on Scotland Road. He for his reasons, and me for mine.

I stared at Daniel's cabin door and nudged it open a bit. The cabin, though very small, looked warm and inviting. I cleared my throat loud enough for him to hear. He covered his suitcase of with a blanket then turned and made his way to me.

"Look," he leaned in the doorway, "I appreciate what you did on board the Ireland, but I've had enough of you chasing me. For your own good, and mine, leave me alone."

"But Daniel I need..." Those were the only words I got out before he shut the door.

I looked up Scotland Road and down, not knowing where to go, and what to do. Only a few stragglers were left roaming about.

Everyone else was busy settling in. That's when it sunk in. Really sunk in. I was alone. Very much alone in a different place, a different time, with no place to go. I clung onto Patsy.

"Oh Patsy, what are we going to do? We've come too far to turn back now. And even if we did, I would not know how to get us there. Razzle-Dazzle, Patsy, how did I get back from 1953? Even if I do figure it out, there's no guarantee we will ever get back again to the right place and time. I-I-I d-d-don't even know what we came to fix—"

I was determined not to cry or carry on as one would naturally do in such a situation. Instead, I bit my lip good and hard and headed back not aft but port, to the only other person who I knew (besides Oscar) that could help us.

Cousin Lexington. She stood outside her cabin doorway, holding her fist up to a group of young passersby no older than I. Their hoots and hollers of, "no longer do we serve or save the Queen...no longer do we serve or save the Queen," filled the hallway. And so did Cousin Lexington's own shouts of protests.

"Keep your dirty little mouths shut," she scolded as they passed by her door. A few elders reinforced her scoldings as the group proceeded down the long corridor in search of their cabins.

I envied the small band of young immigrants. For I was developing the natural yearnings to share life dreams and the curiosities that come with them. And just like the young men and women marching down that corridor that day, my own dreams were just as fresh and carefree, full of the same zeal as theirs; except I had no one to share those dreams with. No one was at my side as I claimed my journey in life. Even if there had been, what would have been the point? No one would have believed me. No one would dare. Except for my sweet, dear old Patsy. And Shamus, of course.

I watched the group move on; skipping, jumping, hooting, and hollering their way to their cabins, each in search for a life other than that offered by family and the country from whence they came. I realized that even though I was not a part of them, in my own way, I was one of them. After all, I had made an equal choice. Mine was to travel not only to a different country, but a different time. Besides, one thing was for sure, no matter how many dreams we might have shared, I, unlike them, had no cabin. And again, I yearned to be with them.

But then, there in front of me was Cousin Lexington, her head poking out her cabin, looking for another group to come along to scold.

"God will always save the Queen!" She shouted, her chubby face royal red with angry pride. "He bloody will!"

"Keep your yapper shut," her roommate bellowed from inside the cabin. "You're likely to get our throats slashed if you keep up that sort of talk. Now hush up!"

"Excuse me?" Cousin Lexington spat. "Are you ashamed of our queen, or are you ashamed of our God? Well, which one?"

I figured Cousin Lexington was a feisty sort of gal, but I never pegged her to be on the side of fist-fighter type of feisty.

"I'll give those ears of yours a good boxing if you keep that up!" She bickered back. "And the good Lord will see me through it!"

I couldn't see the gesture her roommate made but I imagined it was something terrible-due to how Cousin Lexington clenched her large hand indicating she was ready to leave a reminder the queen was above any human on the face of the earth, and would forever hold a most high and special place with the Lord Himself, no matter how many gestures a peasant woman could make.

"Aye, that's better now," Cousin Lexington grumbled smugly, turning her attention back to the hallway. Her face softened as she hung her hands on her wide hips and grinned.

"If it isn't my, 'little mamma.' I suppose your man sent you to explore while he prepares your temporary love nest. I hope it won't be too tight in your quarters. At least you're not being forced to share your bunker with a body or two you don't care for right off the top." She turned her head to her cabin mate, making her words extra loud and clear.

A drawer slammed deliberately hard from inside. "You best be running off now dear. Find your hubby and hold him tight. Better that you do, and not hear the goings-on in here" she said, shutting the door.

A few more passengers staggered past in search of their own cabins and berths in which to lay their heads and dream of their new lives.

Even though Daniel's was a working man's cabin, he made it certain he was traveling alone with no interest in sharing his voyage with anyone other than himself and his strange baggage of dumb old steel marbles.

The Titanic's steam whistle who-whooed low and hollow through the dusk of that early spring evening. It was the ship's way of announcing to all those aboard (and Ireland) it was departing its docking and beginning to forge forward into waters it had never seen before. For it was Titanic's maiden voyage, after all.

The last remaining passengers on Scotland Road scattered into their cabins as if doing so would bring them comfort and safety from the fears of their own fresh journeys.

Yes, truly I tell you, we were alone, Patsy and me.

CHAPTER SEVENTEEN

That first night aboard, I had no alternative but to sleep miserably in a hall cleaning supply pantry next to one of the water-closets meant for steerage usage, third class.

I laid curled on the floor listening to the vile sounds emanating through the walls and vents. With the men's toilet on our left, and ladies on the right, the sounds were quite disturbing to say the least. Most wretchedly worse than one might imagine. Needless to say, the fiasco of it all kept me from partaking in my own meal while Patsy ate his.

I was surprised by how busy a ship is in the deep hours passing in the night. Toilets flushing, stewards yelling out orders, people of all sorts clambering up and down the hall and stairwells, unmarried lovers chasing each other, giggling about in secret meetings, children and babies crying due to unfamiliar surroundings, private conversations finding their way through vents.

During my awake time, I made plans to keep Patsy hidden within the pantry until I was able to make proper arrangements for real sleeping quarters (if it were possible), or until opportunity bared itself to me. Until then the closet would have to suffice. Fortunately, it was just large enough and well ventilated. And with taps right next door I could make sure Patsy had plenty of water.

"You'll be just fine in here until I can find us a suitable place to stay," I reassured him, placing him on a forgotten mop head on the top shelf of the closet. I put my last night's meal next to him. "You have plenty of grub to last you till I can bring you more. And water..." I double checked the soup bowl filled to its rim. "It's fine."

A steward's whistle screamed from one end of Deck E to the other. I stared at the closet door and gave old Pasty a good pat on the head.

"Look alive! Look alive!" a young man's voice shouted while making his way down the corridor.

I opened the closet door just a tad and peered out into the hall. The young man stood but a few feet away and did not see me.

He looked over the papers attached to a clipboard he held tightly in his hands. Work papers I supposed. He was barely more than a boy, and a whisper of one at that. But his words were firm. And he meant everyone of them. Again, he blew his whistle.

"Look alive, look alive. All kitchen crew, look alive!" He yelled out, knocking on each cabin door he passed.

I straightened myself and patted down my hair and skirt, and then carefully slipped out the pantry door. The steward turned and then started on the other side of the hallway, repeating the same call.

"Come forward. All kitchen crew come forward."

Finished, he stopped across from me. I was the only one in line. He eyed me suspiciously as I gave him a nice polite curtsy.

"On your feet, on your feet," he yelled, turning from me to once again patrol the corridor while he waited for the cabin doors to open.

They did and groups of men marched out from opposite ends of Scotland Road. Only a small hoard of twenty-three women joined us, lining up against the white steel walls of the hallway. There was such a mix about us; some tall, some short, some lean and some pudgy-round, but not a one had the softness that came from living a pampered life. For it was Deck E in which we stood. Scotland Road. Truly, it belonged to those who belonged to the third class. The class who worked not for each other, but for those who lived in softer classes of second and first.

Complexions, smooth and rosy were not to be found in this group. Instead, I gazed at faces, some ruddy red from wear and neglect. Each head of hair lacked the common shine and luster of the higher classes. No, the ones standing against that cold hallway wall showed a very different dignity than those soon to be served in first class (and even second class). These folks, the poor, the uneducated, held an air that most all third class held. The look of pride in the determination to complete the task at hand; the hard physical work of preparing, serving, and cleaning up after two thousand and eight people. Not just once or twice a day as on the Titanic, but for a lifetime.

"Vegetable Cooks," the steward said loud and clear. Out stepped five men.

"State your names."

"George Ayling. George Edwin Ayling, sir."

"H.E. Buckly, sir."

The steward stopped marking the names on his clipboard and looked doubtfully at the man, H.E. Buckly.

"Yes, indeed sir. H.E Buckly. That is all. Just plain old H, period, E, period, then Buckly." The steward shook his head and went back to his marking.

"John Bertram Ellis."

"Jimmy Hutchinson. Err, James, James Hutchinson, sir."

"James Orr."

"Very good. Please follow your steward."

We watched the group file down Deck E and up a flight of stairs. I assumed they were being led to their kitchen. I looked at my ticket.

'Cooks Helper-Second Class,' it read.

"Bakers' assistants."

Another group stepped out and lined up as their names were called.

"Albert Barker, Frederick Barnes, Charles Reginald Burgess," the names went on until all eleven were called and stood up front and in line. Then came the last, and maybe most important one of the baking group.

"Head Chief Baker, Charles John Joughin."

Out stepped a rather average young man, not too tall, and yet not too short. His black hair was well groomed and shone with the macassar oil, as was his full mustache. The thick hair under his nose helped call attention away from his smallish chin, and large protruding ears.

"Mister Joughin, please take charge of your helpers. Deck D. First and second-class galleys."

Mister Joughin quickly looked over his new crew. He snapped his head in a quick nod for them to follow him up the same staircase as did the vegetable group. I looked down the line as the steward was getting ready to call his next group.

To my surprise Oscar and Cousin Lexington stood together. Daniel, only a few feet away, was hidden behind a taller man.

I knew Oscar and Cousin Lexington were considered third class, but surely, they could have been mistaken for not first class perhaps, but more second class; a higher second. At least in my young eyes.

And that was where we were to serve. Second class.

"Look lively," the steward yelled out again.

"Cooks' assistant, Oscar Anderson."

"Here," Oscar answered, stepping away from Cousin Lexington.

"The following will line up in front of Mr. Anderson."

"Cooks' helpers, Cooks' helpers', Second class. Listing off. Ruby Drake," he began.

Cousin Lexington responded stepping forward and lively as instructed. Then came the others.

"Henry Ashe...Charles Hogg..."

Each replied, "here."

Then came the dread I hadn't anticipated. The need to explain my name once again. But this time in front of a group of others, namely that of mostly men. And Oscar being one of them. "Michael Braxton..."

My heart stopped pounding.

"Michael Braxton, look lively."

My feet didn't move. I looked over at Daniel who was obviously miserable as I. For I was officially partnered under Oscar Anderson.

"Last call, Michael Braxton, second class, kitchen helper." A few patient coughs rolled down the line. Mine included.

"All right then," the steward sighed, looking at his clipboard. "Next."

"Here," I called out reluctantly lowering my voice just as he was about to put a line through my name, Michael Braxton.

"Good job, mates. Mister Anderson, take charge of your crew, if you will please."

That's when Cousin Lexington burst out.

"Our sweet Lord," she said, folding her hands low in her lap as one does while in prayer.

"Oh, sweet Lord," she repeated several times. "Let us all do our duty serving those who you put before us this day with the same pride and dignity as the queen herself serves her people."

Oscar crossed his arms. "Miss Drake," he chuckled. "I highly doubt a creator of this universe, or any other universe, would take time out of what must be a very busy and complex schedule to see to it that you, or anyone else, should receive a certain position in life, let alone one so meager as the one at hand."

Cousin Lexington turned the color of her name. Ruby red. "I will thank you to keep your sinful thoughts to yourself, young man," she said eyeing him up and down.

"Sinful? You think those thoughts are sinful?" Oscar laughed tapping a finger to his temple. "I guarantee you, Miss Drake, this mind can do a lot better than that."

The steward slapped his pen on his clipboard and pulled himself up, making himself appear taller and larger than his five-foot two frame would allow. He blew his whistle three short times, after which he said, "Miss Drake, Mr. Anderson, I will say this only once. And I want everyone to take note." His sharp young features pinched tight as he stared at Oscar.

"We here on the Titanic will not tolerate any sort of squabbles. Or indecent talk. Each group has a qualified supervisor that we are to address when matters of differences arise. Do you Mr. Anderson in particular, and all others, understand?"

It wasn't truly a real question. And it wasn't even a suggestion. It was a more of a demand. One that Oscar did not appreciate. I watched his arms jiggle against his stomach as he laughed at the steward's ridiculous appearance. I, too, had a hard time not laughing straight out at the awkward little boy-man. For he truly was quite a presumptuous little fellow.

"Seems you need us more than what we need you, little buddy," Oscar mumbled loud enough for those standing near him to hear. Their laughter infuriated the poor steward. Locking his small beady eyes on Oscar and Cousin Lexington, he blew his whistle demanding silence.

I followed my Daniel, Cousin Lexington and against my choice, Oscar, up the same flight of stairs the others had climbed.

They looked odd, the two of them, Oscar and Cousin Lexington walking together up that stairwell. One young, tall, muscular, the other short, considerably older and plumper. From the back they could easily have been mistaken as mother and son.

"Have you ever been blessed by the good Lord with work on such a magnificent ship?" Cousin Lexington asked Oscar.

"Oh, yes," he answered with a chuckle. "Several times."

"I highly doubt that, Mr. Anderson," Cousin Lexington replied.

Oscar grinned. "But never one unsinkable."

"So some say," said Cousin Lexington. "It seems to me that they be tipping the hand of God by making such a claim."

It was a magnificent ship, the Titanic. A ship so wondrous and large I cannot tell of every detail. Nor could the ship's most acquainted stewards. To do so would be impossible. After all, there was no map of any kind to be found anywhere aboard the Titanic, and with ten decks and countless staircases leading this way and that. The Titanic truly was a castle the size of a small town unto its own self. A huge, fancy, man infested, floating maze of a town. To find our route, all any of us could do was carefully memorize every step we took in order to find our way back to our cabins from our destination put forth.

Daniel, noticed I, was particularly careful noting our surroundings. Oscar, on the other hand, was taking more notice of Cousin Lexington's chatter concerning the lack of, "fine and rich first class tapestry on our third-class benches and chairs in our sitting areas. "Seems a might disrespectful, now, doesn't it?" she grumbled.

"Just because the good Lord stationed us as such as we are in life, is no reason for another man to rub it in our hungry faces. I know it helps cut down transferring and breeding fleas and lice, so they claim. I myself never had either."

Oscar laughed. "Now, Miss Ruby, if the Lord is so good, then why pray-tell would He allow one of His beloveds to suffer so with fleas and lice? Hm?"

"You're a young man, Oscar Anderson, and you have much to learn of life," Cousin Lexington snapped back.

If I hadn't despised Oscar so, I would have enjoyed walking beside the two, listening to them share stories and philosophies. Still, I would have kept silent being a traveler different from all other travelers. But perhaps I would have shared what I did know firsthand concerning why we, 'the third-class' voyagers couldn't afford our chairs and such to be covered in fine tapestries or even the simplest cloth. Especially in public sitting rooms. Mr. Hawthorn was the one who taught me firsthand the 'why' for not using cloth coverings.

You see, Mr. Hawthorn's son dropped him off one day and never returned. "Too ashamed and embarrassed, I must assume," Nurse Price had said while we itched ourselves practically raw from flea bites.

Then came The Colonel with the second lesson. That's when Doctor Bayshore ordered any and all articles of fabric to be brought out into the fire-pit and done away with.

That was the first and almost only time each of us got new clothes and bedding (other than when we were in true dire need). It took all of us a good week working together to rid Pine Brook of those nasty lice and bed-bugs.

Actually, I was very surprised Cousin Lexington didn't experience such things firsthand. You know, since she was third-class like the rest of us. And Oscar had so much hairdressing on, I doubt anything could live in his hair. Any bug or other creature would surely suffocate.

We walked on, taking in the ship trying to learn our way through the mazes of corridors and up and down stairwells. Then, just as I was losing hope of ever arriving to our destination, we came to a large open area.

"Note the marking here on the door," our steward instructed, pointing his finger to the metal door plate. He frowned at the confused faces staring back at him. "It says: D Deck Mess Kitchen Galley-Second Class."

Some still didn't understand. Then to my amazement Oscar spoke up. He read the sign not in English but in several different tongues. Each nationality group nodded graciously over and over again, beaming smiles of gratitude. Oscar acknowledged back with a smile.

He looked at me perking a self-impressed eyebrow. I turned my face from him. Cousin Lexington on the other hand looked up at him in the most admiring way.

"The good Lord sure has His mighty hand on you," she said.

Our steward cleared his throat and opened the door to our work area. I must say it was the most massive kitchen I had ever seen. It was larger than Pine Brook's, and at least five times larger than Shamus'. Truly if Nurse Price saw such a room she would have fainted dead away for sure, not only from such a sight but also the heat and strong odors trapped within emanating from food and workers. For it was already half full of busy staff, men mostly. And from the appearance of the crew, they had been at it all night.

Their uniforms were no longer clean and fit, starched crisp and white, ready for a whole new day as one would expect aboard such a fine and elegant vessel. Nay. Theirs were splattered with stains akin to what we had at Pine Brook with one exception. Instead of Pine Brook gray backgrounds theirs were absorbed on Titanic white.

I immediately recognized the head chefs and cooks from the lowly kitchen scullions, soup cooks, assistant confectioners, and all the others called to kitchen duty. It was the chef's Toque Blanche's that gave them their well-earned recognition, as Shamus taught me to call the tall chef hats with pleats. Toque Blanche.

"*Toque Blanche.* The more folds they have in those tall hats, the more advanced up the hierarchy the cook is," I recalled him explaining to me.

"It's said each pleat in their Toque Blanche is the number of ways that particular chief knows how to prepare an egg. Hence, one-hundred pleats, one-hundred ways."

I don't know if I believed him. At least concerning the number of eggs.

Daniel stood against the kitchen wall studying the area as if trying to discover a way out.

"We have five kitchens in total aboard Titanic," the steward crooned." And each of those kitchens have two ranges along with nineteen-yes, I said nineteen, nineteen ovens..." From the size of the kitchen, I did believe him.

I knew our workload was to be heavy, and our hours long and hard. But it wasn't until the steward got done telling us what exactly was expected of us did I fully understand the true extent of our workload.

"It is your job to make sure the galleys on this ship are not only clean and well-kept as you prepare the fine meals that are expected, but that they are also protected as well. Thievery is thievery no matter the amount of extra goods we have on board. You will all get fed well enough, I can tell you that. But you are also expected to work for it, as well."

And what an amount of goods that magnificent ship did hold! We all stood spellbound as the steward rattled off the supplies. Even the most seasoned amongst us stood awestruck at the enormity at hand.

"Remember, each and everyone of you has the responsibility of taking care of, 57,600 crockery items including, pots, pans, baking sheets...127,000 pieces of tableware, including bone china dinner plates, cut-glass tumblers, and fine crystal..."

By the time he got down to the last, 7,500 pounds of bacon and ham, and 25,000 pounds of poultry, I was exhausted.

Jeepers creepers, how in the world would a mere mess crew of sixty-two keep up with all that? I thought.

The steward answered my question before any could ask it.

"We need to depend heavily on all 322 storekeepers and victualling crew to complete our daily tasks. All of them. That personally includes each and everyone of you. After all, we do have 2,224 mouths to feed, three times a day, plus what will be consumed in-between meals by the privileged passengers."

Now, being a cook's helper meant just that. To help wherever we were needed. And because of that, I couldn't help but feel sorry for Daniel.

As the assistants to the head cooks looked us over deciding which one of us they would take to help in their unit that day, Daniel pressed himself against the wall as if trying to melt into it. But for Cousin Lexington the picking was different.

"Dibbies on that one right there," the baker's assistant yelled, pointing at Cousin Lexington to such an extent no one would steal her. She was one of the very few women allowed to help in the kitchens.

The vegetable clerk mumbled something to Oscar, and off went he went to the vegetable tables and bins.

And then he turned his attention to me and looked me over as well. I felt myself wilt. "You'll do. Come forward," he said most un-enthusiastically. I, to say the very least, was a bit insulted. Worse yet was Daniel.

I looked at him, pasted tight against the wall purposely hiding from the cook's picks. I was sure his special physical situation would keep him from the draw. But nay. They decided he was the most useful to work with the soups. He avoided me and walked off with the soup assistant.

"State your name," the clerk said to me.

I sighed. Doing so I would have to repeat my story. So I did, repeating it for all to hear.

"Fine," the vegetable man said, eyeing me up with great doubt.

"You got this far. Who am I to question?" He led me to the bins and tables next to Oscar.

"You should be quite comfortable there," he said, pointing to a long, wide table surrounded by large metal tubs filled with assorted vegetables, and empty ones yet to be filled.

"Is there any way I can perhaps be placed with a different group? Say maybe, oh I don't know, maybe the soup, or the bakery?"

Vegetable man gave me a hard stare. “Look. Either you do your work as given or you can spend the entire voyage in the brink. Take your choice, *Michael.*”

I took a deep breath and tried not to look at Oscar as I marched forward to my place at the station.

The smell of rutabagas, onions and cabbages, and other crude vegetables filled the air. Some roasting, some boiling, and some lined up neatly, cut into the prettiest shapes resembling some of my favorite things like, flowers (roses in particular) chunks of diamonds, and some sat on silver platters formed into actual art resembling real outdoor scenes (mainly forest and mountain). Nurse Price and Little Margret Jean and I oohed and ahhed plenty of times over such lavishly prepared fruits and vegetables featured in Mrs. Beeton’s Book of Household Management.

I stood by a rather tall man who smelled scrumptiously of butter sauce and asparagus. It helped snuff out the pungency of human perspiration mixed up with the bitters of cabbage, onions, and turnips simmering in the huge stockpot in front of us.

“Potatoes,” a man shouted through a screen of steam floating in front of his face.

“I need more potatoes,” his hands too busy to stop chopping and dicing the vegetables in front of him, he pointed his forehead at me.

“You, peel those potatoes and keep them coming.”

“Me?” I jabbed my finger to my chest.

“No, the person standing behind you. Yes, you. Now get moving.”

Oscar stared at me, grinning. The anger inside me radiated to my checks making him smile even all the more. I reached down inside the bucket next to my legs and grabbed a potato and squeezed it.

Oscar’s cooking cap sat crooked to one side; a blonde strand of hair curled to the side of his forehead. I hate admitting I wanted to brush the curl aside, not because it lay so bothersome and irritatingly close to his silver eyes, but that it teased me in a rather provocative manner. For a moment, just one fleeting moment, I wanted to touch it, and him. The hat made him not only handsomely good looking in a gentlemen sort of way, but also a devilishly-roguish way.

"You'll need an apron and a net," he yelled to me.

"He's right, you know," said the tall man. "Grab one and a hair net over there at the clothing pantry before the head cook sees you." Oscar raised his eyebrows, nodding his head in agreement.

"Potatoes," the vegetable cook demanded again behind his veil of steam. "Potatoes, now!"

I skedaddled to the pantry and grabbed a freshly starched white apron and slipped its opening over my head. Twisting my hair into a knot on top of my head, I covered the loose bun with a hairnet. It sagged to the side from the heaviness of my hair. As I flopped the bundle of hair in place, Oscar took hold of the straps of my apron. I turned stiff as the cloth.

"I don't bite," he said, giving the ties a good tug. "Matter of fact, I'm quite a delightful person. Most helpful, too."

"I th-th-think I c-c-can do it myself, th-thank you."

He pulled the straps (and me) closer to himself and began tying the ends nice and tight. Before I could protest his 'helpful insistence,' he bent down to my ear and whispered something I would always remember.

"I will guarantee you, in the long run you will be very glad that you kept company with me." With a last yank of the straps, he was gone and standing back in his area.

I stared at him. He tentatively began to place the platters of finely carved fruits and vegetables depicting nature, in neat and tidy rows in front of him.

I ran to my own table and grabbed a knife, for the man behind his veil of steam had grown very impatient.

"Hurry your ass up or you'll be scrubbing them toilets and chamber pots with the other worthlessness in The Glory Holes."

"Y-y-yes sir," I spat, knowing what horrors awaited those cursed with such a job.

"Here now. What did you have planned for that?" Oscar nodded at my short, steel knife. My knuckles turned pale, gripping the knife tight in my hand.

"If you're going to do a job, do it right. I have something that surpasses that by far."

He walked over to a machine that looked like some sort of winger clothes washer with a self-rinsing vat attached beneath it.

"You have only two simple chores. Peeling potatoes and washing them. That's it."

I tried not to play the idiot attempting to figure out just what in the heck the damn machine was, let alone what was I expected to do with it.

"It's a potato peeler," Oscar said plugging its end into a generator socket. "It's electric. Watch."

He stuck his hand in the sack next to the machine and pulled out a hefty potato and placed it on the belt attached to the machine. "Press this button right here and..."

The potato passed through a space between a double-sided knife that slid up and down. Not fast and not slow, and no longer than one full minute of spinning, and sliding, and the potato was clean of all its rough, dark brown skin.

"The potatoes automatically fall into the vat of water. See?" The spud plunked into the tub of water beneath it. "And it gets a good washing. The water is flushed through an oxidation filter returning it back into the vat nice and clean, see? Ingenious, don't you agree? When the vat is full, pull the potatoes out and put them in those buckets."

Putting aside it was Oscar who was showing me how the machine worked, I was amazed at the process.

By the end, the spud was clean and fresh. I thought of Nurse Price and promised myself if I ever made it back to Pine Brook, I would somehow bring her such a marvelous machine.

"So, all you're needing to do is place your potato here, and take them out there, and put them here in these buckets. That's it."

Oscar watched me pick a spud from the open sack and placed it on the slider plate.

"You can put two on at a time, you know. Even three or four if they're small. It speeds things up. Here, I'll show you." He pulled a big spud from the sack.

"See, like this," he said placing it next to mine on the sliding plate. "Easy, see? Two at once. Both get peeled equally." They plopped into the washing vat.

"Machines are wonderful in the way that some are able to get us from one point to another, just like all those dirty potatoes in that sack on the floor. They get peeled here, and end up there, all nice and cleaned in the vat, all ready to be prepared and served.

"But sometimes machines aren't so good. Like when they put things where they shouldn't be." He put another two potatoes on.

"Do you know how much coal and man power it will take to get us across the whole Atlantic Ocean? Six thousand, six hundred and eleven tons of coal and one hundred stokers. After all it is Titanic's job to race against time. But I'm sure you know that already." He stared at me hard and steady.

"You do know what I'm talking about, don't you? How we're racing against time."

I looked away and at his hands. They were large and strong, yet appeared to be gentle as was the man in the garden of 1953. He placed another two potatoes on the peeler.

"That was one fine story you conjured up, *Michael*. But one word of advice. For your own good, and the sake of everyone else, take care of your deeds and let others attend theirs."

The machine rolled on. I said nothing.

"But there is just one small thing concerning your task," Oscar added.

"Cook won't find much use for a few dozen. He expects hundreds, and hundreds, and more hundreds. The job will take you hours, if not the whole of our journey. So, you, little mademoiselle is hereby sentenced to be the potato queen. It will keep you out of trouble. Well, at least for today. Hopefully. Your throne awaits, your highness."

Little mademoiselle? Why did he call me that? Only Shamus calls me that! And what did he mean concerning letting others do their own deeds?

Before I could ask him, he removed his cap and bowed before me. Grinning his boyish grin, he pressed his cap to his chest, waiting for me to comply to his instructions.

For a moment, just one moment, I realized my hate for him was not true hate, but envy. His pretentiousness stemmed from too much wisdom given to someone too young. For he wasn't much older than me and yet he knew so much more than I. And from what I saw, even more than his superiors.

The air about him was not of that type of sophistication held by those with much money handed down from generations past until it flows through them, and becomes their blood. Nay, Oscar was one born naturally with an air of sophistication, like how he was born with his silver-gray eyes. He had the class that Shamus often talked of. The sort of class that money cannot buy, nor poverty stifle.

"A person is either born with class, or they are not," Shamus oftentimes reminded me. And Oscar and Cousin Lexington were just the sort of souls to prove it.

Given the task as bakers helper, Cousin Lexington was doing just that. Helping the best she knew how. She was heard across the kitchen from bakery side to soup side and every place in between.

Her scolding's to the head baker and his assistant made even myself cringe. Cousin Lexington was not impressed with the much experienced head baker nor his insistence to use what he said was the automatic whisk and bread kneader.

"Bread needs the human touch," Cousin Lexington argued. "Not some hunk of metal twisting about in an oversized washbasin. Same with them eggs. No machine can do what the human hand can. It's in the feel of it, too, you know, not just the looks, you know."

She went on with this for quite some time until the master baker put his hand up, flagging a steward over to his side. A few mumbles later and Cousin Lexington was escorted quietly out the galley door. Some moments later she returned taking her post once again, red faced and silent. This time her hands took hold of the electric machine in front of her rather than the dough sitting in the vat.

But it was Daniel who I kept watch on the most. I strained to see him standing past some of the most complicated kitchen items I had ever seen. He was his tight-lipped self. Not talking, not asking questions like the others; instead, he stood quietly at his stove stirring the massive soup kettles in front of himself taking in his surroundings and fellow coworkers.

His job in the soup division seemed an easy enough task: adding the head soup master's pre-measured ingredients into the correct broths at the correct time. After that, he was to stir each stock making sure none scorched. It was a welcomed duty for any one-armed man, and a much needed one for the soup cook who was busy chopping poultry, beef and other meats (some of which to this day I still do not recognize).

I watched Daniel place a colander full of what appeared to be soaked peas, into a very large stock-pot. The soup simmering inside stopped, then slowly started again. The broth bubbled like blobs of green rain dancing in a small, thick bright green puddle. Daniel began stirring it, all the while looking about the kitchen as if fixated on finding a way out. He hadn't noticed me watching him, and reached into his pocket pulling out one of his steel marbles.

I wasn't at all sure what he was going to do with it. At first, I thought he was going to place it in one of the cooking kettles of soup.

"Potatoes, keep them coming. I need more potatoes," the vegetable assistant shouted out.

Another helper came and took the ones washed and cleaned and set to go.

"Th-thank you," I said, setting another two to be peeled.

"Tis' fine, mum, but you must not dally. Cook has little patience." I smiled at the little fellow giving him a nod of appreciation.

I looked over at Daniel only to find him gone.

At first I panicked then realized how silly I was. After all being on a ship out at sea meant he couldn't go far.

I looked down at the spud vat. Only half filled. I put a few more through, then some more until the next load was full.

"Sir," I shouted at the cook. "Say, sir."

"What is it," he snapped keeping watch on his work.

"M-m-may I visit the l-l-lavatory, please s-s-sir?" There came no answer.

"S-s-sir, p-p-please sir, m-m-may I—"

"Stop all that blasted hissing! It's downright painful hearing you utter even one word."

"B-b-but s-s-sir, I—"

"Blast you! We haven't time to dilly-dally."

The expression on his face was so soured a person would think raw lemon juice poured from his brow instead of sweat.

"Oh darn," I said, dropping a potato on the floor. No one noticed. Not even Oscar. He was much too busy with his own tasks. I bent down to retrieve it and didn't come up. So, making my way past the potato man, I began searching for Daniel and his steel marbles.

The floor was strange as strange could ever be. It was made of some sort of thin rubber with grooves running in hexagons, like the shape of honeycombs. I assumed it was to keep us from slipping about during rough seas.

It was cold, and dirty as I crawled past the workers feet. The floor, littered with all sorts of food, some old, some new, some rotten, smelled of rancid grease and lard which had soaked into some of the fryer workers shoes and pant legs. Despite gacking, not once or twice, but a third time, I managed to keep moving without detection.

Passing the fryer area with a few yards to go, I rested under a table. That's how I spotted Daniel slinking against the wall. A few more yards and he would be in the serving pantry and out the door and in the dining room. I stood up ready to chase after him. He saw me and bolted. And so did Oscar.

"There's our potato girl," he said making his way to me. "How did you get way over there without me seeing you?"

His smile was bright and cheerful. And I despised it.

"I n-n-need to indulge the l-l-lavatory, if y-y-you please," I stammered watching Daniel make his way out the pantry doors. I tried glimpsing him. The doors sprang open and shut so quickly I had just enough time to hear a piano and cello duet floating about the dining hall. It was no use. Oscar had won. Daniel was gone.

CHAPTER EIGHTEEN

It had been an extremely long work day. Twelve hours and how many to go I had yet to find out. And due to Oscar's watchful eyes, I was unable to procure an observance of Daniels whereabouts and, do-abouts. I was weary thinking how to get away from Oscar and his blasted potato machine in order to find Daniel. It seemed impossible.

And so, with breakfast and lunch well beyond, and first supper shift beginning, I stood diligently at my station. And with nothing to entertain myself I continued to take in my surroundings while working on my own chores. The entire scene was a festive ruckus as if an unexpected holiday were upon us.

"Better than they ever ate for more than one day," good old Cousin Lexington boasted loudly from her corner of the kitchen.

"Poor lambs. I been aboard many ships, I've eaten many meals alongside them all...first class all the way down to the firemen and stockers, and I'm telling ya', as God is my witness, this food of theirs aboard this ship here...it be fit enough for second class, even first, by any standard, ship-wise that is."

I was learning that only a few incidences were to be shared between first and second classes (third class being excluded, of course). Meals served in shifts was one of them.

Second class dining took place first and in their own dining saloon with a three-course meal. Then came the first class, of which I was informed earned ten-course meals and always ate later and in a much more formal format in their own private dining room. That is unless they chose to engage with the other classes. And for the third class, they did very well in their own private, cafeteria style eating saloon.

And so came the sound of pots and pans banging and clattering while soups and sauces brewed and hissed to delectable perfection, mashed together with strong demands of, 'this and that' from the head cooks and chefs. Heated arguments between meager kitchen scallions and assistants added to the brew.

I watched what I believed to be potato number, four thousand-four hundred, spin clean of its skin, and then plunk into the vat of churning water. And just as my own escape scheme was formulating in the furrows of my mind, a commotion began to commence from across the kitchen.

Shouts from wait staff and demands from the stewards could be heard clear back to my area, the vegetable area. I looked up from the potato machine to investigate the eruption.

"Hip, hip—Hip, hip," the maître d's prepped the waiters, marching in the most best of manners to and fro from the serving pantry between the kitchen and dining room.

The evening garsons were far more sophisticated than the breakfast and lunch crews. For these fine fellows were like ballerinos, all properly starched and groomed. Their suave movements back and forth from pantry to the dining room were well practiced and in perfect precision with the ice and beverage boys, and busboys, and those serving fresh wash cloths with rose water basins, and everything else fine. Truly, it was as if I were watching a fine ballet.

I watched with delight as each food item was placed strategically on large, silver serving trays. Heavier items in the middle, lighter on the outside. I knew the reason for this placement due to my own training instructions given to me by none other than Shamus himself. That, and I did hear the lead waiters instructing their crews to always double check their tray loads for menu accuracy and balance before encasing them with their silver domes.

First course: Consommé with tapioca, second course: Baked haddock with sharp sauce, curried chicken and rice, spring lamb with mint sauce, roast turkey with savory cranberry sauce, green peas, pureed turnips, boiled rice, boiled and roast potatoes; Third course (desserts): Plum pudding, wine jelly, coconut sandwich, American ice cream, assorted nuts, fresh fruit, cheese, biscuits.

Except for the roasted and boiled potatoes, my tongue danced for a taste of the succulents beneath the silver domes bobbing out the serving pantry and into the dining room. Out went the trays of food above the waiters' heads, but not so far as to lose control.

"Braxton, Michael Braxton, scullion," a steward addressed, coming up along the work tables. I turned from the commotion to find the voice belonged to very same steward as that morning calling my name.

"Allen, George Allen, scullion," he went on calling out more names in his pinched manner.

"Ball, Percy Ball, plate washer...Bradshaw, John Bradshaw, plate washer..."

Finally, all were called and he blew his whistle. Three short trills.

"Those kitchen helpers called may take a thirty-minute break and will then report back to me to begin clean up. You may eat and toilet during this time. After your return a new list shall be called for their relief. Until then, those not called at this time for their relief are to remain here with cooks and chef assistants to help serve."

Three more short trills and he was gone. I sighed with relief and immediately removed my soiled apron and cap and headed for the serving pantry. From there I would survey the dining room and with any luck I would find Daniel.

So as not to be a menace to the flow of servers' and stewards' comings and goings, I held myself against the oak paneled wall of the serving pantry and stared into the dining hall. The ambiance of such finery was that which one reads of in the most romantic of novels.

And for a moment I pretended to be Nelly Dean from 'Wuthering

Heights' hiding behind a curtain watching as a splendid meal was about to be set forth for Heathcliff and Catherine.

Long mahogany tables and swivel chairs upholstered in deep crimson leather were bolted into the flooring. *To keep them safe from the thrashing of rough seas,* I reasoned.

The deep raspberry colored linoleum tile flooring with its creamy octagon shapes matched the chairs and tables beautifully, providing the room more than justice.

The tables set in perfection (of course) held fresh red roses and white carnations vased between small crystal hurricanes with burning candles inside. Electric lights inside cut-glass cages hugged the walls, casting a soft, warm glow onto the gold lining of the dining rooms white honeycomb ceiling and walls.

Just past the pantry to my left, sat a man at the piano, a cello player accompanied him. Their music sweet to my ears, floated past the low chatter of a young couple to my right and filled the room.

The two were very much stylish; she in a green velveteen gown with black fur trim I would have died for. The buttonholes, surrounded by a tapestry of white doves in flight, made me think of Huston and his chalk drawings. The eyes of the doves suited as buttons were nothing less than mother of pearls.

Her jewels, a perfectly matched assemble of emeralds, caught my eye with every slight movement of her neck and hand. The earrings, necklace and dinner ring sparkled and glimmered like miniature chunks of smooth transparent green ice showing just the proper hint of green to let those around her know that her emeralds were the most highly desired of all.

And he (her escort) complemented her well. His black hair well-greased, matched his black dinner suit and tie. His stark white shirt showed him to be a well-bred gentleman. But the manner in which the two held hands across the table told me they were not lovers, nor sweethearts. Their conversation proved me right.

"I don't fit in, I just don't fit in, Franklin. Can't you see that? No matter how much you groom me with the best of consultants. Even if Lady Duff-Gordon were at my side guiding me every inch of the way. Even she would be unable to design me to be a suitable heir surrounding Mr. Butt and his people. No, Franklin, I still would not fit in, both outside of me, or the inside of me. It just isn't possible. Besides the name does give me the giggles. Imagine being addressed as Mrs. Butt for the rest of *your* life."

The young woman was not younger than myself, nor older. Her hair was dark as mine and just as thick and wavy. The length was a guess for she styled it as all the rest of the woman in the saloon. High and loose, held with a soft netting of pearls and tiny gleams of emeralds. Her face was not beautiful. But drawn with sweet simpleness.

She had declared her personal misgivings in such a modest manner that, though being of the same age as myself and of such wealth, I wanted to rescue her from her predicament and the overconfident man across from her. For he was overly persistent, disregarding her obvious insecurity of being a step down from those above her. And well was her understanding. For they were dining in second class, after all, not first.

"Oh, my sweet, sweet adoring Maisy. What matters as for a last name? Even with such a name as Butt..."

They looked about, stifling their giggles.

"Just stay shy of chocolates and other confectionery and you will be fine." Franklin cleared his throat, straightening himself.

"See, even you cannot contain yourself."

"I am so sorry, sister. I mustn't jest so. Truly, I am sorry. If you could only see what everyone else sees when they look at you, certainly you would not think such a way, least say such things. You know it was Mother's dream, and Father's for the most part, that you and I become all we might become. It was not their wish for us to stay in such poverty as that we were born." He squeezed her hand.

"Now listen to me, my dear sister. I ask you, am I not your loving older brother? Have I not looked after you all these years? Provided for you the best way manageable? Come now, answer me."

She recoiled her hands from his. He grabbed them back, gently.

"Maisy, you are beautiful, both inside and out. It is not fair that one with such a good heart and of such good character should go through life scorned upon simply due to economic status. Why Maisy, there are hundreds, perhaps even thousands, of men and women with pockets so lined with notes and money that they have no room for a warm hand, or heart. Not even their own, as cold as they themselves might be.

"I cannot think of anyone more deserving of a fine life than you. Mother and father so wanted it to be that way for you, and for me. Why not allow them their dream come true to be seen from Heaven?

Why deny them even in death? Why deny yourself in life?" Franklin's eyes danced with endearment.

"Oh, Maisy. If you were evil and full of malice and harvested hatred toward man, any man or woman or child no matter their station, I truly would greet such a marriage arrangement with disgust. Not encouragement."

"Franklin, I don't know this man no more than I do our uncle from childhood. And you, what shall become of you, dear brother? I cannot breathe a day without you, not one. And I shan't. I will simply hold my breath till I burst if he sends you away. Or better, I will run with you, leaving the cold-hearted scoundrel to his own lonely death.

Promise me, dear Franklin, promise me you won't leave me, not for one day, not for one moment."

Franklin laughed. "I doubt Major Archibald Butt can be considered an old uncle lying on his deathbed. Nor is he a scoundrel, and a cold hearted one at that. You exaggerate so well. If he were, do you believe I would allow you, my dearest one, to seek out his interest in you? He has proven himself a loyal and true friend, and a great military advisor. Not only to myself, but also the president of the United States of America, Taft himself, and Theodore Roosevelt.

Maisy, his affection for you is an honor. A true honor.

"Just stay clear of that W.T. Stead. No matter his questions, simply turn your cheek and answer him not. He might just write you and the major up in one of his articles. He's always on the lookout for a good rag."

Franklin laughed. There was something familiar in his laugh. It warmed me with an inner warmth I hadn't felt since I was a young girl.

I was drawn to him and Maisy. They reminded me of what I and Huston would have been. And as I listened close to their conversation, a light for my existence on the Titanic began to flicker and dawn.

"Franklin, what if he finds me dull and rather boring? What if he doesn't view me as you do, my dear brother? What if I find I am truly remorseful marrying a man that I have no feelings for?"

Maisy turned her face from Franklin. Her voice lowered, barely audible.

"Franklin, I-I..."

"Have no experience?" he asked gently, taking her hand. Maisy sighed. Her face seemed on fire.

"Listen Maisy, I do wish Mother or Aunt Lanora were here to help with...your...natural needs. I'm afraid all I can do is inform you...to let you know...well, as far as it goes...for a man, that is..."

Franklin looked down at his plate and picked at his food, his blush was deeper than Maisy's.

"Have no worries, dear sister. Trust me. It matters not. A true gentleman is a gentleman no matter what circumstances are set before him.

"And if all goes as it should, I shall be a proud uncle. Within time, of course."

Franklin chuckled. Taking Maisy's hand, he gently kissed it. "Be well, sister. Let no worries come to you." He wiped away her tears as I did mine from my own eyes. And my heart again ached for Huston.

"Oh, my beloved brother, Franklin. How I adore you. Still, I do wish Mother were here," Maisy said. "Perhaps if everything does pan out well, and do find myself in a few years with children of my own, and if one were to be a girl, I shall name her after Mother."

Franklin grinned with delight. "Jeepers creepers! That would be absolutely wonderful."

Maisy laughed with relief. "You sound just like Mother did." My ears perked. *Jeepers creepers?*

"Yes, and if a boy, he shall carry Mother's beloved brother's name."

I held my breath and looked at Franklin and then Maisy. I looked at them close and hard. "Jeepers creepers," I said almost loud enough for them to hear. *"Jeepers creepers!"*

I held tightly to a bread cart perched in front of me and held myself up, for my knees had gone weak and buckled as Franklin said the name.

"Huston. Yes, Uncle Huston and Mother were close as you and I. It should do both them proud." My heart danced.

Could it be, could it really and truly be? But how, how could such a thing be possible? My mind raced thinking that in the realm of time anything is possible.

I checked behind me making sure Oscar (or any member of his troop) hadn't spotted me.

The kitchen workers had returned and were performing their tasks most diligently. Naturally I was unable to contain myself to join them. For my mission was much larger than that assigned to me after all. I hadn't traveled into the future to man my position of sitting at my throne-my throne of potatoes. I had to go forward and discover as much as possible. So, with bread cart in hand, I cautiously as possible advanced toward the two, Franklin and Maisy, hoping to catch more of their conversation.

"Who would ever think it would be Mother to provide our family wealth, and not Father. Her servitude to Shamus was a blessing not just to her, but us and our future children as well." My heart pounded so fast I could not breath.

Shamus? My Shamus? Shamus P. Fitzgerald?'

I had to make sure. And once I did, what would I do? What could I do? For if Franklin and Maisy were my children, I was there aboard the great Titanic to protect them, that I knew. But from what? And how? Would I reveal to them who I was? Would I disclose my time travel to them? Why, they'd think me a crazy woman for sure.

Oh, how I wanted to run to them, hold them in my arms, talk with them. I could not take my eyes off them.

"Though Shamus was not our blood uncle I always felt as if he were," Maisy was saying. "And Aunt Margret. I always looked forward to her visits. She was a wonderful playmate and companion.

Don't you miss them so, Franklin? Oh, don't you miss them?"

"Yes, yes I do. And Grandmother Price, and Grandfather Bruce. I miss the whole lot of them, yes, I do. Even though they were not blood family, I do not believe anyone could have asked for a finer crop to have been taken in by.

"Yes, our mother was very fortunate indeed."

"I do have one regret, brother. That Father was not home often.

Always gone somewhere, doing things us children and the others, except Uncle Shamus and Mother, were to know about.

"Oh, how I hated the secrets. All the secrets! To this day I can't help but wonder about them."

"Yes, we could ponder such things till death takes us, that is true. But now we must go on and fulfill Mother's dreams and hopes for us; to keep in societies' good graces with good money. And your marriage to Major Butt does insure us of keeping that promise to her. After all, Shamus's estate cannot last us forever. We have only but another year to keep us from the streets.

"And Maisy, if it were me, I mean if I were female, I wouldn't see any harm looking at dear old Archibald every day. He is quite handsome you know. And kind. That we must give him also."

"And boring," Maisy turned a deep rose color. "Oh, I am so sorry, Franklin. I mustn't think such things, let alone say them, even to you." "Maisy," Franklin whispered, leaning close to his sister, "rumor has it, he had an audience with the Pope and carries with him a letter from Pope Pius X to the president. That's another reason to stay far away from that yellow journalist, William T. Stead. No Maisy, I cannot disagree more. I am sure the major has many good stories to share, and with being Mrs. Archibald Butt, your life shall never see a dull day. I promise."

And so, it was confirmed. The two beautiful people sitting at the table were in fact my children. My very own children. But where was I? Where was their father, my husband whose identity I knew not in order to grieve for? My mission, as far as I could see, was to save my dear little Maisy from the life of a marriage to someone she was not in love with, but would merely tolerate in order to save herself and her brother, my son, from a life of poverty.

I questioned if I should approach them. Pushing the bread-cart forward, I made my way to their table ignoring requests of wantings from others along the way. The delicate scent of lavender and rose surrounded Maisy in a most favorable manner. I smiled. For apparently, I had taught her well. I stood for a moment taking in the two of them. Yes, in Franklin I could see my own beloved Huston, his features gentle, not sharp as many young men, except his nose. That he won from his mother. It was longer than mine, ending in a sharpness that was stern, but yet very much attractive.

And in Maisy I saw my own mother. The color of Maisy's dark hair, and tufts of soft curls framing her face belonged to me, but every inch of her fair and soft complexion with its apple red checks and lips belonged to my mother.

The face of an angel, I thought reaching to touch her shoulder.

"Is everything fine? Have you any requests?" I asked, removing my hand from the cart and passing it over the soft green velveteen of Maisy's gown. Feeling the realness of the heat from her shoulder, I pulled my hand away. Yes, she was real. And so was Franklin. Blood ran through them as it did me. My blood, and the blood of a man I did not know.

"Yes, is there anything you might require?" My heart dropped to my stomach. Oscar. It was Oscar. He stood in front of me, before Maisy or Franklin had time to turn and face me. I flushed.

"No, none at the moment," Franklin answered. "We are fine. Our meal, or the first portion thereof, is superb. Especially these potatoes. Our compliments to the chief."

"Fine. Very well then," Oscar said, looking at me unrelentingly. "Perhaps we need to move on to the next guest, but first let's freshen up your cart, shall we?"

He gripped my elbow, forcing me (and the cart) into the serving pantry. I pulled myself from him, and leaned against an empty cutting table. He took deep breaths, letting each one out slowly and deliberately. I glared at him.

"Look, I know you're new. I know you're anxious to learn things.

But right now is not the time. Not this time. Not now. There's just too many, too much..."

I fired back. "Who are you? And wh-wh-who do you think you are? I don't know you, a-a-and I-I-I don't c-c-care to know you. The truth is, I-I-I don't l-l-like you! You're bossy, a-a-and arrogant, a-a-and..."

Oscar rubbed his face. "Look kid," he said, "I'm not here to play the, *Who's Most Popular,* game. I'm here on business." I kept my glare.

"Alright, tell you what. Let's call a truce," he said. "Obviously, neither one of us is going anywhere. Like it or not, I am not the enemy, I assure you."

There was something captured in those silver eyes of his that conveyed a sense of sincerity.

"Alright," I said. "I-I-I'll give. I won't like it, n-n-nor you, but I'll give. U-under one circumstance. Th-that you stop bossing me around. You're not my b-b-boss."

He grinned. A spark of amusement flashed in his eyes.

"Yes, I can understand that," he said, looking down at his shoes, chuckling. "You're right. I am not your boss."

"And you are not my f-f-friend, either."

He continued staring at his shoes. His light laughter ended. "I am so sorry you feel that way, Little Mademoiselle. Truly I am. I do understand it though. But would it be too much if I may suggest that you reconsider that, I am not your enemy." He looked up from the floor, searching for a spark of acceptance.

"Little Mademoiselle," I repeated. "W-w-why would you call me that? Little Mademoiselle?"

He arched his eyebrows. A grin grew on his lips. "As I say, I am not your enemy. We shall leave it at that for now. But, I do need to warn you. We cannot in any manner, in any way, in any form, communicate anything beyond what is considered normal hospitality with those patronizing this ship. To do so can be, shall we say, catastrophic."

The sternness in his words was not that of belligerence but a seriousness, giving me a sense of concern. I thought of Franklin and Maisy.

"Wh-what if a person knows another person, or thinks they do, th-then wh-what? Would they not think a person a *snob* if th-that person refused to indulge th-them in conversation?" I waited again as Oscar rubbed his face.

"Well?"

"Just don't. Trust me," he answered. "Just don't."

CHAPTER NINETEEN

I pondered Doctor Bruce's diagnosis. Perhaps I was mad. Perhaps for some unknown reason I was experiencing what Doctor Bruce and Nurse Price referred to as a relapse of my Psychosis Absorption, leaving me with a loss of all my senses and allowing my overactive imagination to take over. It certainly did seem much more plausible than time travel. Especially into the future, and especially meeting one's unborn adult children.

I snuggled deeper inside my blankets and handed Patsy a buttered biscuit. His huge claw snatched it gently from my hand.

"But they are real, Patsy, just as real as you and I and everyone aboard this ship, and as real as all those back home."

I pulled the blankets around me, stroking Patsy's soft, black feathers.

"Boy, Patsy," I said watching him eat his buttered biscuit. He held it in his claw and nibbled it with his beak, keeping his sharp eyes on every crumb letting not a-one fall to the side. "If it gets any colder in here I'll see my breath. Yours, too." I tested the air. Nothing but an ever so slight of a mist.

Digging deeper inside my blankets I listened to the strong and steady rumbles of the ship's engines that I, and all aboard, had grown accustomed to. Now, only when concentrating did we hear their rhythm.

I thought of Cousin Lexington and how grateful I was to her especially after learning we were to be at sea for five more days.

You see, it happened our dear Cousin Lexington found out I was sleeping in a pantry closet and due to that, I lost the baby which in turn led to the loss of my husband (that I never had).

Being empathetic, she had used her vociferous self to arrange with the purser that I, *'Michelle'*, should have my very own private cabin. And second class to boot. Scullion or not.

I chuckled, reconstructing the vision of her holding her arms tightly across her full, girdled bosom as she looked over the growing crowd of passengers whom themselves were discontented with the temperature in their rooms.

Her emotional pursuance left the purser with only two choices. Either give into Cousin Lexington's demands, or be charged with the most unrewarding review that might cost him his job, plus that of the steady reputation of the White Star Ocean Liners, and Harland and Wolff Shipbuilders.

"I'll take this matter straight to Thomas Andrews himself. He is in Cabin A-36," she threatened. "And I shan't be shy to pound on his door. I am sure he is looking over his blueprints to this ship of his, as we speak, and therefore knows what extra rooms are available and where."

She continued, turning to the group gathering around us. "Everything this poor dear lamb has been through. Putting a little missus like my Michelle here in with a band of working men," she said with a disapproving sneer.

"And because of it, she has been sleeping in a pantry closet, next to the water closets! No wonder she lost a child from within the womb. And still she performed her duties like everyone else, and spot on at that. Why, I would think such a fine and fancy ship as this would be able to accommodate one little person like our Michelle here. Don't you agree?

"Besides, it's common knowledge that not all rooms are filled. A good many are empty, especially second class. I would hate to think how many ears will hear such tales as to how Mr. Joseph Bruce Ismay and his great and mighty White Ship Builders refused a poor lassie in such dire straits such as the soon to be, ex-Mrs. Daniel Coxon. And not by her choice, if you should need to know. Shameful. Mighty shameful. No woman deserves to be, well, that is not for me to tell. The shame I am talking of belongs to you, not her. Not allowing a poor, hardworking young lassie a bed in which to rest. Causing her to sleep in the hall. No wonder she lost her child. Shame on you. God help you. Shame on you!"

Tsk's and scorns of disapproval from the crowd hissed around us and the purser.

"Well, me and the Missus here needs to wear long johns even with the extra blankets you gave us," an elderly man said.

"Some might think this ship to be unsinkable, but it sure as hell is miserable cold," another grumbled.

"Well," Cousin Lexington said." That is very easy to explain. You see, the ship builders in their haste to complete this floating maze, somehow forgot to connect the duct work leading into all but three of the one-hundred and sixty-two second class cabins.

"And those three cabin rooms are unbearably hot," she explained to the passengers standing about, full of complaints concerning the miserable chill in their cabins.

"And what's more!" she went on, knowing she had the group's full attention. "It's a bloody pity! All those poor, Black Gang workers unflaggingly filling and stoking all those furnaces...twenty-nine of them bloody furnaces! Twenty-five which are double ended! That makes a grand total of one hundred and sixty-two boilers that need to be fed, when all are in use.

"And with the coal shortage going on means this ship and all other ships are using a lower grade of coal, which means it burns much hotter and much quicker, which in turn means those poor old souls are shoveling, and toiling, sweating from heat and exertion twice more than the average stoke, probably thrice."

"And how do you know these facts, Mademoiselle?" The purser asked with as much bulky defiance as his body structure.

The onlookers stared at Cousin Lexington, waiting for her answer. "Why," she said even more defiantly than he, "no one other than Mr. Thomas Andrews himself told me so!" she gloated. "Cabin A-36."

The crowd gasped. The purser gave a doubtful eye roll.

"Yes, it's true! I met Mr. Andrews on deck. Our deck! Deck B!" She exclaimed. "He claimed to be touring the ship personally in order to make sure all was well and satisfactory for everyone aboard, even us poor rascals traveling steerage. After a reasonable and agreeable conversation with the man, he insisted that I use his name if I need anything. So, I am."

She looked at the nameplate on the counter and ran her finger across the name. She smacked her lips and grinned.

"Now Purser Hugh Walter McElroy, may Michelle have her own cabin, a nice private one, with plenty blankets? Or shall I make way to A-36?"

The purser cleared his throat. "It's highly irregular for a meager kitchen worker to have—"

Cousin Lexington crossed her arms again, holding her ground. "I am stepping forward. I shall take another step and another. Now, do I need to knock on cabin A-36?"

"Oh, very well," the purser snapped, grabbing a new set of keys from the key peg. "Deck D, cabin number ten. It's a double berth. Close to the service door. I assume that *ought* to be agreeable."

Cousin Lexington turned to the group of passengers huddled together, eyeing up their fine clothes and manners. "Imagine that," she said with such arrogance that it caused me to see an exclamation mark written in the air above her head.

"Who would ever think the day would come when the lowly steerage would have it all the better than the class higher than them?"

"Yes, well, concerning all that," the purser said, turning his attention to me, "you will be sharing the same area with many of our upper-class passengers. I'll take it for granted that you do understand your..." He looked over the passengers hovering about.

"Your, social obligation," he smirked. "Well, just in case you've forgotten, I'll freshen your memory.

"You may not socialize with our guests. You, after all, are hired help and not on earned holiday as our real passengers. Keep that in mind." He smirked again and handed me two blankets.

"Hmm. I do believe she is to have another blanket," Cousin Lexington stated. "And if you don't mind, I shall require an extra myself."

Begrudgingly, the purser turned to grab the extra blankets.

"Are you sure you will be fine without heat? It is brisk," she asked, turning to me with a smile as he shoved them into her arms.

"Y-y-yes, I do believe so," I answered. "The extra blankets will do just fine."

And that is how I acquired my own private cabin, double berth at that.

It was quite meager, with nothing but a view of half painted walls and under the bed, sliding dressers drawers but with no drawers. For you see, the launch date had been set before the ship's completion, leaving many other cabins in the same disarray. After all, no matter how glorious a ship it was, it was still a ship, not a hotel with private boarding rooms like back home.

So, there I was laying on my berth, deep inside layers of blankets, stroking Patsy's soft, black feathers thinking and wondering what turn of events was ahead of us. Patsy truly was a great comfort to me. The warmth of his body assured me that even if everything I was experiencing those last few days were not real, at least he was. And so was the chill in my cabin.

Patsy had free reign. And with a sink full of water and plenty of biscuits and hard bread and assorted vegetables and fruits, he was quite content. But I, on the other hand, was restless, even with a long hard day behind me and the gentle loll of the chugging and churning of the steam engines below me. Restless to the point of needing to take a stroll in fresh clean air. Salty ocean air. After all it had been two full days since I last took in any sort of Mother Nature. Besides, my curiosity to explore outweighed my tired and wearisome body.

I had seen the ocean only twice in my life; once, during that disastrous family outing to New York, and the other when arriving magically in Queenstown Harbor.

To view the sea from its center was a once-in-a lifetime endeavor, one that I could not decline. So, anticipating what I might find, I eagerly tucked Patsy deep inside my jacket, and covered us with a blanket.

"It's a might chilly out there," I explained to him. "And neither one of us can chance taking to a cold."

He rustled a bit then settled nicely; our closeness added warmth to my body.

Opening the cabin door, I peeked up and down the corridor. I would walk the deck at my own pace this time and not rushing in haste down Scotland Road with the lower class, kitchen scullions and other workers. For I was now on Deck D, the deck I was to call home. For a few days, anyway.

And it was nothing like Deck E, third class Scotland Road, with its narrow, concrete floors and bare walls exposing pipes of all sorts and uncaged light bulbs that hung by their electrical wiring.

Despite Deck D's narrow hallways (as cabin corridors are on any ship unless one is traveling first class) second class was exceptional. It was fair to consider it to be that of first class on any other ships. Its hallways, coated in a creamy white, were elegant, as elegant as the finest of hotels. The smell of fresh paint seeping from cabins not yet completed gave the whole area a wonderfully clean scent. I stood taking it all in.

The linoleum under my feet spread before me like a river of frozen vanilla custard topped with splotches of Mrs. Thompson's canned raspberries. Feet forward, I made my way down the hall taking note of the mahogany woodwork turned to perfection.

On the ceiling the steam pipes ran the entire length of the hallway and were held in place with shiny sheets of metal and steel rivets.

Strips of gold gilding surrounded each air vent, electrical fixture, ornate protective plate, and all the light globes. They glistened as if freshly polished.

Passing the servers' staircase, I came to a vestibule. To my left was a reception room. I peered inside the doorway window. An exceptional carpeting of tapestry of deep burgundies, forest greens and warm yellows was beyond anything the Spring Green Mercantile could ever dream of laying beneath any of our feet.

Stark white, carved paneled walls fit perfectly with the decorative honeycomb patterns of the inlaid ceiling. I stepped away and continued to look for the way out onto the promenade, all the while heeding the purser's warning to, "*avoid anyone that might come my way.*"

I did so not to obey his demeaning, arrogant insistence that I was to avoid anyone in the upper classes, but to keep anyone else from involving them self in my journey. After all, there was no need for me to complicate matters further than what they had become. I needed to think, time to breathe and clear my mind.

I nodded to the few passing me, keeping my distance as I continued down the nearly vacant hall. Turning the corner, I came to yet another vestibule with another staircase. I was lost. For the ship was too large and too much for one to explore on their own.

I knew not to venture upward, for it would bring me too far up, possibly to the first-class promenade.

But there, a few yards before me, was a door. "Promenade Deck D," I said, reading the sign above it. I took the chance and pushed it open.

The heavy steel gave a slight screech. I stepped out and found myself to be correct. For I stood under a sky that had unfolded from day into night with stars so plentiful they shone beyond any number I could recite.

They glittered and sparkled like zillions and zillions of diamond nuggets, and appeared so close that I resisted the urge to reach up and grab one. The wind though slight was crisp, carrying a fresh damp whiff of salt that stung the inside of my nostrils. Not in a raw manner, but in a welcomed invigorating way. I listened to the ship pound itself against the waves. The rhythm of boat and water danced together. I hastened me forward into the blackened night. And that's when I saw him. To my left, a man ran past me like a mischievous goblin trying to escape the ominous glare of the lights of the deck.

"A member of the Black Gang," I told Patsy, knowing he was from the belly of the ship. "I'm sure of it."

He was just as Cousin Lexington described stokers to be. With his stokers' kerchief tied about his neck, he was blackened with sweat from the greasy coal dust shining on his face. In his hand he carried a metal shovel, its scoop nearly burnt through. He stared at me for a moment then traveled on. Within that moment, I sensed I knew him for somehow, he was familiar. I followed him.

We passed an open cove. Inside, rows of wooden chairs and sunning loungers stacked in needle straight order stood ready for the next day's novel readers and sun-filled day dreamers. Along the cove wall were sets of windows stained in the most delicate pattern of blue and yellow Persian flowers. It was the dining saloon I had peeked into. And it was there I spotted the man running to the right side of the deck. Passing the restaurant, he was out of my sight. I knew what I had to do.

"Patsy, I need to let you go till I find that man and see what he's up to. Maybe that way I can find out what's going on. Where do you think you should go till I get back?"

Patsy searched the promenade. He cocked his large, black head back and forth, up and down. A shine high above the very top deck caught his eye. Thick cables ran from one pole to another like a clothesline, transferring the ship's Marconi telegrams from ship to inland, and inland to the ship.

I uncovered Patsy. "The wind might be a bit rough up there, so try and stay put until I return."

I stood watching him fly to one of the poles. He flapped his wings several times, then settled and tucked them snugly against himself. With Patsy perched safely on top of the pole, I turned my attention to the man and began to pursue him.

Turning the corner outside the dining saloon, I came to the other side of the deck, port side. The left side. The stoker and his half-burnt shovel were nowhere in sight. He could not go around for there was nowhere to go except to cast himself into the ocean. The only conclusion, he went up, not down. I spotted a ladder that leaned against the pentacle of the bridge leading up to another promenade deck. Promenade Deck A. First-class.

"He had to go up, since no ladder leads down," I thought out loud. "But where? Where was he going, and why?"

I hid my blanket under a chaise lounger to ensure no one would steal it away from me and Patsy. We would need it later for not only warmth but a way to smuggle Patsy back inside.

Placing one hand on the ladder, I grabbed the bottom of my dress and pulled it up to enable my feet to climb safely up the ladder without tripping. The moist cold sea breeze made the metal doubly miserable with cold causing my hands to stick and the bottom of my boots to slip. I climbed ten of the cold, round metal rungs making it to the top: I peered over the railing. The wind stung my face like hundreds of pins made of ice. I wiped them against my arm trying to protect my face.

I was met by a row of lifeboats. I stayed on the last rung to evaluate my situation before moving forward. That's how I caught sight of the man's pant legs and boots as he dashed into a covered archway.

The dull sound of his fists banged on something solid. *A door,* I thought. *And He's trying to get in.*

So, with his attention intently held to gaining access within the doorway, I pulled myself off the ladder and onto the deck and snuck carefully past the lifeboats, one foot at a time.

Ten steps, I counted. *Fifteen, twenty.* His banging became louder and more persistent with each step.

Thirty steps, Thirty-five steps, forty.

So close was I, I could hear his muttering. And I could see he was standing in front of a cabin door. I shivered from deep within as I held myself tight against the bridge wall and hid behind the boats hanging next to the cabin. A thin, layer of salty ice made the steel on the deck unbearably cold and slick. I was glad Patsy was not with me but safe high above on the wire rigs that carried messages to loved ones and business associates across the ocean. I thought of Mr. Hawthorn, and the S.O.S. he taught me. Three dots for S, and three dashes for O.

Save our Ship... Save our Ship... I heard Mr. Hawthorn repeat in my head. All the while the man with the half-burnt shovel in his hand frantically pounded even harder on the door just as Mr. Hawthorn had on the arms of his medicine chair, with his own scarred hands. Three long pounds, three short pounds, then three more long pounds. *Save our Ship?* I questioned under my breath.

"Captain, aye, Captain!" The man shouted, attracting the attention of the few passengers strolling along the deck beneath us.

"What goes on up there?" one of them shouted up at the man.

"None your concern, sir," the stoker called down. "None your concern, at all. Enjoy your evening, sir." He went on again, banging and calling out for his captain.

"If none's the matter than why is that gal spying on you so, and why are you so frantic?"

"Again sir, beg pardon, none of your concern. Please sir, do move on and enjoy your evening with your Missus. Do beg your pardon."

The stoker stopped his pounding and looked down at the couple. "Beg pardon, sir," he yelled to them. "But what girl are you referring to, if I might ask?"

The man and his lady halted. "That one, right there," he said, pointing up at me. "The one around the corner from you. Hidden among the boats. She's stuck to the side of the ship like a salted kipper in a can."

My heart raced as the couple moved on, laughing. I had been discovered. The lifeboats were strung too high for me to climb into in order to hide inside them. I had to find another escape route. Fast.

"Thanks kindly," the stoker called after them. The air went still.

I heard nothing except the waves pounding against the massive hull of the ship, and the steady hum of the steam engines. No pounding of fists on the captain's door, nor the running of feet and boot clopping on the deck. Patsy let out a cry. The man was coming, heading to me. I held my breath as if doing so would force me to disappear.

"Who in the Lord's name is out there," a strong voice demanded, coming from the captain's cabin.

The wind gave a nasty, brisk shift carrying the sound of the man's heavy boots pausing then running back to the door. It was the wind that brought his answer to my ears.

"Please sir, "I need a word with you concerning a happening in the coal bunkers. It seems we have a problem."

"Who are you?" the captain asked suspiciously.

"Please forgive my filthy self, sir. I'm a fireman down in the hull. Please, Captain, sir. It is my concern that our lives be at stake."

"Whose lives?"

"Why, our lives, sir. Yours and mine. And everyone's aboard this ship. Please sir, if you will, I need to explain. I think my captain would appreciate this being discussed where no ears might hear."

The captain hesitated, shutting the door behind himself. "This spot is fine," he said, his tone guarded. "I'll have you know I give no unannounced audiences in my private cabin."

"Alright then, I shall spit it out right here and now. Though me guts tell me different.

"Sir, Captain, we have a fire in the belly of your ship. Bunker number six, section ten, just fore of the first stacker. And she be burning something ghastly hot to the point we might not make it across the sea. The hull is already weakened alright, and coming to the frigid waters, well...I fear the steel won't hold and that she just might crack in two.

"It's been burning down the middle of the ship's guts before we even left the shores of Southhampton, Captain, sir. A bunch of us informed Mr. Ismay, and Mr. Andrews, and when we insisted that Mr. Clarke and his crew take another look during inspection, we was told to shut our yappers or get off. A bunch did, and a bunch didn't. I be one who didn't, but now I think me a fool listening to them fancy men in them fancied up suits.

"I hate's repeatin' what's already been said but, you see sir, we be in trouble, and if'n we keep up the speed we be going at, we has'ta burn up more fuel, makin' that big stretch of burnt steel running down the middle of the ship's hull weaken her even more. And with the water temperature coming against that...well sir, she likely to split in half...right down the middle.

"That Mr. Clarke and his bunch reassured us we'd be safe, that no fire was to stop your Titanic...no fire, no bergs, or ocean waves or storms. But Captain, I be here to tell you...they be liars sir, and we be goners if we don't make it to them States soon. Truth be told sir, we've not enough coal to get us there, not if we has to keep up this speed.

"And then there be the issue of them bulkheads. There be sixteen of 'em, sir."

The captain's voice was so uncompromising I guessed his face to be sea rugged and stern, and without the meagerest glint of compassion. "I assure you," he said, "that I am very much aware of what my ship has to offer in the way of safety. We *are* unsinkable. Fire or no fire. We *are* unsinkable. If you knew what you were talking about, you would know that we are, due to the fact that we have sixteen bulkheads to keep us afloat if anything were to happen. That is why we are not sinkable but *unsinkable*. And let me assure you that I will not be lectured on such matters. Am I making myself clear? Now if you will excuse me—"

"Aye, yes sir, very clear. That is why I am here, sir. It seems them inspectors and engineers weren't too honest with their reports, sir. Them bulkheads, they's not tall enough, sir, not tall enough at all to keep the water from flowing in n' over them bulkheads, flooding out the whole hull specially if'n she cracks down the middle. Only four of the heads will come down and hold, only four, sir, only four.

"And sir, with all due respect sir, them bulkheads ain't going to do us no good. 'Specially with one be set in the middle. That one is the one to crack us in half for sure. Sir, with much respect I tell you true, we be in trouble if that bottom cracks and we begin filling...sir."

The captain began pulling his door shut. The stoker slammed his foot in the doorway, speaking to him through the slit.

"I be beggen' you, sir, them bulkheads. They be too short. If water comes in it's only a matter of time before we all be swimmin' about in two separate glasses filled with water. That is if the temp of the water don't kill us all.

"Your ship, sir, she don't carry enough lifeboats to save everyone. There be only twenty of them and with two thousand, four hundred and thirty-five of us passengers...Well sir, we sure be goners when Titanic's belly rips open. And I assure you, sir, it's sure to happen." The fear in the man's voice was not held back. Nor did the captain hold back his annoyance. He cleared his throat.

"I am fully aware of the circumstances. I appreciate your concern, and I do assure you that we are all quite safe on this big gal. Now then, if you don't mind, I would like to get back to my duties. Thank you again, err...what did you say your name is?" "Dilly sir, John Dilly," he said proudly.

"Mmm...Mr. John Dilly. I thank you for keeping this confidential. I suspect you shall continue not to rouse our guests and other hires, with this nugget of knowledge? Good fellow, now might I bid you good evening? Oh, and Mr. Dilly, by law, all we need are twenty lifeboats. No more."

Before Mr. John Dilly had a chance to face away from his captain, I snuck back around from the corner of the captain's quarters and repositioned myself tightly against a lifeboat, third from the ladder. I would wait for Mr. John Dilly to pass by.

And as I waited, it was then and there in the distance just over the horizon that I saw another ship. Oddly, the vessel had no lighting but even in the depth of the night it was still quite visible. Its shape cut through the brilliant stars, leaving its huge silhouette on the canvas of blackened sky. I knew it was not an iceberg for the air had no scent other than chilled sea salt.

I looked about the lifeboats and deck. Mr. Dilly was gone, but not thoughts of fire in the belly of the hull of the magnificent Titanic.

I slipped down the ladder, and back onto promenade Deck D. It was deserted. Grabbing the blanket, I called to Patsy.

"I don't like what I heard, Patsy. I don't like it one bit! And I didn't like the sight of that ship I spotted on the other side by the captain's quarters, ether. It looks abandoned. Jeepers-Creepers! Patsy, I have to find Daniel. I believe him and those damn steel marbles of his has something to do with all this. I don't know what, but I intend to find out."

I pulled the blanket tight about myself and Patsy and looked past the deck and railing, and into the night surrounding us. All I could see was water. Black shiny water with the reflection of the of stars sparkling above our heads. The ocean, so deep as it was far, miles and miles far and wide, with no land to be found.

The man, Dilly, his words haunted me...*she be burning something ghastly hot to the point we might not make it across the sea. The hull is already weakened...I fear she might crack in two...frigid water...we was told to shut our yappers or get off...*

Then came the, *three long pounds*, and *three short pounds*, of Mr. Dilly's fists on the captain's door. And I thought of, *Mr. Hawthorne...S.O.S...*

"Jeepers-Creepers, Patsy! I hate to think what it would be like drowning out there in that freezing saltwater. Miles deep...so deep the bottom never sees the light of day. The mere thought makes me shudder with fear. And cold. Bet it's colder than anything anyone ever felt before. I bet if a person took in a big gulp of that freezing saltwater before dying, they would lose their mind.

"I bet it burns the throat and lungs something so awful, it has to make a person go insane, surely it has to."

'The hull is already weakened...frigid water...might crack in two...told to shut our yappers...three long pounds...three short pounds... S.O.S. Save our ship...Save our ship'

"Patsy, there's a lot of people on this ship. Over one thousand, my very own children included. I can't fathom the thought..."

It was too much to bare. No longer was there any doubt as to my mission for coming to the Titanic. Not only to save the lives of my very own children, but all our souls aboard. Yes, all two thousand-four hundred and thirty-five souls. I had to do something to save those poor souls. And fast.

We strolled across the deck, Patsy and I, while thoughts of the thousand heinous deaths about to take place at one time followed in my mind. I felt certain Patsy understood all of what I had said, for his demeanor turned as dismal as that of mine.

We found the entrance door again leading back inside the ship, and we went in. Immediately what warmth was to be had, both myself and Patsy enjoyed. Still, I kept him wrapped in our blanket so as not to draw any extra attention from the few passersby that were to be had. Our room was down the hallway past the staircase and down yet another hallway.

It was hard to imagine such a wonderful place with all its splendor, and all its wonderful passengers (including my own children) would soon be prisoners, forever entombed at the bottom of that gelid of dark, cold liquid called the Atlantic Ocean. Unless I could stop it.

CHAPTER TWENTY

"You know what I have to do, don't you." It wasn't so much a question as it was a statement of reassurance that I finally knew what my mission was. Now the only question remaining was, "how to do it."

I placed the last of Patsy's leftovers on the nightstand next to the extra berth and filled the sink with water. I, of course, would not sleep that whole entire night but would venture about the ship in hopes of conjuring up Daniel and, with his help, save all those aboard.

"You just hold tight until I get back," I told Patsy, kissing the old bird on his big black head. "I'll be back as soon as I can."

Except for the steady sound of the steam engines, the hall was quiet and empty. The curious passengers with their curious conversations were tucked safe and sound in their own berths. Warm or not. I headed for the stairwell I knew best, the one used by the ship's crew, stewards, and us, the kitchen victualing staff. For even in the future,

Edwardian societal manners were still insistent upon the old standards of the Victorian ways. The ones I learned from Nurse Price. The ones I was accustomed to: *No staff nor any party of its branch shall confront or come into contact with anyone outside of their status and class quo.*

I whispered a quick, "thank you," to Nurse Price for diligently ensuring I would know such harsh and fashionable rules before leaving Pine Brook and that no matter how hard I tried to fight such laws of society, I would acknowledge and execute their use one day.

So, just as I had done at Shamus's, I would do also aboard the Titanic. No use of the ship's splendid staircases, nor its lifts constructed for privileged guests would I use. Instead, I continued to use the stairwell used by us, the less fortunate class and workers. The same ones I had been escorted, up and down with Cousin Lexington and Oscar, and Daniel to fulfill our kitchen duties.

And just as my first night aboard, I found the stairwell quite lively. Kitchen crews and stewards running back and forth between decks were getting that morning's meals prepared and tables set for breakfast.

Stewards serving every class, coming on and off duty, carried towels, bed sheets, and linens, for what dumbwaiters were to be had were busy, thus leaving the stairwells as the main way of getting back and forth.

As I passed fellow co-workers, I could not help but want to yell out warnings to each and everyone of them.

Stop, please stop and listen everybody... S.O.S....S.O.S....our ship, this beautiful ship is due to sink! Please...S.O.S....Save Our Souls!

But to do so would surely cause a panic. Besides, only a very few would know the meaning of those three little letters, and even fewer would believe me if they had. After all, Titanic was much too large and beautiful for such a thing to happen, being known as unsinkable.

My first and utmost concern of course was my children. Then

came Cousin Lexington, and Daniel with his one arm, and then (without much passion) came Oscar. After all, once the ship went down and our little group was safe and sound, I do not think I could bear the thought of not having at least alerted the man.

I knew not what cabin my Maisy and Franklin were in, but I did know they would be second class. After all, that is where I first saw them. The second-class dining saloon. Although that was a good start, to search all one hundred sixty-two, second class cabins would take a week, and we had not a week but perhaps a few days, or perhaps just a few hours. To find them I needed to go through the second-class purser and, thanks to his encounter with dear Cousin Lexington, he did not like me. Not one iota. But if anyone could get information out of him surely it was Cousin Lexington. But I had to be careful how I put all of it to her. After all, telling her the fireman's story might well set her off on a wild praying tangent, or worse, a one woman rescue crusade.

Jeepers creepers, I thought, visualizing the ordeal. The Master At-Arms would be called and that would be the very last thing I needed. Yes, the very last thing. The both of us sitting in the brig all the while as the Titanic goes down, and all those loved within her.

Thoughts came to my mind of the rogues whom a few nights ago were hell-bent on caroling how they obtained their new found freedom by severing ties from Queen and State.

They laid peacefully asleep in their berths. Their dreams, I imagined, consisted of a sweet new life, treasures filled with nothing but happiness and prosperity; for thus far, theirs had been lives filled with nothing more than handfuls of bleak opportunities ending in nothing more than ash heaps of burned out hopes and struggles. So, to imagine finding the final destination to all new hopes and dreams born, far beneath the ocean alongside other sunken treasures is more than dismal, to say the least.

I made my way down the staircase and crept down Scotland Road. With Cousin Lexington's cabin only a few yards away I wondered what would I tell her. *Jeepers creepers!* What would I tell her?

We're going to die! We're all going to die; at any moment we're all going to die! All of us, my future children included. It will be a horrible death...First we will have to fight our way through a mob of two-thousand four-hundred and thirty-five horrified, panic stricken passengers as we try to find our way all the way up to the boat deck, the highest deck of all where the lifeboats are...If we're lucky enough and make it and don't get trampled to death along the way, we will have to wait our turn and get in one of those confounded deals with all those strangers...if we make it that far...if the ship hasn't gone under...if...'

There were a hundred, *ifs*.

I had gotten no more than ten feet from Cousin Lexington's cabin, with my next *if* formulating in my mind when, lo and behold, I happened upon no one other than my Daniel.

To say the least, I was overwhelmed with curiosity as to what he was doing roaming the halls at such a late hour, especially toting such a large, heavy sack. I had to guess its contents to be nothing other than marbles. Metal marbles. And lots of them.

I quickly hid myself in the shadows of the nearest side hallway and waited. My slyness paid off.

Being sure enough distance was gained between us, I crept out from the darkness, staying a safe pace behind his. This gave me the advantage. For his well-founded suspicion of being followed caused him to turn sporadically and check his backside. Hence, I retreated into the next nearest side hall, avoiding his spying me. If I had been a child, Little Margret Jean and I would have spent hours of fun dodging from one another in this manner. But alas, this was not a game by any means. It was real life and many people were depending on me (whether they knew it or not).

We forged on. Daniel hurrying at an incredible speed lugging his hefty bag, and I barely nipping the shadow at the edge of his heels.

All that chasing and dodging pushed us past the usual working man's stairwells. I trusted Daniel knew where he was going. For the confidence in his pace appeared to be that he had traveled that hallway not once or twice, but many times before.

He arrived at the farthest end of the ship and could go no further. He turned and looked down the hall. Again, I ducked from his view. He must have felt safe from any watching eyes for he did the oddest thing. He opened a panel of green wall, a secret door hidden from passersby, and with one last look, my Daniel heaved that heavy sack of his into the hidden passage. He pulled a clean kerchief from his pocket and tied it around his nose and mouth, then slipped through the entrance and closed the wall behind himself. I waited, and when I too felt it safe, I took pursuit after him.

I opened the green door just as Daniel had and I peered inside, but stairs I found not. Instead, a metal ladder built into a shaft led up and down the decks. The top of Daniel's capped head was descending into the mighty belly of the Titanic itself.

His head tilted back. I quickly ducked from his view just as he looked up. I assumed he was checking for anyone following him, or perhaps he was looking for reassurance that the way back up had not disappeared.

Three glances up for him, and three quick ducks from his view for me, and out he went out from my sight.

I squeezed through the small green door, and with the hem of my dress in hand, I took a step downward, my foot landing on a thin round rung. Immediately I was compelled to look upward just as Daniel had. That's when I discovered we were in the fourth funnel. Needless to say, I was grateful its only purpose served was Mr. Andrews' way of extending the appearance of the girth of the ship, which in turn allowed him to use it as an extra air vent and an extra hidden route for the men working below.

Each step on the rungs brought me down, closer to them (the men) and Daniel, and the very innards of Titanic.

Looking upward one last time, my eyes followed the line of metal cages anchored into the wall. The light bulbs within glowed dull and dim all the way to the top of the funnel. Past the opening I saw a round patch of black the size of a large fist. It was the night sky, black as night ought to be. I barely made out the speckles of white pin holes splattered in its darkness. I perched for a moment and studied them.

"Stars," I whispered. "Glorious, wondrous stars."

Thoughts of Pine Brook and long summer nights of Little Margret Jean and I trying to count the dazzling sparks washed over my mind.

"I miss you, Margret Jean," I whispered up into the dark heavens. "I wonder, are you still alive? Is Dr. Bruce, and Nurse Price? I sure wish I was with you and Nurse Price, and..."

The sounds stirring in the ship's belly pulled me back to reality.

I looked down the funnel's ladder. I was nearing its bottom. I stopped thinking of them, all of them back home. For I had to stay focused in the here and now. If I succeeded, there would be plenty of time to celebrate being with all of them again. But if I didn't succeed, there would be no reason, and no one to celebrate with for I would not exist, except as a salted corpse on the bottom of the ocean.

I listened to the hissing of the steam engines and the pounding tempo of the thick, wet steel of the massive cylinders hammering against one another. The pounding rhythm so intense, it tremored my inner being. It was as if I had discovered not just the heartbeat of the ship, but its very soul itself.

Heat and steam from the coal burning in the boilers rose to where I was perched. I continued making my way down to the very last rung.

At last, I stepped off the steel ladder and into the searing heat engulfing the belly of the ship. And it was frightening. For the heat and steam was so dense it fought for what air there was.

The oily silt formed by the heat and filth that gave life to the mighty ship clung to the sides of the funnel and ladder, also clung to my hands and dress.

The men manning the filth and blackened grease wore handkerchiefs like bandits stealing the very last gulps of fresh, clean air. For the strong smell of engine grease and hot coal cauterized with human sweat had already begun to swaddle the inside of my nostrils. Choking, I covered my nose and mouth. It was then that I realized the glorious vessel we all had fallen in love with was fueled not by heavenly wings but the fires of hell itself. For the hull was hell's corridor, and the men toiling within, its warriors.

I spotted Daniel making his way through the steam and mist pouring from the vents of the boilers. The heat, nearly unbearable, was as hard to comprehend as were the size of the boilers. They were huge. Huge like everything on Titanic. Each boiler stood as tall as a two story house, clear up to the ceiling of the hull, and covered four city blocks. The entire system went on and on, past what I could see. And above it all laid Scotland Road.

The men looked pathetically small and meager as they shoveled hunks of black coal at a practical pace, keeping a steady feed into the mouths of the furnaces which fueled the boilers, which fueled the ship. One would think a place with such high humidity would keep everything and everyone washed clean and Titanic white. But I dare say not so.

It was the intense heat that created the steam that fueled the Titanic. And it was that very steam's humidity which caused the engine grease and oil and fine coal dust to stick in the air, which in turn stuck to the men like miserable, nasty, black glue. Even without their handkerchiefs tied to their faces, it was hard to distinguish the men's features, for the poor creatures were slathered from head to toe in all that black, wet, oily coal dust. Their sweat did little to rinse them clean.

I dared to moved forward. Tripping, I caught myself as I fell to the ground, ruining my dress. It too was covered with the thick, greasy soot and coal dust. How was I to explain such a pitiful mess to Cousin Lexington, and Oscar and anyone else I would come in contact with. For it was my only dress, my work dress. And Oscar, with not one iota of indecisiveness, would know where I had been. And if Cousin Lexington found out, I would certainly get a very unhesitating scolding from her for sure. Lectures and elaborate prayers were not what I needed. What I needed was to pursue Daniel and find out what exactly he intended to do with the contents of that darn bag of his.

I looked through the bellows of steam. And there, a fourth of a boiler away, standing in the mist hissing its way into every recess of the hull, was Daniel. He was talking with a gentleman leaning on a shovel. He flopped the sack of steel marbles onto the sodden floor, and though it was difficult to see, I believed the man to be none other than Mr. John Dilly himself.

Wiping the greasy black sweat from his brow with his handkerchief, a streak of chalk white skin showed from head to toe, how respectfully filthy he truly was. There was no doubt. It was Mr. Dilly for the scoop of his shovel was missing, burnt away from the fires.

Nodding in agreement to that which they conversed, Daniel also wiped his brow. He listened intently to what I, myself, desperately needed to hear. So, dredging up the bottom of my dress, I slowly walked along the wall opposite of the great furnaces. Tiny chunks of coal crushed under my boots.

Guardedly, I stopped and hid among the giant steel ribs supporting the integrity of the mighty vessel. But even from that distance away from the boilers I could not escape the heat, for it was everywhere. Absorbed into every inch of the steel of the hull.

The stokers continued to shovel their coal into the mouths of the furnaces, allowing me to continue slinking unnoticed, between the hull's steel ribs. Closing in on Daniel, I stood as still as a beam of wood in hell. And I listened.

"I tried reasoning with the old man but seems to me he refused full acknowledgment of the situation. At least to me face. He said all was well, and to never mind such things. I don't know, Daniel. I myself was there when them mates colored up that melted molten line with black paint. If they hadn't, them inspectors surely would of spied it out and put a stop to Titanic's launch.

"Gives me the damn willies, Daniel, the damn willies. I gave him my name as John Dilly, seeing that's how I'm registered. I almost slipped and called me my real name. Imagine how much troubles that would be if'n I had and he went checking." 'Mr. Dilly' chuckled.

"Yep. That would be a problem," Daniel laughed. "He never gave an inkling as to what is going on? No memories at all, huh?"

"Nope, not a one, Daniel, not a one. Amazing how's they never does."

"I know. Odd, isn't it? And you're sure nobody seen nor heard you speaking to Smith? I can't very well say I can give him respect calling him Captain. If he knows of this, that is."

"Nay, Daniel. Not a soul followed me. Not one." Mr. Dilly looked at the floor. "I take that back. 'Twas a couple strolling about the bridge. Said something to me 'bout some girl standing close by watching me, but I did not see one. Even if so, what could I do? What was done and said, is done and said."

"Damn it," I heard Daniel cuss. "Damn it. She's going to mess it up again.

"Listen Christopher, we can't take another risk, you know that. This is our last chance. We're only allowed so many tries. The Thread for this Time Line is too thin as it is. It's amazing it didn't snap this last time." Daniel's eyes narrowed, weaving his brows together.

"I know it's a risk, but right now I can't think of any other way around this. And we don't have time to sit and think this through. Not like last time. Not this time. We have to get in and fix boiler room six and holding tank number ten. If we don't...damn it, Chris, I thought for sure the Doctor was taking care of her, keeping her out of the way.

He promised." Again, Daniel's brow pinched together. "It's my guess Fitzgerald has his hand in this. Somehow, he got around the Doctor and our arrangements...somehow, he managed to get her back. Somehow he found a way of convincing the doctor...then manipulating her—"

"It is puzzling," Christopher answered. "Daniel, when she talked to you, did you at any time suspect anything? Had you seen or heard anything at all to point to the Doctor's disloyalty?"

I gasped. What I was hearing? What they were saying was impossible. He was talking about me...

Me! And about Shamus and Doctor Bruce! Arrangements? Shamus getting me back? Manipulating me? What did he possibly mean?

I stared hard at Daniel trying to place his face. *Who was he? Why did I feel attached to him? What about Christopher? Was I supposed to know him? I thought I did...*

Daniel looked down at his bag. "Well, we have no time to spare for speculating, so putting all that aside, I brought what I could. I'll have to go back to the storage bunkers and keep bringing down what

I can till we have it all here. Plus, there's plenty more in the storage bunkers. It's a matter of time, and as long as no one gets in our way we just might do okay."

"Well, sir," Christopher said seriously, "we don't have much choice now, do we? Do or die, as the saying goes. Do or die. And I sure don't wish the latter on any of us."

"Long as nobody gets in our way, we still stand a fighting

chance this time," Daniel said, handing off the bag of steel balls to Christopher.

I, in turn, held tight to my dress and scuttled forward fast as I could, passing three of the hull's ribs. From there, through the haze and steam I watched Daniel and Christopher nod to each other like two ghosts passing down, deep inside the ship's innards.

I knew where Daniel was going, and I knew what he was bringing back. What I still didn't know was, what he and Christopher had planned for the metal marbles. All I could do to find out was wait patiently in the hot mist rolling through the belly of the ship for his return.

CHAPTER TWENTY-ONE

There were five different forms of workers in that ship's bottom. So I learned. For the only tales I heard of them were within the walls of the kitchen. Cousin Lexington (leading most of the gossip) explained the differences between them, which was a good thing. Until then I hadn't any need of knowing such hardened laborers, and what demands were put on them. And truth be told, upon seeing just one (and only one) I would have thought all the positions same. For under the protection of their soiled and grungy handkerchiefs, the stokers, firemen, trimmers, greasers, foremen, and the engineers, were just as filthy and miserable as the next. These were the fearsome workers known (on all steamer ships) as, The Black Gang.

Although the foremen (and engineers) blasted out an order here and an order there, they paled in comparison to the real boss. For the beastly black ash in the ship's guts was the true boss, giving no preference or concern to a person's name or station in life. It settled where it wanted and in what crevices it chose.

I noticed a red light mounted on each of the frames of the boilers. I counted twenty-nine red lights in all. Every twenty minutes the lights blinked off and on, and then like the changing of the guards in some far-off kingdom, the stokers and trimmers and firemen changed position with the other workers, who were resting, while waiting to take over.

Twice and a half I watched the grimy men switch their stance. Some hastening about, hauling barrow after barrow of coal from the coal bunkers, then hacking the chunks into pieces suitably sized for the furnaces. Some hauled, some hacked, and some shoveled. And some yelled out orders.

"You there, speed up, and you...slow, *slower...*"

As I watched and listened, I recognized Christopher walking through the haze, wheelbarrow in front of his ragged self. He tugged his soiled cap, giving an indiscreet nod to those passing by. Keeping my watch on him, I stepped back into the shadows, melting closer to the wall.

He passed by giving only a rushed look in my direction. I wondered, *had he seen me? Did he take me for another worker?* Staying tight to the ship's rib as possible, I snuck a look around.

Daniel was back and carrying another sack of his marbles. Quickly, Christopher cleared a spot in his barrow, pushing the coal to the side. Without a word, Daniel dumped the bag inside the barrow and exited straightaway, leaving Christopher to shove the mound of coal back on top of the metal balls. Christopher checked behind his shoulder and the catwalk above our heads. At this point I, being just as dark black as the others, blended well with my new comrades and the wall. It was no surprise that he hadn't noticed me as he turned and traveled back down past the furnaces.

Laden with grease, and coal dust, I took courage and stepped out from the shadows. As long as I remained in the hull I would be regarded as nothing more than just another member of the Black Gang.

Now, allow me to tell you this; even though I was young, I had seen many dejected and discouraged faces, primarily those arriving through the doors of Pine Brook. For theirs was a look acquired through either the breaking of the human spirit due to the overburdens of life, or gained naturally through a wrongful and wounded birth of sorts (such as that as Little Margret Jean). But never had I seen such wretched, ominous faces as those of Titanic's Black Gang; souls smothered in such filth that one cannot imagine a living, breathing human soul could exist beneath.

But strange as it was as I slinked about the bowels of that ship chasing after a man I knew, but did not know, I took notice of something pure and radiant within those men's eyes as they met mine. A spark. A spark deliberately contrived from heartiness and pluck. And the living Spirit of Hope.

It is the straight, forthright determination of hope that a person sees in another when a goal set forth is within their grasp and is nearing completion. Yes, hope. Wonderful, glorious hope.

Knowing their new lives existed and was waiting for them just a mere thirteen days away, fertilized the fruit of their soon triumph: a superior life far greater than that of the conditions momentarily barred by them in the belly of the Titanic. And yet the sight of the joy of hope in their eyes broke my heart. For I was soon to learn the secret that lay in boiler room six, and holding tank number ten. The answer to the secret that had brought me so far from home. And so I needed my fellow workers' hope as much as they did.

An arm of steam rushed out at me, shoving me close to the wall. I wiped the sodden droplets of water from my face. I must have smeared coal dust about my brow and checks. For when I looked down at my hands, they were also black and greasy as tar as the faces before me.

I accepted the fact that I had unknowingly surrendered to the ship's hell. Just as the Black Gang had at the start of the Titanic's voyage.

I tried avoiding the eyes that began to take notice of me.

"Can't work with those fancies on," one gang member chortled out at me.

"Hey, we all do our equal share of work down here," another, not so friendly, shouted.

"Stole away pretending to be a priest...ain't you got no shame?"

I looked down at myself and saw what they saw. I could explain that I was no priest, but they might then think of me as a dandy, especially naturally having a soft, high girl's voice. These men were rough, with not a gentle corner on them. Perhaps it might have been easier if I truly had been a stowaway disguised as a priest for, alas, I could bear their comments no more.

I turned and faced the wall. Their demands that I remove my feminine attire and join them nauseated me. It was not the hardness of the labor or thoughts of joining them per se, but the removing of my dress that left me verklempt. With as much delay as possible, I carefully, and ever so slowly unbuttoned the top of my dress.

My hands shook, slipping the second button through its loop. Then the third and then the fourth. And as if I had eaten something gone bad, a small bubble of bile rose from my stomach, spreading in my throat. I swallowed it back down and continued to slowly undo each button.

"A priest!" Again, the word spat out someone's mouth like a piece of rotten fish.

"You could have worked for your transport just like any of us. Coming on board as a stowaway disguised as a priest...God help your soul!"

I pressed my palms to the wall, not wanting to let go of the security of my dress. But alas, I could bear the men's comments no longer. For a hard crew they were.

Under the coal dust my face blazed with shame and embarrassment as I slowly unlatched my last button. Then it happened. My dress fell open. And I prayed to the God that I did not believe in, hoping He would hide my breasts from the men standing next to me watching me undress. I prayed the men were ignorant as I concerning the undergarments lying beneath the gowns of His own appointed spokespersons (His priests) leaving the usage of my corsets and girdles, and foundations to one's own imagination and not facts.

And so, looking down at myself, I thanked that God for the whalebone corset that Nurse Price so did shun. For it saved my dignity. It was there under its protection and my undershirt that the crests of my breasts were hidden. And I thanked Him.

My '*vestment*' slipped from my shoulders and waist onto the ground. I was left stranding me with nothing to cover myself but my long stockings and garters, corset, and my boots, of course. Some men gasped, some spat, some whispered vulgar words depicting a '*dandy priest,*' as they left my side.

From what I could decipher, the Black Gang held their energy in check, spending it not on pointless arguments and brawls, but for the toils of shoveling and sweating their way to their new, glorious lives.

"You will need this," the last remaining one said, placing a shovel against the rib of the haul. "And this."

The man, though rough as the others, had a decency about him. For he pulled a kerchief from down deep inside his shirt against his chest and handed it to me. It was half used and not nearly as black as the one around his neck.

"Use them well and you will get along just fine, '*Father*'."

I nodded a rough, '*thank you,*' as I had seen men do toward each other. The fellow moved on and I knelt down on one knee. Picking up a corner of my now sodden dress, I dropped it. For it was useless, enmeshed with the wet, black coal.

I tied the handkerchief around my mouth and nose and began

pulling the lacing from one boot and then the other. Discreetly as possible, I rolled up the lace and ruffles on my leggings and tethered them down. Soon enough, like everything in that hell-hole, pretty or not, they would soon be drenched with soot and become unidentifiable.

Christopher passed by me, his barrow full of coal. He was meeting up with Daniel and would be passing me again soon enough. I stood straight and took myself in, strangely grateful that I now was just as filthy as the rest. Being so I would surely escape the men's eyes (even in my underthings) especially the eyes of Daniel. For only upon a very close and intimate exam could anyone detect me as female. So, I waited like a spider anticipating a fly. A fly named Daniel. And sure enough he came.

I grabbed my shovel and began stabbing the spade onto the floor here and there as if looking for chunks of coal. I worked slowly and steadily, all the while watching Daniel dump the steel marbles into the wheelbarrow, and Christopher covering them with his black nuggets of coal.

With their mission completed, they turned from the other and set forth yet another round of their plan. They would meet again when most movements of the crew would be at its greatest.

"At the changing of posts," Daniel instructed. "When the red timer lights blink twice."

I pulled my handkerchief up, not daring to make eye contact as Christopher passed by. With shovel in hand, I trailed behind him as if we were a team, he the lead, and I, his gopher.

We traveled past several of the mammoth boilers and huge bunkers filled with the enormous pieces of coal. Workers in groups of three stood inside the bunkers and out, each man chopping and slicing, splitting and tossing the boulders of coal, turning them into suitable mounds of efficient pieces.

Some of the men hurried to fill their wheelbarrows of the stuff, then scampered off like black mice stealing morsels of burnt toast.

Except their homes were not nests of cottony comfort but raging boilers ranting for more fuel.

I followed Christopher to the next boiler, three stories high. It was connected to a coal bunker. *Bunker No. 10,* I read on the plaque. And, *Boiler 6. The ones he told the captain about.*

I clung to my shovel, digging mindlessly into the floor, all the while keeping Christopher in sight from the corner of my eye.

Checking his surroundings for intruders, he took very little notice of me, for I was much too busy performing 'my duty' to be of any danger to him.

Christopher slid his hand inside a small divot between the bunker and the boiler and pulled out a new shovel, replacing it with his half burnt one.

Now, allow me to be honest with you. If I could have turned and run right then and there, I truly would have done so. But alas, I could not. For I came much too far, and knowing so many lives, including my very own children, depended on me I had no choice but to stay and fulfill my duty (to the best of my ability, that is). But, before we go on, I must sincerely apologize for sounding so preposterous but as you will see, what I am about to tell you is so truly outrageous, so truly incredible, that you very well will be inclined to label me a liar, a true professional beguiler. Or perhaps, a person truly, undoubtedly, undeniably insane. But no matter. What I saw, I saw. And what I did...I did.

And what I witnessed was one of the most remarkable feats that science could ever muster. If indeed it was science.

I stood silent and still, watching Christopher place his new shovel inside the wheelbarrow on top of the coal. He stood staring at the steady, solid glow of red, and orange, and yellow, and white coal blazing within the furnace. The black chunks were no longer separate nuggets but one huge, thick mass of orange and white. They looked cold and harmless. But the tremendous heat within said, "Not."

Christopher pulled his stoker's handkerchief down from around his nose and mouth. And with a heavy sigh, as if preparing to perform the same task countless number of times, he stepped inside the cavity of that furnace. Furnace No. 10. Taking with him wheelbarrow, shovel, steel balls, and all.

I so badly wanted to scream for him to, *stop!* to call out for the assistance of fellow stokers, and would have done so, for my mouth was a gap to do so when I realized to my double amazement that he did not catch fire. Nor did he cry out, screaming, gasping for life, begging for mercy as one would. But nay, he did not.

Nor did he melt, or blaze into eternity. He didn't even spark. Yet the furnace and all inside raged as Christopher comfortably began scraping his shovel on the floor, clearing a path.

I stood transfixed at the mouth of the furnace and watched him heave away coal and flames to the middle of the furnace, feeding Boiler No. 6. Then, giving no warning, he jerked his head to see if anyone was about.

With my now blackened handkerchief held snugly to my face I quickly busied myself, pecking the floor with my shovel. When I felt assured he found me to be of no concern, I took a chance and glanced his way. This time he was half hidden by the flames within and was busy shoveling. That's when I saw it. The secret of Boiler No. 6. The secret that Captain Smith said didn't exist. The one the inspectors insisted overlooking for fear of impeding Titanic's mighty and furious voyage of glory. A voyage that would bring the great Titanic and her passengers, both great and small, young and old, down into a grave of black, muddy soot waiting patiently for them beneath the freezing saltwater of the Atlantic.

I gasped at what I saw. Christopher was right. An extensive line of coal did sag in the ship's floor so deep it indeed had weakened the steel underneath. And that steel was the only thing between us and the endless, forever and ever depth of the unforgiving, frigid waters of the Atlantic.

Though the burn line was not wholly exposed, I could perceive its massive proportion by the line of sunken coal running from the boiler to the wall and under, and into the coal bunker next door. From what I could see, I guessed the burn ditch to stretch a good thirty feet long, and at least a good six feet wide, and three inches deep.

I did not ask myself *how* such a deathtrap could be purposely overlooked, for it could not. It was much too large, making it much too obvious to do so. Instead, I asked, *why* its failure to be properly dealt with was done deliberately so. Unforgivably so. And so, Mr. John Dilly (aka Christopher) was right. The fire was causing the ship to split in the worst possible area, right in the middle, rendering the shortness of the bulkhead doors useless. Ocean water would rush in both aft and forward, filling the ship just as Christopher described, as if it were two separate drinking glasses turned on their sides in a tub of water.

But it would not be ordinary water that would come streaming in, and easily drained. No. It would pour in, as an uncontrollable deluge of a flood. Like a dam breaking, bringing with it the entire Atlantic Ocean, freezing and wild.

I watched Christopher heave a mass of the steel marbles onto a small section of cleared flooring. It would take too many of them to fill such a gorge than what I had seen Daniel manage to haul down. I wanted so desperately to tell this to Christopher, that perhaps his and Daniel's efforts were futile and other options were needed, and that with my assistance perhaps the three of us could somehow manage to evacuate the ship. We could gather everyone on deck and row them in shifts over to the abandoned black ship. It would take time, but it could be done.

Putting aside all the men had said and thought of me, I stopped pecking the ground and headed directly for the mouth of the boiler.

The heat was tremendous and I backed away.

"Christopher," I shouted inside the furnace. The heat dissolved my words. "Christopher," I yelled again. I have to tell you something."

"Problem?" A voice came at me from behind. "You there, what's the problem?" Despite the heat, my hands froze defensively on my shovel. "I say, is there a problem?"

I remained still.

"If you don't answer me I will see to it you answer with the help of another fellow."

I cleared my throat, getting ready to lower my voice in the most masculine manner I could muster. "Aye, nope."

"Nope? Nope what?" His reply was quick and sharp. I winced.

"Ah, no sir? No problem here?"

"What's wrong with your voice? You ain't got some sort of those spreading diseases, do you? The kinds that does ya' in?"

"Ah, no, no sir. No case of any sort-a disease here. And ahh- no troubles neither, sir. Thank you, sir." I turned away and started stabbing that floor harder than any black gang member there.

"Where you from? Your accent is that of an American. Why are down here doing such work, and where are you coming from? And what are doing over here, down in this area? Well, answer me."

I drove my shovel even harder into the ground, past the inches of hardened coal dust and into the steel bottom floor itself. Deliberately making as sharp of sounds as possible, hoping Christopher would hear the steel on steel, giving him the edge to evacuate the boiler.

"Stop that," the man growled. "You're wasting precious energy. I think the coal dust crusted your brain. Stop it, I say."

But I did not. I stabbed that floor all the more. And I stabbed it again and again. The pitch of the shovel scraping the cement pierced our ears.

"Stop it! Stop it this instant!" the man demanded. And I '*demanded'* not to obey.

I kept chipping away, refusing the urge to look over at Christopher. For I knew if I did, so would the man, and all would be lost. Finally, the man stopped me with his hand.

"I warned you," he said, taking hold of my shovel.

Until that moment I'd never known the force of a man's hand and the power it holds. For before I could say, Jack Sprat, I found myself laying on the ground, my face throbbing with such a miserable searing pain, it turned my head one way and at the same time, turned it another way. And for the first time in my life I was able to see the stars everyone described when discussing a powerful blow to one's head.

"And you in there," he yelled. "What are you doing? Come out of there instantly, right this moment!"

I pulled myself out of the ashes and the muck and the mire of that hell hole owned by the great and wonderful Titanic. And that's when the bad thing happened. The thing I never should have done. I charged the man.

He lost his balance, tumbling with a dull thud into the black sod and dust. His eyes glowed at me, hot with anger. My legs weighted with fear, refused to move.

"Alright. You wanna' fight, I give you a fight. Then I dump you in the ship's slops and watch you float out to sea...and she be a terrible might unforgiving, that sea..."

I was frozen, not knowing what to do.

"Christopher!" I heard myself shouting, hoisting my shovel over my shoulder. I was in a daze of sorts. An uncontrollable daze. I had absolutely no control over what I was doing. I was someone else hearing my voice shouting, "Christopher! Christopher! Christopher!"

The man rose from the dust. A sensation of fear shot through me like I had never experienced before. The hissing of the boilers, and the roar of the steam engines no longer existed. Nor did I hear the grinding and clanking of metal against metal coming to a halt. It seemed all sounds in the ship's belly disappeared, sucked up into some sort of secret vacuum. My lips moved, forming the name Christopher. But alas, his name too was gone. For all was still. And all that remained around me was the sound of my own breath, bellowing in and out my lungs—and the man and his face.

He stood talking, his eyes and mouth twisting in such anger that I knew what I had to do. He left me with no choice.

I focused on him as he made his way to me. He was already wounded, crouching like some sort of two-legged creature ready to charge its prey.

Calling out for Christopher a last and final time was pointless. He, nor anyone else could hear me for I had no voice to yell. Clinging to my shovel, my muscles tightened, ready to swing.

"Come on you dirty devil," I shouted. My words were not heard, but merely whispers that perhaps only I could hear. "I'll swat that bloody ass of yours..."

I took one last glance at Christopher.

*God save us! It's worthless, all of this...worthless...*I thought, seeing him pick through the burnt coals, heaving the last of his steel marbles onto the crack of Titanic's floor.

That is all I could think. And that was it. And I did what I did. The bad thing.

I swung my shovel. I swung it hard. I swung it so hard I felt a thick, heavy thud as it smacked the man. I watched, stunned, as he slumped to the ground and laid in a heap as if he were one large clump of that damp, black coal. The wet seeping about his head caused the ash to glisten, blackening it even more. What I had done to that man left me much too frightened to call out for help. For all I was capable of doing was to stare at the poor-joe. And watch. And listen.

He squirmed about, as if strings were attached to his limbs forcing him to dance like a giant, black marionette in the dark, damp ashes. His groans, barely audible over the hissings and spits of the steam engines, stopped his breath midway. And when all was complete, and all his motion and groaning had stopped, a snow angel of black-ash tracked where his movements had been.

I gripped the handle of my shovel and stared at the ill-fated man. Had anyone seen me cause his death?

Quickly, I looked about the hull through the steam. The workers were much too busy to notice anything but the unquenchable appetite of the demon furnaces before them. I checked Christopher. He, too, was absorbed in his own task of heaving the last of his worthless marbles onto the floor and burying them under the white-hot coals and ash. I wanted to cry out to him, truly I did. But nay, I could not. For my voice was stuck deep down somewhere between my guts and my throat and would not move. As quickly as the accident happened, so came to my mind the alternatives handed before me.

I could turn from the mess and make my way through the steam room and back to my cabin and Patsy, leaving all behind me as if it were what I wanted it to be—nothing more than a bad dream.

Or, I could draw deliberate attention to the man and put the blame for his death on Christopher, as I was the only witness to the incident. Or, I could (God forbid) dispose of the body in the same manner as Christopher was disposing of his marbles. And with that, I was left with the very least choice of all: tell Daniel what I had done.

I had but a fraction of a second to make up my mind, for the heaviness of a man's hand weighed on my shoulder. I sucked in all my breath, and with my stomach spinning up into my throat, I turned to face the one person I never expected to ever see again, (especially in the belly of the ship).

"I see you have found out the dilemma. Ships sink when filled with water," the captain said. "Now, if you don't mind following me back to my cabin, in a nice peaceful manner, I can see to it that your big mess here becomes a very small matter."

I looked at Christopher. With all his steelies seeded, he was in the midst of undertaking their final burial. My mouth gaped open. My words calling to him to, '*help me*' were ready to march out.

"I wouldn't do that," the man said. "Not unless you plan to create even more havoc than you have already. I believe a little chat is in order."

The pressure of his hand on mine forced me to let go of the shovel. He grabbed the handle (and my arm) and led us through the geysers and veils of steam. I felt weightless, as if I were floating, and not walking across the black ash and loose lumps of coal. The heat I despised so badly when first I arrived down deep in that engine hull no longer attacked me. Fear had taken its control of me, leaving me to feel nothing but its dull sense of being. It was as if I were walking through a dream, escorted by Death itself.

"I-I-I... I-I-I... I didn't mean to...i-it w-w-was an accident. Really it was." My stammering's were of no use. He couldn't hear me, nor did the others as we passed them by making our way to the ladder leading back to the upper decks. For the captain and I had become the ghosts passing in the belly of the ship.

"My-my-my dress, s-s-sir," I stuttered, looking down at my blackened, half naked body. Still the Captain paid me no mind.

He held my arm tight, forcing my hand to take hold of the first rung. Clenching the rails, I pulled myself up. Little by little I climbed that damn ladder, each rung becoming cooler with each step. Behind me, Captain Smith followed, the condemning spade in his hand clumping its way with us. With each step we took, the shovel clanked against the metal rungs. But deep within my mind what I heard was Mr. Hawthorn tapping out his three dots, his three dashes...three dots, three dashes.

Save Our Souls...Save Our Souls...

I looked up hoping the stars were still clustered in their tight little circle beyond the smoke stack. They were still there but beginning to fade. And so was the hope I previously found in them. My hope of going home.

The tiny twinkles of anticipation shining out that everything would be fine and done and all would be well, and that I would be home soon, were replaced by doom and gloom. And death. Not only did I not know what was to happen to me, but to my children as well and all those aboard that ship.

The closer the captain and I got to the top of the tunnel the more I thought of them; my children, Maisy and Franklin, (and all the people). For their sakes I had to find a way to finish what I had started. That's when I knew then and there, I would die trying if need be. And I think I just might have.

CHAPTER TWENTY-TWO

The captain gave me a sturdy poke with the handle of the shovel. "Don't you stop. I know what you did," he said giving me another jab in the rump. "And I have the evidence to prove it, right here. Not that I need it." I turned and glared down at him.

"Well, sir," I spat, "If you know wh-wh-what I did, th-th-then you must know wh-wh-why I did it."

"Just you keep going. We'll have the constable handle this."

With the loss of all dignity and pride, I marched half naked, covered from head to toe in the filthiest of all filth, down the halls and onto the lifts of what was hailed as *the* most glorious and prestigious ship man ever built.

Neither of us spoke. Not a word, not even a jeer of malice as we headed to the captain's quarters.

The cabin was not small and stuffy and cramped like Oscar's and the others. Nor was it overly large.

I detected the familiar smell of whiskey and snuff lingering about the sofa and chairs and the captain's desk. It was the same odor I smelled on the doctor who attended to my needs aboard the tender America. Except this time the scent was not stale, but fresh, carrying with it with a hint of mint.

A plaid flannel coverlet covered the davenport. The captain snatched it up and tossed it at me aggressively.

"Place this on my chair before you slide your dirty ass on it," he demanded, nodding sharply at the chair farthest from the door. He said not another word, but went to his closet and pulled out a thick bathrobe.

"And here, put this around yourself like a respectable woman; murderer or not, I don't want any talk coming from anyone that I molested you."

He didn't bother looking me over as perhaps Oscar might have (or any other man). There was no room for lust in his eyes, for it was disgust and anger that filled them to the rim. I pulled the robe around my shoulders and slid my arms into the sleeves hoping to find some comfort within. I found none. None was to be found.

I wanted to sit back in the chair for I was well spent, but knew better. I was not a welcomed guest after all, but a murderess. A scared, nervous, cold-blooded murderess. The edge of the seat would do just fine.

There tucked away in the corner of the end table next to me was half a cigar, snuffed out and smoldering in a copper ashtray. A wisp of white smoke swirled around a set of heavily framed photographs of the captain and what appeared to be his wife and children. I leaned toward them seeking a closer look.

"So, you are a murderess, are you?" The captain said, grabbing my attention. A wave of shock surged through me. I glared at him.

"A-a-a-a murderess, me?" Saying it out loud made the accusation real. Much too real. The fear of facing the fact wasn't just for myself, but also for those in the photographs, as well.

The captain stepped to his desk and opened the humidor sitting next to his name plaque. *Captain Edward J. Smith.*

He plucked up a fresh cigar then pulled a fancy lighter from his coat. He lit his cigar, the tiny flame reflected deep within his black eyes. They glared at me like hunks of lit coal. No words, no sounds came from him except the soggy sucking on his cigar. Puffs of white-gray smoke circled his head as he turned from me to watch the sun rise in the orange glow of the morning. I stole another look at the photographs.

The people stood straight and secure, and were dressed ever so neatly; their smiles communicating to the viewer just how comfortable and grand life had been for them. For gone were the lost and worried looks shared by those inhabiting Scotland Road.

Captain Smith cleared his throat to warn me to shift my eyes away from the photos. My silence was best my friend (at least for the moment). Questions I did not ask, and silent I kept concerning what I knew.

"It is best you say nothing," the captain said affirming my silence. "Though I am curious as to why you were down in the coal bunkers and boilers with the Black Gang. How did you manage to get yourself in with them without being discovered? Ugh, never mind. If you're smart enough to do that, you're smart enough not to answer. Besides all will be answered shortly. For the both of us, I'm sure."

He lifted the phone from the receiver cradled on the wall, gnawing his cigar as he spoke. "Constable. My cabin. Bring the doctor." That's all he said. That's all he had to say.

My mind raced trying to connect everything and everyone I had come against, from the time I was but a child losing my beloved family, to those whom became like my family at dear old Pine Brook, to my arrival with Miss Gavin at Shamus's and Patsy's. And now here, on the Titanic. For lo and behold, the pictures on the captain's end table told me the connection was so.

My finger shook as I pointed at the photos. "Are th-they *your* family? Wife and ch-children?" I asked.

The captain stopped puffing on his cigar. His lips pinched together. "What business is it of yours? You want to kill them too? I must admit I have never come across a murderess before. Plenty of gentlemen murderers, yes, but no women murderesses."

He picked up the middle photo and stared at it. The one I could not take my eyes off.

Oh, how I wanted to blurt out everything! How I wasn't a real murderess any more than he himself were a loyal and worthy sea captain. That I was a woman, and a mother, but not a mother, not yet, but soon to be. And the photo which he held was one that I also held many times as I laid in my warm bed at night, wondering who they were and why I felt such a tender bond to them. It was the very same glass-plated picture that Nurse Price had taken extra care to graciously wrap and tuck away for me with the other photos I cherished in the shoebox.

I wanted to tell him that unless he let me go, the ship, his ship and all aboard would not survive to see the next light of day. Himself, and those in the picture included.

I'm here to save the Titanic and all aboard, including my very own children, the ones in the picture that you hold...

Yes, that is what I wanted to tell him. Maybe then he would believe I was not a murderer on purpose but out of necessity...nay, No! I could not say a word of any of it.

Surely, he would think me insane. But...maybe, just maybe I am insane. Maybe that's why he called for a doctor.

"S-s-sir," I stammered. "I want to inform you of s-something.

S-something that concerns..." I pointed at the picture in his hands. "Them."

Gray smoke rose past his pinched face. He took a heavy draw from his cigar, and squinted at me as he placed the photo back on the end-table. I looked again at Franklin and Maisy, and the older woman standing between them. She wasn't beautiful, nor was she overly plain. In her hand she held a parasol. The very one I recalled adoring in *Harper's Bazar*. Yes, the woman was familiar. All too familiar. I looked at the captain.

"C-c-captain, th-th-the people in your photographs...a-a-are they *your* children?"

The captain's answer came out dry, and agitated. "I'm the one to be asking questions, not you."

I wiped my face with the arm of his robe and again looked at the lady in the photo with her children. I looked at the picture next to it. My breath left me. I quickly looked at the captain. "You-you-you—" The knock on the cabin door drew my words away from his ears.

"Well, who was it?" the captain asked. Then came the name of the man whose life I had taken.

"Barrett, sir. Frederick Barrett." It was Oscar who answered, and his voice was strained. "Lead Stoker, Boiler Room 6."

The captain continued to chew his cigar. "Yes, yes, I am very much aware of who Mr. Barrett is, or was," he said letting his stogie rest for a quick moment.

"Good man," Oscar said. "Knew what he was doing. He was widowed, sir, and remarried. Just had twins two weeks ago, a boy and a girl. He has three others, two from his current wife and another from his previous marriage. He had quite the burden to carry. Now his new wife has to carry it all.

"I'll hold off notifying the Missus or any of his relatives. No use causing them any more grief than necessary. There'll be plenty of time for that."

Captain Smith narrowed his black eyes at me and turned to his cabin window. He stood steadfast, watching the ocean waves lick the horizon laying against the distant sky, now a pale blue. His stogie now long burned was nothing more than a stub. He removed it from his lips just long enough to bark out his order to Oscar, then shoved it back into his mouth. He chewed its end with even more fervor.

"Get her outta' here."

"S-s-sir, i-i-if I may, I-I-I did not do it on pur-pur-purpose. Th-th-the ship is in d-d-danger, sir. And you know it." My words drifted past him like the morning waves rolling past his magnificent and fearless ship, Titanic.

"Come on you." The disgust in Oscar's voice took hold of me as firmly as his hand on my arm. He waited patiently alongside me giving me time to realize no response would come from the captain. Finally, Oscar tugged my arm and began leading me down the hall past the few early morning risers, and those in service to them. They stared at me, terrified of me as if I were some mad woman that was coming for them, if not for Oscar.

Clinging to each other, they all moved to the other side of the hallway and waited for us to pass. Their mumblings were hurtful guesses as to my crime. And in a strange way I was glad it was Oscar at my side, guiding me through the maze of corridors, protecting me from what might have turned out to be brutal physical attacks on my personal self from the others aboard. And before long, to my surprise, I was delivered not to some jail with bars in an obscure portion of the ship, but to my cabin. And within to where my comfort was Patsy, my beloved Patsy.

I watched Oscar pull a clustered ring of keys from his coat.

"Oscar, may I please, please have a bit of food. It isn't for me. Ii-it's for a f-f-friend. A very dear friend."

"For Patsy, I assume," he said unlocking my room.

"Yes," I nodded. "Th-th-thank you, Oscar."

The door swung open. He looked inside then motioned for me to sit on my berth. He flagged his hand for Patsy to come to him. As I had done, Patsy obeyed, landing on Oscar's arm.

"Oscar, I think I'm in trouble."

"Yeah. I should say so," he chuckled, stroking Patsy.

"N-n-no. I mean real trouble. If I t-t-tell you something, something th-th-that sounds crazy, d-d-d-do you promise not to laugh?"

"No," he laughed, handing Patsy to me. I held Patsy extra close to me. "Well, it depends on what it is."

I stole a glance at Oscar. He was studying me as I nervously pet Patsy. There was something about Oscar's silver-gray eyes. They appeared to be incandescent. That's when the thought truly came to me, flowing through me. It was as though Oscar's eyes reflected the echoes of life caught in the ripples of times.

I took a deep breath, trying to hold back the insane words. The moment they came out, I wanted to take them back. Just like the murder of Mr. Frederick William Barrett. But alas, I could not.

"I-I-I think you are a...a time traveler like me. A-a-a-and s-s-so is the c-c-captain. I-I-I want to go home, but I can't. Even i-i-if I could, I w-w-w-wouldn't-wouldn't know-know h-h-how. Please, d-d-don't laugh."

To my surprise he did not. Nor did he crack a smirk or a grin. He stared at the clutch of keys dangling in his hand. His voice was graveled.

"Why didn't you listen to me when I told you to leave everything alone. Yes, you are in trouble. Oh, how I wish you would have stayed up in the kitchens with Ruby. If only you had stayed...I have other matters to tend to." He turned and faced the door. "I've already seen to Patsy's needs. He's all taken care of."

Oscar hesitated. I thought perhaps he might have thought better about his words and was thinking of a way to undo them, for he heaved a heavy sigh and without regret, he turned the knob to my cabin door and walked out, locking the door behind him. And with that, he was gone.

I cuddled Patsy, burying my head on his. And I cried. Flashes of Mr. Frederick William Barrett rushed into my mind.

I tried to stop the pictures from repeating over and over like a cheap nickelodeon, but it was no use. I, Camarilla Rae Berkelman was, as the captain put it, a murderess. A true, cold-blooded murderess. Self-defense or intentional mattered not. My own hands had taken the life of another, and for that I could find no excuse. My punishment:

Mr. Barrett's look of horror flaring before me. His brow lifting then knotting from the pain of the shovel bearing down on his head; his eyes staring at me in disbelief, his black, greasy face giving acknowledgment that his death was a mere breath away. I watched it again and again and again.

Then came forth his soul fighting, convulsing, squirming as it fought its way out his body. I laid on the berth, beyond sick in my stomach, weeping just as I had when I learned of the death of my mother and father, and that of Huston.

The guilt of killing someone else's father, husband, and brother was too much for me to bear. I had taken the life of another human. It was heinous. I screamed. And I did not stop. Yet, I knew the worst was yet to come. The death of my very own children.

Through my grief, I did not hear the door unlocking, nor did I hear the soft padding of feet passing through the cabin. With the familiar smell of cigar, old mint, and stale whiskey filling the cabin came a hand resting on my shoulder. Before I could turn to see who it was, a sharp prick and a sting of warmth spread from my forearm downward and upward. The liquid inside the needle flowed through my body, warming me to a sweat. I opened my mouth to beg for mercy, but I could not. I turned numb and began to slip away. Away from the horrors of Frederick Barrett and my mission on the ship. Away from Franklin and Maisy, Christopher, Cousin Lexington.

Away from everything and everyone. Even Oscar. For I had been injected with a serum that caused my mind to become tired and unstable.

I hung tight to what little thoughts I could, and to Patsy. I fought to stay awake, hoping to make sense of what the doctor was saying before his words disappeared. And before my own words went unheard.

"I-I-I...I have to tell you..." I mumbled, not sure if I were talking with my mouth or, if my plea was only sounding in my mind. "This ship...it's-it's-it's going to sink...if we don't save it. We're all going t-t-to, t-to, to die, all of us...my children, Maisy and Franklin...Daniel, Cousin Lexington...Oscar...all of us."

"So, you are worried about Oscar?" the doctor laughed.

He was the same doctor who attended to me on the tug, Ireland, for I recognized his scent. It was the same scent there, and the very same that lingered in the captain's cabin.

"Oscar...he, he told me once that, that, he, he, is not the enemy. W-what did he mean? W-why did he say that? Where is he, were did he go...?"

I forced open my eyes and looked about. I had already begun to sleep. The man in front of me was as blurry as my thoughts. "Oh, really? Did he now? Tell me more." I swallowed. My tongue was as thick as my words.

"I-I-I, I-I'm a...time traveler. And I'm telling you, this ship is going to sink. I don't know w-w-when, but it will. Soon. Very-very soon. That's why I'm here. To...to save my own children and everyone on th-th-this ship."

"Yes," the doctor chuckled. "That is a possibility, the ship sinking and all. After all, there is a very weak spot in Boiler Room No. 6, the one Mr. Barrett was helping to fix. You see, what you did was slow down the progress of repairing it. So, logically, you helped speed things up. That's why I'm here. I wanted to come by and thank you personally for going to such a great expense to do so.

"And so, when the good Captain Smith called asking that I tend to you, I couldn't very well ignore his request, now could I?

"You see, Camarilla," the doctor said, ignoring Patsy and his attacks. "Mr. Barrett knew exactly what to do to fix the problem and you interfered with that. But as far as being some sort of time traveler, that is very much true. But I'm afraid I have assigned myself to be the bearer of some very bad news. This shall be your last travel. You see, the time line is extremely fragile at this point, and it shares the same destiny as yourself. When you discovered it, perhaps you should have been a tad more discreet as to whom you shared its existence with.

"No dear, dear Camarilla, there simply isn't enough of it to go around for everyone. Not without it snapping forever. This last time jump is like a game of Russian Roulette, for all of us, if you will. Some shall make it just fine, and others, well...not so fine, shall we say."

I heard Patsy cawing, fighting a mighty fight as the doctor took hold of my arm. He injected another needle. "I must say my goodbyes now, for I do have much to tend to before we leave this great and magnificent vessel they call Titanic.

"Such a shame. She is a magnificent work of art by any standard. Oh, well, que sera sera." The doctor released my arm. I struggled to move away from him.

"Now, now, my little black lamb. Please try to relax. You should sleep very well. Though, I do have a concern about this bird here. He is rather vicious. And I'm afraid he violates our health regulations. Besides, it's doubtful it will be allowed to accompany you where you're going, you naughty little lady."

Again I prayed to the God I did not believe in. And all fell dark.

CHAPTER TWENTY-THREE

"We don't have much time." It was Oscar. He was sitting on my berth. His words were short. How much time had passed, I do not know. He shifted himself a little to the left, closer to my legs. "So, Doctor, when did you get here?"

"Soon as Edward called. He gave me a key. He will be here any time."

The clanking of metal jingled in my ears. The doctor's words, rough as sharers of steel, his breath wafted the smell of his stale cigar and whiskey downward to my nose.

"Yes, our time is limited," he said. "Seems the little mademoiselle here made quite the confession." Oscar sighed. "That does complicate matters, now doesn't it."

My cabin door opened, and try as I might, I could not pry my eyes open to see who it was.

"Yes, it does, gentlemen," the voice said, it belonged to the captain. I assumed he remained standing at the door directly across from me, for the cabin was small, and the captain was large.

"Her admittance, after all, to make a confession on both counts of crime, murder *and* Time Interference does complicate matters. Constable, it is my feeling that your prisoner here should be kept under lock and key," he said.

"Though I do greatly respect her for being a fellow Time Traveler, that doesn't mean she isn't dangerous, obviously. So, as you can see, I took the liberty of having the good doctor prescribe a relaxant to keep her calm and subdued. We can't have her running about screaming and calling attention to us, now can we? Not that anyone would pay her any mind, other than to call her a crazed wild woman, but it is better to be safe than sorry, as the saying goes. I want no more interference from her. Do you understand? No more!"

I dared not flinch even a brow alerting them to my consciousness. Besides, I could not do so even if I wanted. My body was limp, and strangely heavy. Too heavy to move. All I could do was lay on my bunk and listen, hoping to remember all that was being said.

"So be it then," Oscar said. "But whatever you do, don't kill her with that crap. After all, we might need her again down the Line. That is, if she should somehow miraculously survive."

The doctor lifted my arm, letting it flop against the berth. Oscar must have shown his concern. "It's okay," the captain said. "The doctor knows what he's doing, don't you, Doctor?"

"Your just too soft, Oscar," the doctor said. "Always have been. Of course, I know what I'm doing. I've been doing this for centuries after all, haven't I? See, she is completely sedated. She will be of no use or harm to anyone. Especially us."

Centuries? Wait! Did he say, centuries?

I wanted to yell out to them. I wanted to tell them that, like Oscar, I was not the enemy but a very confused and tired mother trying to save her children, and all those aboard the Titanic, as well as they should also be.

"And make damn sure you get rid of those other two. That damn Daniel Coxen and Mr. Dilly," said Captain Smith. "When the constable here questions them, insist on them receiving something to help calm them down, too. Permanently," the captain added. "Once the ship goes down, we can't have them telling tales and casting suspicion on any of us. Besides, they've chased us enough throughout all these years. Their time has finally come. After all, we did agree this would be our last time. Our Dividing Time, did we not?"

"Yes, The Dividing Time," Oscar repeated. "Yes, we did."

"Aye-aye, Captain," the doctor agreed. "The Dividing Time."

*The Dividing Time...Shamus...*My mind raced backward, back to Shamus and that dreadful tea party.

'For it is you, Little Mademoiselle, you, yourself that managed to break through the gravity field that holds time. It is what you call The Dividing Time. And now, it is upon your very own request that I have brought you back here to weave Time back to what was once normal.'

"She'll be out of it for some time. And when she does wake up, she will be quite drowsy, long enough that we needn't worry 'bout her saying anything to anyone 'bout anything," the doctor said.

"Even when she does come around and manages her way to the top, I doubt anyone will have a willing ear to lend her," Captain Smith chuckled. "What, with all the confusion and such that will be occurring."

Oscar shifted on my cot. "Well, if a murder is to be conducted, intentionally or not, now is the best time as ever to do so, wouldn't you say?" he chimed in.

"Oh, say now, has someone changed their attitude?" The doctor asked. "Might I quote, *'I am not the enemy.'* Tell us Constable, what do you mean by, 'you are not the enemy'?

"Why, that's easy enough to understand, isn't it?" Oscar replied. "Given my position, I find no delight in doing away with a life. But as we all know, sometimes it is necessary, and it is my duty to make it as comfortable as possible. Trust me, just like the both of you, I'm looking forward to having a little rest and relaxation. By myself, in my own way. And with her and Coxen and Dilly out of the way, we will all get the final rest that we earned. But I must insist on completing our mission in my way. Not yours or anyone else's. When it's her time I will let you know.

"I'm glad you understand," said the captain. "We are we in agreement, then? That this is our final Time Run. Our Dividing Time. Once this is done, so are we."

I managed to open my eyes into slight slits, just enough to see the mighty Captain Smith standing next to the door, covering it with his large, plump frame. I thought of Doctor Bayshore and how many times he had stood at my door waiting for me to awaken, or fall peacefully asleep. Closing my eyes, I continued to listen, knowing I had to fight the sleep that was overcoming me. It was a fight that under no circumstances could I lose but had to win. With my eyes slipping shut and my mind wondering, I screamed inside myself to stay awake.

"Let's run through the plan one more time. Like the constable here says, we don't have much time," said the captain.

"Aye-aye," the doctor agreed. Oscar said nothing.

"We will leave one lifeboat in place next to my cabin; we shall meet there at 2:00 am. This so called unsinkable, big gal is set to sink precisely at 2:20 am. That gives us a good twenty minutes to be let down and row ourselves away from the suction and to the Black Ship. Once out of range, we will all board the Black Ship together, which as we speak, sits portside.

"And thanks to our fine constable here, and our good friends back in Southhampton, Cherbourg, and Queenstown, the Black Ship is stocked with the finest troves of jewels, the finest art collections, more currency exchanges that we can count...compliments of our fine and wealthy passengers. Yes, my fine friends, there is plenty to keep us all well satisfied for the rest of our, *natural* lives, living higher than any king that ever lived on earth. The monetary compensation that we each shall receive is well beyond that which was promised us for the speed breaking success of the great and powerful, unsinkable, Titanic. Think men! No more having to hustle time, wondering and worrying if we have landed in the correct place, at the correct time."

"Aye, Captain. Worrying if the Threads will hold; each time they are used they weaken," the doctor added. "Or if they might tangle. Remember that time back in—"

"Come now, men," Captain Smith interrupted. "We haven't time to play nostalgia games. Save it for when we're safely aboard The Black Ship and heading to our new homes. We do have quite the voyage ahead of us.

"Just think. This opportunity is being handed over to us due to man's foolishness for believing that God Himself cannot sink this ship, or that He looks over us so lovingly that He will never allow bad things to happen. Garbage. All of it! This is the time we have been waiting for all these years. It is our chance to cash in *our* Time.

"Speaking for myself, it has been many years at sea for me. And by tomorrow morning, when we are on the Black Ship, I will be more than grateful to submit my soul to *my* Dividing Time. How 'bout you, doctor?"

"Yes, Edward. Yes, it is the perfect time," the doctor agreed. "More than willing!"

"You certainly have earned the right, Captain," Oscar interrupted. "Being entrusted by the Royal Navy itself and being the cherished and adored sea captain that you are, it's only natural that you have been chosen to pilot the Titanic's maiden voyage. Why it's the perfect set up. Well done, my friend. Well done indeed!"

"Here, here," the doctor clapped, agreeing with Oscar.

"Now, now gentlemen. No need for such adulation," Captain Smith grunted. "It's simply our time to take advantage of man's naivete so that we may now sit in the lap of luxury as we live out our lives. Natural lives, that is. We Travelers have done our duty. Some have chosen our way while others, like the little Mademoiselle here, and her two mates, Daniel Coxen and Dilly, are free to continue to follow their own path of time in their own way. *If* they are to survive tomorrow morning, that is. I, for one, am tired, gentlemen. A rest is long due me. I am so glad you both have chosen to join me in our rest. "Once on board the Black Ship, we will head south for Puerto Madryn, South America, and from there, the world is our playground.

"Yes, it will be glorious. Simply glorious," said the doctor. "But I do have one concern. Your dead sister's children. The girl, will she be willing to leave her fiancé, Mr. Archibald Butt, behind?"

"Oh, please doctor. Put your fears to rest. I assure you, they will prove to be no trouble. No trouble at all. Will they, Oscar?"

'Your dead sister's children...' I held the statement in my head.

The captain and the doctors' laughter were cold as the freezing waters on which we sailed and would soon be sleeping under. I did not want to hear anymore. I wanted them to stop their madness. I wanted them gone. I wanted time to be no more. But only in my head could I beg for such things. For though my eyes were shut, my ears remained open. And the only way I could fight for my Maisy and Franklin was through remembering what I was hearing. But sleep was calling me like a mother calling to her child. I struggled. I struggled hard to keep my mind alert and awake.

The awful stench filling the cabin was not only from the doctor's whiskey and snuff and the captain's cigars, but the filth of the men's vile intentions. And having my Maisy and Franklin a part of it set my most inner being on fire. I would fight them. Patsy and I. *Yes, we will fight them. After all, I killed once. I can, and will kill again.*

My head hurt. My body raged with anger. *This man, this horrible, vile man standing before me...surely cannot be of his blood. He cannot be my mother's brother. He cannot be the one we had traveled so far to see. Mother would truly be heartbroken...*

"With a few little bribes here and there, that burn mark was covered up very well," Captain Smith boasted. "And the bulkheads being constructed shorter than what was useful. Brilliant. Simply brilliant. Such a well-orchestrated mission.

"Say now, you're awfully silent, Oscar. What thoughts hold you so captive?"

Oscar chuckled. "As fun as this has been, gentlemen, we best get a move on. The ocean, she will be rising faster than we think. We shall have plenty of time to discuss all matters later."

"Very well, gentlemen," said Captain Smith. "Till we meet again."

"Yes, till we meet again. In the morning," Oscar said as the last of their farewells came, my tears rolled down my checks following me into a sleep that turned black as the ocean depths beneath us.

I awoke not knowing how much time had passed. An hour? Two hours? A day, a night? I tried sitting up. My body, still limp and heavy, was impossible to move.

I called for Patsy, but to no avail. For I had neither a voice nor a sense the old boy was in the cabin. Then I remembered. The doctor. And the nightmare came back to life.

"'*I shall take him with...*'"

Groggy and cold, I watched a strobe of light pass under the crack of my cabin door. It was much like the light under The Green Door in Nora's room. But the other side of this door, in the hallway, were the ship's stewards pounding on cabin doors, politely shouting out their orders. A scream now and then followed a few cries and sobs.

"Hurry, Missus... Don't dawdle... No need to bring anything

'cept yourselves..." More pounding, more crying, a scream. Passengers scrambled by. A scudder of light passed under the door.

"Hurry now..." More pounding. I tried to make sense of it all. The cabin was dark and exceptionally cold, its walls creaked in a miserable manner. The mighty ship engines had ceased their rumblings leaving only the demands of the ship's stewards, and the outburst cries of passengers fleeing the lower deck.

The chill inside the cabin grew a bleak, frigid cold, a cold deeper than a body can withstand. For it was the chill of death that I felt. And with it crept in the knowledge that the time I traveled so far for had finally come. And the worst of that time was upon my children and myself, and all those aboard the great Titanic.

I called out to the stewards walking the hall chanting for us to leave. My voice, weak and frail, was nonexistent except to my own ears.

"Step lively...Step lively! Yes, that's it...keep moving!"

The passing feet gave way to more flickering of light under the crack of the door. Then more pounding. It was louder this time, closer as well as the young man's voice.

"Come forward. Very well, madam. Come forward"

My head was clearing, giving way to the calling of the familiar voice of the steward. It was that of the young man I had so unrightfully disliked and mocked just a few days before. No longer did he sound smug and infuriating, but concerned and frightened.

"You in there! You must come out!" he yelled, this time knocking firmly on my door. "Captain's orders..."

"Help," I called out. I swallowed trying to wet my throat. "Help. I-I'm-I'm here. Help." Try as I might, nothing came out but a mere, raspy squeak.

He knocked again, this time louder and with as much desperation as in his voice. "No time to dilly-dally. We must be quick now. We haven't time."

I tried crying out again. "P-p-please sir. I'm here. I-I can't move. Help me." The door handle jiggled. More knocking. Another jiggle.

"Yes, I'm here, right here. Don't give up. Please don't give up!" I cried, for I knew he could not hear me. And I knew we were sinking.

"That cabin be empty, mate. The doctor said so. No need to struggle. This deck be cleared. We best be off ourselves. Captain says we be lucky if this big girl don't go down under in an hour. God-speed, mate."

"Yes, you, as well," the young steward answered." It's been a fine privilege serving with you, sir. Godspeed."

"No! D-don't leave me, please, d-don't leave me." My voice was now nothing but a mere whisper in the dark. I looked at the wash basin hoping against hope to find my beloved Patsy, though I knew he was gone.

A brush! A hair brush! I spotted its handle barely hanging over the sink. Tightening every muscle within, I forced my arm to reach it.

"Wait," I cried shaking, struggling to grab the hard, hunk of metal. I could feel its handle on the tips of my fingers. I forced my arm further, pushing it upward with my whole body. I opened my hand. The hard bristles poked into my palm. Without a moment's hesitation I closed my fingers around the stiff stubble making sure it held firm in my grip. I carefully shoved it into my mouth, and I bit down hard, ignoring the thorns poking the roof of my mouth. Then, using my hands, I reached down and pulled my numb legs to the side of the bed and sat up and took the brush from my mouth.

"Oh God, *please wait*," I tried calling out. "Please wait." I threw it. I threw the brush at the door. It fell onto the floor with a light, plunk.

"Very well. Give my best to the Missus," the steward was saying. His voice faded fast away, as did his feet from the door. I stared at the last stream of light that guided those above me to safety. Then came the silence. The deafening silence as sometimes Gods voice can be.

And again, I prayed to the God in which I did not believe. "Lord, that is the name those who believe in you call you by. Lord. Lord, I do not know why you allow such tragedies to come upon us people, especially those that seem to take such pride in claiming you as their Lord and Savior. Like Cousin Lexington, err, Ruby Drake. And the children, Lord, why? Why do you forsake all the little children? To me, you are a cruel and vicious God. A God quick to anger, and quick to forget those who love you the most, especially in their time of need such as this. Or when a little girl's mamma and daddy and brother are taken away forever. That is why I never claimed to know you, and more so never claimed to love you, not like Mama and Daddy did. But before I die, if I might, I have just two simple requests for you, if you do exist, that is.

"The first request is quite simple since you are supposedly God Almighty. Please see to it that my children, and all children make it out of this alive and well, as well as the old and incapable like the ones I saw coming on board before me. See to it that no harm comes to any of them.

"My second request is, give me the answer as to why you are so mean. Why do you make us mere humans suffer so? With illnesses both inside and out, like that of Little Margret Jean, and the Mr. Hawthorn, and everyone coming and going from places like Pine Brook.

"I think that is all I want to say to you. For now, anyway. I don't know if I will meet you and gain my rewards by seeing my mama and daddy and Huston, like I've been told happens when a person dies. I'm inclined to think not. Since I hadn't ever really cared about you like the others did. Chances are I will probably end up way down inside the Earth to be burning forever in that damn lake of fire that you made for people like me. After all, I am a murderess. Either way, I just wanted to let you know how I feel about you.

"Well, that's it for now, I guess. Just remember, take care of my children, and all the others. Amen."

It's strange the way I did not cry or carry on the way most folks would in such a dire situation as I that early morning aboard the Titanic. I knew I was going to die, and in the most tragic manner I could possibly think of, and feared for so long. Drowning in the murky depths of the freezing saltwater in the middle of the Atlantic Ocean.

Above me I could hear the screams and sobs of women and children and the cries of some men. It was happening, and I knew it. The end was coming too soon, taking with it the lives of too many.

The cabin walls, creaked and moaned, warning me they would not hold for long. For the water that God made, God forsaken water, had found its way inside the hallway and its abandoned cabins.

Under my cabin door, it came flowing, slow at first, in a trickle of a stream. I stared at it, watching it grow into a babbling brook searching for new boundaries that had no end. But alas, it found its way to the walls of my small dark cabin and rested, waiting for more to flow so it could rise.

I laid down, struggling to pull the blanket at the end of my cot over myself. For the breath of death was breathing upon me. And I cried.

I cannot tell you what thoughts came to me that day, at the hour of my death. For there were many. Both regrets and delights of a life that was just beginning, and ending much too soon. Those thoughts, bad and good, were like the frigid ice water refusing to stop rising, which had collected and began to cover my bed.

I choked. A tiny stream of cold, dribbled into my mouth. I swallowed the liquid salt and choked again. It burned as it flowed down my throat and nostrils and ears as well. It stung so terribly bad, I knew that if I didn't get up I would never do so again for I would drown, just as I feared. That's when I had to decide. Life or death.

The warmth of a tiny spark of hope smoldered deep inside my gut and in my heart.

My Thread. My Thread of Time...

I spat the venom from my mouth and sat up. I shook my head. My legs. I could barely make them out within the darkness. It was as if they were no longer a part of me. I tried moving them. Nothing.

The water was rising and I could not wait for the doctor's medication to wear off. To do so would mean certain death.

"Move, move you damned things, move..." It was a raspy demand as I grabbed hold of one, forcing it onto the floor. I seized the other and did the same. I could feel the freezing water surrounding them. The water so cold it would cause permanent damage if I did not move quickly enough to the dry decks above.

"Cold," I chattered, sitting fully up." I'm so cold. I-I-I just need to sleep for a moment and then I'll be fine." I looked at my bunk. Water covered it and my blanket like a bed of ice. A few more minutes of laying down and I would be underneath it, unable to get up.

"No! I will not die. Not here, not like this. I have to...get out of here. I have to find Maisy and Franklin. I must..."

I reached down under the water and moved one leg forward then the next. The water, the water so frigid it numbed my hands as they worked their way through, maneuvering my legs and feet. I pulled my hands out and blew into them, rubbing them together to gain circulation. Even my breath was losing its warmth. I looked about the cabin and sobbed.

There was no denying my actions. It was poor Mr. Frederick Barrett who laid on a bed of ice somewhere deep inside a part of the ship that only the doctor and a few others knew the whereabouts. The ship's morgue. I shuddered at the very thought. For I knew, I too, along with the many others onboard would soon join him.

I took a deep breath, and again I plunged my hands back into the water and took hold of my shins. I stood up, fighting the nearly impossible stiffness that had taken control over my body. The doctor had done his work well.

I stood and gasped for strength. The sea was now past my knees. I fought every muscle to move my legs. Five steps. I took five laborious steps and stopped. I yanked up my hands trying to warm them. The cabin walls groaned, waiting to buckle under its pressure.

"Just a few more steps...then...I shall find my Maisy and Franklin...just another step or two..."

Hope. It was not too late to save them and Cousin Lexington, and Patsy, and all those I cared for, were just a few feet away.

"I will find them, all of them...I will bring them with me...back to Shamus and...Netsel...Miss Gavin and..."

I rubbed my hands one last time and again I reached into the water. I found my legs. This time I refused to let them go.

The cabin walls creaked louder, and moaned louder and groaned heavier as I moved through the shadows of murk. The walls bulged, then cracked.

"Hurry, Camarilla," I encouraged myself. "Hurry. One more step. One...more...step." Exhausted, I fell against the door.

Go on, grab it, grab the knob...you can...do it...do it now; let's go, Camarilla. We have a mission to fulfill.

Again, with renewed hope and new found faith I turned the handle and sobbed. It was locked. I raised my arms and pounded the door.

I pounded and pounded, and pounded some more.

"Open, open the door," I shouted, beating my fists with less strength each time. "Open the door."

I had grown weak, my hips and waist I could not feel, for my legs had long lost all sensation. The ocean water was past them, and now hostile, making its way to my waist. Soon its grip of death would take hold of my heart.

And my heart broke. I realized that I had no choice but to abandon my dear Maisy and Franklin.

For now, I thought. *Dying aboard a ship that had yet to come to pass made no sense.*

"I'll go back. Back to a different time. Back before they were born. Back before Mama and Daddy's accident. Back before the Captain, my long-lost uncle leaves his shoppe. Yes, that's it. I will..." I harked-back and was horrified. Tears escaped from my eyes. The Thread of Time would hold but just one more travel and no more. Going back was impossible. And I wept. For my soon to be death was meaningless. After all, I was there, and the captain, with the others, were there. I was alone.

"Anyone," I sobbed quietly hugging my cabin door. If anyone at all...anyone can hear me... I'm here...I'm in here..."

"I can't." A voice answered. It was as if God once again came to mock me.

"Oh, you *are* cruel, "I cried. "Giving Life and taking it as you please with no regard to those it affects. You could have sent an angel. Would that be too much to ask?"

"What? What are you saying? Has the water frozen your brain? I can't open the door."

Was it, could it be? It was not the angel I had wanted, but one that would have to do. It was Oscar. And with the rising water ready to pass my waist, I had but only one way out. And that was up to Oscar.

"Oh, please hurry...the water, it's passing my waist and heading for my chest."

"I can't," he yelled back. "The water is too high. The pressure is too great against the door. I can't do it."

"Try, oh please try. I-I-I don't want to die like this. Please, Oscar, please. I'm so cold. I can't feel my legs. The doctor, he...he did this to me. And you. You did this to me too! I'm sleepy. I want to sleep."

"Oh, now it's *please*, is it? A few days it was, '*go away Oscar. I despise you, Oscar.*' I didn't say I wouldn't, I said-oh never mind. Very well then. I must get an ax. I will be back. I promise. And please, whatever you do, do not fall asleep. If you do, it's all over. You hear me? If you do, it's all over! Move your legs, move around. Move every part of your body to keep it warm and think. Think of Maisy, and Franklin, and those back home. Promise?"

"Yes, I-I-I promise. Back home, why did you-you-you say back home?"

That thought raced through my mind as I waited for Oscar's return. I listened to the walls whimper and sob as if being tortured along with me. I picked up my legs with my hands and moved them about through the piercing water. It was as if I were floating through a pool of a thousand searing knives. The pain burned and was much too unbearable to endure. I stopped all movement and fell against the door and rested.

"God, if you do exist as claimed by those like Cousin Lexington, and Mother and Father, why are you letting this happen? Why are you to let so many die so tortuously this night. Where, where are you? *Where?*"

I was tired. And the only thing I was able to move were the sweet thoughts of Franklin and Maisy, my Little Margret Jean and Nurse Price, and yes, as Oscar had instructed, all those back home.

How old would they be? I wondered. Visions of Little Margret and our special hallway and games we played so long ago made me smile. I giggled. It was home, that I knew now. It didn't matter, not one iota did it matter where home was. What did matter was all those who made it a home.

And Doctor Bruce, how old would he be? Would Mr. Hawthorn still be alive? Was it possible? Oh, how I wished to show him my interpretation of Brahms. He would be pleased, very pleased. And Shamus. What of him and Netsel. Dear old sweet Netsel.

"How he loves his horses," I whispered, feeling the cabin door against my cheek. I rubbed against it as if it were Mokey and Lucy.

"If only I would have known how to use the Threads of Time

better. It would have brought us home. All of us. Patsy! Oh, where is my dear boy, Patsy, and Maisy, and Franklin...?"

"Who? Who loves horses?" It was Oscar. His tone was eager.

"A dear old friend of mine. It matters not. Not anymore."

"Step back," I heard Oscar say. "Get away from the door as far as you can."

"The water, i-i-it feels thick. I-I can't. It's too thick. The water, it's so thick. It cuts me like a dagger. Hundreds and hundreds of sharp...shiny, hot, daggers..."

"Listen to me, Camarilla. And you listen good! You mustn't give up. Not now. We are close, Camarilla, so close. Do what you must to remove yourself from the door. Do it now. I demand it of you."

No longer did I feel the cold. No longer did it cut through me like searing knives of fire. I began feeling warmth again. For bending down, I picked up my legs and tried wrestling away from Oscar and the door. I don't know how I managed, but I did. It was as if I were floating through the water like on some sort of raft. All pain was nonexistent.

"Alright, I'm away," I yelled out.

Then came the slicing and tearing down of the door between me and Oscar. He had found the ax by the fire door and, piece by piece, like an Angel of Mercy, Oscar was taking the door down.

With his final stroke he made enough room for himself and I to get through.

"We haven't much time," he said breathlessly. He took my hands and pulled me through the water toward the door. "We have to hurry."

"Oscar." I looked him straightaway. "Why?"

"We need to go, *now*," he snapped. "We don't have time for the why's. Not now."

I couldn't help it. I started to cry. "Oh, I made such a mess of everything."

"Yes, yes you did," Oscar said, taking hold of my arm, forcing me out the cabin and into the hallway. "Now trust me. I won't let anything happen to you. I will explain everything to you when it's over. I promise. I really do. But right now, we must *get out now! Look!*"

He pointed to the other end of the hall. A dirty brown wave was rolling toward us.

"Run, Camarilla, run," he shouted, yanking me toward the stairwell. *"Move it!"*

I tried desperately to reach the stairwell. Really and truly, I did. But it was too much, and I was too weak. The water rolled like a dam that had busted open. It was a sickening brown, and angry-mad as if it too were on a mission. It rushed past me, pushing me. My arm slipped from Oscar's grip, thrusting me a good ten feet back. Oscar was ahead of me and was moving further away.

"Am I moving?" I called to him, for I no longer felt my body. "Am I moving? I'm tired," I whispered. "So tired. I-I-I think I'm going to go to sleep now. Just for a while. I can't help it. I-I-I'm sorry. Really, I am, Oscar. Truly.

"T-T-Tell them, t-t-t-tell my Maisy and Franklin, Cousin Lexington...t-tell them how I tried. How far I came."

"It's hypothermia, Camarilla," Oscar shouted at me. "You have to fight it." His words were muffled, barely audible.

"Damn it," he cussed. "If only you would have listened! If only..."

What happened next was odd. And unless a person were to experience the same situation, it is impossible to clearly explain what happened next. I assure you, no matter how badly the next is described, it is true. Sincerely.

No longer did I fear the ocean and its biting cold, evil saltwater. For it was warm and was becoming a part of me, and I a part of it. Closing my eyes I sunk downward, beneath it.

No longer did I shiver with a thousand pains as it filled my ears and poured down my throat and into my nostrils. I had no want to fight it, but welcomed it as if it were tucking myself into my warm, soft bed on a cold Wisconsin winter's night. It was then that I began my sleep just as Mr. Frederick Barrett had begun his.

My Dividing Time. This is my Dividing Time. Mama, Daddy, Huston, if you can hear me, I want you to know I now understand. I am ready for my Dividing Time...

For God was answering me, answering me as perhaps He was answering all the others onboard that great and magnificent ship called The Titanic. And as He did, our Angels came. I saw them, each and everyone, reaching out to us, the ones of us underwater. The old couple I stood behind on the plank were the first I saw touch the hands of their Angels. Then, came the Angels belonging to Tillie and her children, and Drew, her husband.

Not an ounce of terror or distress captured their frozen faces. Not a tear shone in their eyes. For the glorious rays of Heaven and all its splendid wounder replaced all that had been.

We were no longer frightened, the lot of us. And like Mr. Frederick Barrett, we were turning, twisting, reaching for our Angels as they also reached for us.

I felt sorry for those still alive scrambling about, crying and screaming, carrying on as if the very end of the world was upon them. Which it was. For their Angels had yet to come.

But it was the others that my heart broke for most. For their Angels were not so loving and kind. I watched, horrified as blackness surrounded them.

I paid Oscar no mind. I wanted not. I could not. For a light much brighter than he shone down on me. And I took its hand. And all fear had passed. And with it so did the ship and all its screams and howlings, and all its whimperings and sobbing. For it, too, was dying. And I, I was going Home.

CHAPTER TWENTY-FOUR

The air was cold. Freezing. Enough to halt one's breath before it had a chance to escape one's lungs and chest. The frozen salt from the water and air burned my throat, my eyes, my nose, my very skin ached. I cried, wishing my Angel of Death to release me once again from the torments of life. But nay. It was not to be.

Alas. Oscar stood over me, just as handsome as I had remembered, and shivering. People around him ran, screaming for mercy. Others cried out prayers to a God I now knew existed. For it was through His Angels that I touched His hand, and that He held mine. I had touched. It was His hand that brought comfort in death.

And it was through Oscar's that He brought me into the lifeboat. He was not Oscar, not any longer, but the man I once knew and loved so long ago. He was my Angel. The Angel God Himself sent back to watch over me. For the veil had dropped between us.

"Huston..." I reached to touch him.

"See, I told you I was not the enemy, didn't I? But I had you fooled. Pretty good, huh?"

I laid staring into his face. Drops of ocean water sparkled in his hair like the stars above him. They dripped on me, warmed from his body.

"I have some people here that want to see you," he said, smiling as he wiped the drops of salty ocean water from my face.

"Hello, Camarilla. I am so sorry about the doctor, and having to put you through everything. It was our only way of finally putting an end to his reign. I hope you can forgive me."

The captain placed something warm in the crook of my arm. It nuzzled close to me. It was Patsy. My Patsy. He opened his mouth, baring his stiff brown tongue. I smiled back at him, rubbing my face on his generous, black head.

"Love you, old boy," I managed to whisper. He was safe and sound, faithful as ever. As was my mother's brother. The one we ventured to visit so long ago.

"Promise you will stay put, next time. You have your job, and we have ours. And we mustn't be crossing each other again, can we? At least not until our Dividing Time really does come and we can all finally, Go Home."

"Yes, I-I-I do promise Uncle. I am sorry."

"Now, child, you be strong now," Cousin Lexington joined in. "We've lots to do ahead of us and you need your rest. God be with you. We will see you soon enough now." Cousin Lexington bent down and kissed my forehead. I reached up to touch her. She was soft and warm, just like Patsy. "You can call me, Mrs. Thompson if you like. And tell old Shamus that he can't get away from me that easily. Tell him I went dress shopping; for a nice white one with lots and lots of lace and ruffles." She giggled and grabbed my cheek, giving it a good firm pinch.

"Tell him we have a lot to discuss when I get home. Patsy, I will see you soon. You did well. Again."

"Daniel, can you help Ruby here get on board, please? And Franklin, you help your sister." Huston's orders were sweet as the air of life that filled our lungs.

I managed to sit up and look into the faces of those I had come to fight for, to give my life for. My children. My wonderful, beautiful children, and all the others that had gathered there (and the ones whose names and faces I did not know.)

"Huston, are they, are they one of us?" I mustered my thoughts to speak. For my throat was raw from salt and cold. My nose stung. I could not smell the fresh clean sea air I had enjoyed. Nor could I bear to look upon the stars so bright.

"No. No, they are not. They are normal, and they will have a most normal, and happy life. And Franklin, he will become an uncle. And very soon."

I looked over to see her soon to be beloved, Major Archibald Butt take Maisy from the care of Daniel. He diligently placed her in the life boat hanging from the ropes and pulleys.

"Don't worry, my love, I will be right behind you with Franklin."

My heart leapt with joy as he kissed her hands, releasing her into the boat. Together we watched as she was lowered away to safety.

A blanket was pulled over my shivering body. I watched as the young steward's hands tucked it tight around me.

"I-I-I'm sorry," I said to him, the young and wonderful steward. Despite his short stature, he truly stood tall as a man.

"No worries, Missus. No worries," he said giving me a smile and a wink. "All's well." Confused, I looked to Huston.

"It's part of the Time Line. Some things we are not to know," he said, looking out at the ocean.

"You see, if we know too much it disrupts those things we need to have come about on their own. We never know who might be our Angels in time. Maisy will not recognize you. Not now anyway. Nor will Franklin. As you can now understand, it's for the better. Trust me."

"Huston, I-I am so sorry. I am so sorry for doubting you. I have so much to tell you."

"And I you, my love. But right now, right here, is not the time. I have to go now, and so do you. My mission is not quite completed, I'm afraid."

He paused and stared at me, then bent and kissed my forehead. "I need to go now, he said, pulling away from me."

"Wait, Huston, don't go, *please.* I miss you so. What about, about all these people? Will they all...are they all going too..." He stopped and turned back.

"Yes, some will die and some shall live. That is part of life, is it not? And Camarilla, life never ends. It goes on forever. It just changes form.

"Now, you really do need to be careful as Uncle Edward warns," he chuckled. "Remember the garden? The one Shamus started so many years ago?"

The garden, I thought. "Oh Huston, I could never forget the garden. That was you, wasn't it? The man with the children."

"Yes, yes it was."

"And the little boy and girl, the ones who chased me, they were..." I looked over at Archibald and Franklin. Huston smiled and nodded.

"Yes, your grandchildren, Camarilla, they are your grandchildren. I happen to be watching them that day. It's synchronicity brought about due to, connectamaltrie. You know, part of that old saying, 'being at the right place at the right time.' Synchronicity.

"When the time is right, meet us there. Meet us in fifty-three. Nineteen fifty-three, that is. We'll be there, I promise. Oh, tell Shamus I send my greetings and not to worry. His Little Mademoiselle had done her job well. I promise."

Huston held up a golden thread and a vial of liquid.

"Here. I mustn't forget. Don't lose them this time. When you get back, you'll know what to do with it."

"The Golden Thread of Time," I said, taking it from him. "And Shamus's polio medicine."

And with that, I watched Huston, and everyone, and everything, fade away. For as much as it hurt my heart, I knew that their time, was not my time. Not yet. But like all those we love and lose in life, one day, soon enough, we will all be together once again. For the circle of life, and love shall never truly be broken.

And so, as I once again began to wake, the voices around me were familiar. And I was happy. For the hand that held mine was as right and as good as any I could have prayed for.

"She's coming around, Doctor. She's coming around."

Truly, I tell you, the God I hadn't believed in answered my prayer. Truly, I was happy. For I knew I was home.

And so as promised, I, Camarilla Rae Berkelman, told you my story. And, if you choose to believe it, then I have done my duty well. And perhaps, just perhaps, it is still being written somewhere.

Somewhere Behind the Green Door.

THE END

ann m. andrashie

Author of
Dog Island

You can visit Ann at
Amazon.com
www.facebook.com/ann.andrashie
https://www.linkedin.com/in/annmandrashie/
www.ann-m-andrashie.com/ GoodReads.com

Reviews are always warmly welcome

About the Author

Ann was born in the Chicago area. She and her family moved to the Wisconsin Northwoods when she was thirteen. Living in both locations has given Ann a useful insight as a writer to both city life and country.

As the years flew by, Ann's dream of becoming an actress was not to be. In its place she took the advice of instructors from long past, and put the characters dancing in her head loose on paper.

Her knack for writing (along with an active imagination) gained Ann employment consisting of writing newsletters and advertising for several businesses.

Forever writing unshared stories, it wasn't until her twins were raised and with children of their own, did she finally find time to get truly serious about her stories. With the help of a very dear friend and a few family members, Ann found the courage to share her fictional writings which led to finishing her first novel, *Dog Island*. Now retired, Ann completed her second novel, *Behind The Green Door-memoir of a time traveler*, and is looking forward to writing its sequel, and other stories as well.

Ann's own life, filled with happiness and joy, sorrow and hard times, blends the perfect combination used in her novels that readers carry with them long after the last page is turned.

www.ann-m-andrashie.com

CPSIA information can be obtained
at www.ICGtesting.com
Printed in the USA
LVHW030149271222
735871LV00001B/23

9 781737 047940